Christmas Pact

To Love an Imperfect Man

WELL OF LIFE
PUBLISHING

Christmas Pact

Christmas Hotel Series Book Four

by

Saundra Staats McLemore

Christmas Pact
To Love an Imperfect Man

Christmas Hotel Series Book Four

by

Saundra Staats McLemore

Paperback ISBN: 978-1-7336122-0-3

Also available as an eBook
eBook 978-0-9826750-9-0

First published by
Desert Breeze Publishing 2015
© Saundra Staats McLemore 2015

This new and revised edition 2019

Content Editor: Chris Wright
Cover Artist: Gwen Phifer
Photography by: Taria Reed Studios

All scripture verses are taken from the KJV of the Holy Bible. *The Old Rugged Cross* (George Bennard 1912) and *Standing on the Promises* (Russell Kelso Carter 1886) and *Shall We Gather at the River* (Robert Lowry 1864) and *When the Roll is Called up Yonder* (James M. Black 1893) and *Just as I Am* (Charlotte Elliott 1836) and an excerpt from *The Village Blacksmith* (Henry Wadsworth Longfellow

1840) and *Destiny* (Edwin Arnold 1832-1904) and *She Walks in Beauty* (Lord Byron 1813) quote from: (Alfred Lord Tennyson 1809-1892) mentioned: Johann Strauss 1825-1899 and an excerpt from *The Way We Were* (Alan Bergman and Marvin Hamlisch 1973)

Published by

Well of Life Publishing
Ohio
United States of America

http://www.saundrastaatsmclemore.com

Other Books by Saundra Staats McLemore

The Staats Family Chronicles Series

Abraham and Anna – Book One of Staats Family Chronicles Series – Available now
Joy out of Ashes – Book Two of Staats Family Chronicles Series – Available now

Christmas Hotel Series

Book One: Christmas Hotel
(New Edition) Available now
Book Two: Christmas for Lucy
(New Edition) Available now
Book Three: Christmas Redemption
(New Edition) Available now
Book Four: Christmas Pact (New Edition)
Paperback available now
eBook available October 11, 2019
Book Five: Christmas Love and Mercy
New Edition)
Available November 01, 2019
Book Six: Christmas Hotel Reunion
(New Edition)
Available November 15, 2019

Dedication

I dedicate *Christmas Pact* in the memory of my brother Specialist Four Gerald Martin Staats United States Army. He was killed in battle during the Vietnam War. Born: December 06, 1949 Died: February 26, 1970. You will always be loved, missed, and not forgotten, Jerry.

A special dedication was later added in memory of my mother Christine Dailey Staats. She passed away just thirty-four days shy of her ninety-sixth birthday, which would have been September 21, 2015. That date is Desert Breeze Publisher's original release date for *Christmas Pact*. Mother, I know that you and Jerry are together again for all eternity.

Acknowledgements

A thank you to my cousin Patricia Parks, CRNA ANP (Certified Registered Nurse Anesthetist Advanced Nurse Practitioner) for providing the extra medical advice and reviewing two chapters for medical accuracy.

I would also like to thank Tony Staats for reading *Christmas Pact* and helping to find all those typos!

I thank Franklin, Kentucky historian, Gayla McClary Coates, for the needed information regarding Franklin, Kentucky in the Christmas Hotel series. She graciously answered my questions, and much of the information I was able to use for the accuracy of pertinent information.

I would like to offer a special thank you to Sid and Jill Broderson for granting me permission to have my characters Christopher and Jerilyn Wright and their children, reside in their historical home at 210 South College Street in Franklin, Kentucky.

This beautiful home is known in Franklin as the *Montague House* or the *Malone House*. The Italianate structure was built around 1860 by William Clement Montague.

Another special thank you to Barbara Beasley Smith for allowing me to have her father Dr. L. F. Beasley "visit" the story.

As always, I thank my husband Robert E. McLemore for his complete support, as I enjoy the passion I have for writing.

I would like to thank our Lord and Savior Jesus Christ for the inspiration He provides for every story I write.

Chapters

Chapter One: At Christmas Hotel 1

Chapter Two: Staff Sergeant Andrew
       McConnaughey 6

Chapter Three: Getting Acquainted 11

Chapter Four: Destiny 20

Chapter Five: Dating and Beaus 28

Chapter Six: Secrets 40

Chapter Seven: Mistletoe and Ice Skating 44

Chapter Eight: Intentions 52

Chapter Nine: Shopping in Nashville 62

Chapter Ten: Igloos, Snowmen,
       and Snowball Fights 68

Chapter Eleven: Memories 76

Chapter Twelve: The Proposal 79

Chapter Thirteen: The Wedding 89

Chapter Fourteen: Goodbyes 99

Chapter Fifteen: Interruptions from Memories 104

Chapter Sixteen: A German Reunion 107

Chapter Seventeen: Blessings and Goodbyes 117

Chapter Eighteen: The Valentine's Day Flowers 122

Chapter Nineteen: The Visitors 127

Chapter Twenty: The Survivor Assistant 132

Chapter Twenty-One: Nighttime Visitor 136

Chapter Twenty-Two: Andrew Michael
........McConnaughey 144

Chapter Twenty-Three: A Revelation 150

Chapter Twenty-Four: Marcus Taylor 155

Chapter Twenty-Five: A Marriage of Convenience   163

Chapter Twenty-Six: Teaching Again 168

Chapter Twenty-Seven: Changes 172

Chapter Twenty-Eight: Bellingham, Washington ... 181

Chapter Twenty-Nine: Unequally Yoked 200

Chapter Thirty: Return of a Night Visitor 209

Chapter Thirty-One: Angela Dawn 215

Chapter Thirty-Two: Vacation Suggestion 220

Chapter Thirty-Three: Danger 225

Chapter Thirty-Four: Emergency 231

Chapter Thirty-Five: Divorce 238

Chapter Thirty-Six: The Unsigned Papers 243

Chapter Thirty-Seven: The Awakening 248

Chapter Thirty-Eight: Behold Your New Life 257

Chapter Thirty-Nine: Pastor Mattingly 261

Chapter Forty: Harrison Chapman 266

Chapter Forty-One: Veteran Therapy 272

Chapter Forty-Two: Thanksgiving Day 279

Chapter Forty-Three: Decisions 287

Chapter Forty-Four: Comfort 293

Chapter Forty-Five: The Medicine of Laughter 297

Chapter Forty-Six: Confessions 304

Chapter Forty-Seven: Questions and Answers 314

Chapter Forty-Eight: Mt. Vernon
    Missionary Baptist 319

Chapter Forty-Nine: Counseling with Christopher 324

Chapter Fifty: Advice from a Wise Mother 335

Chapter Fifty-One: Visiting Angels Revealed 341

Chapter Fifty-Two: Letter of Hope 348

Chapter Fifty-Three: Healing Decisions 354

Chapter Fifty-Four: New Beginnings 361

Epilogue 367

Author's Notes 369

As of This Writing 374

Family Assistance 376

Christmas Pact Discussions and Questions
for Book Club 378

Sneak Peek of Christmas Love and Mercy
Book Five of the Christmas Hotel Series 382

"For out of much affliction and anguish of heart I wrote unto you with many tears; not that ye should be grieved, but that ye might know the love which I have more abundantly unto you."
2 Corinthians 2:4

Chapter One

At Christmas Hotel

"Hear me speedily, O LORD: my spirit faileth:
hide not thy face from me, lest I be like unto them
that go down into the pit. Cause me to hear thy
loving kindness in the morning; for in thee do I
trust: cause me to know the way wherein I
should walk; for I lift up my soul unto thee."
Psalm 146: 7-8

The Present Day
Early Morning,
Monday December 02, 1974
Carrie Emeline lay on her back on the bed in Room #7 at Christmas Hotel and cried out in despair to God. "My life is a mess, and I'm only thirty-two. Dear God, I never thought my marriage would come to this. I never expected to be in this situation. I always thought I'd be married 'until death we do part'. I expected a fairy tale marriage ... like my parents' marriage ... like my siblings' marriages."

Sitting up, she blew out her breath and grabbed another tissue on the nightstand to wipe the tears that streamed down her cheeks and into her ears. Snatching several more tissues, she blew her nose and threw the tissues into the overflowing waste basket with the others. She stared at them; disgusted with herself. *I've got to pull myself together. My parents are worried. How can I possibly tell them about all the horrible years since I married? I never let on to them that anything was amiss. I led them to believe the marriage wasn't perfect, but it was satisfactory. Anyway, they discovered it was far from perfect when Angela was born. I'm going to have to tell them I've been living a lie. How do I break the hearts of the two people I love so much?*

Rising from the bed, Carrie Emeline grabbed her robe, and quickly pulled it on, tossing her long, brown, wavy hair over the collar. While tying the robe, she strode across the room. Opening the heavy drapes, she peered out the window. She unlocked the french doors and stepped out on the balcony, escaping the claustrophobic room. Gripping the railing, she looked down onto the square of the town's park-like setting. Although the sun had not yet risen, she could tell from the streetlights that the square was decorated. She knew from past experience, the Christmas decorations had gone up the day following Thanksgiving.

Although the still dark morning afforded no light except the light poles in the square, she could see in the dim light, the poles had holly wrapped around them with a red bow at the top. With the security lights over the doors of the businesses surrounding the square, she could make out the Christmas wreaths attached to all the doors. Not much about the town had changed in her lifetime. Some of the businesses had come and gone, along with the people of Franklin, but love from the townspeople prevailed. She sighed, looked down at the balcony, and back up again. "Is there hope for me, Lord? Will I ever be happy again?"

She thought about the final divorce papers she'd received at her Louisville home in early November. Although she knew the papers were coming, actually holding them and reading the fact that divorce was inevitable caused her misery.

Was our marriage doomed from the start?

Down below, an elderly bearded man sat on a bench inside the square under a dimly lit streetlight. She frowned when she couldn't place him among the townspeople. He didn't look like the other men that congregated on the square, sometimes whittling or simply shooting the breeze. Wearing farmer's overalls, a heavy plaid shirt, and a large floppy hat, he sat feeding the pigeons and the doves. One of the doves took flight and landed on the railing around her balcony. The bird watched her intently, and Carrie Emeline stared back. Human and bird locked gazes for about thirty seconds, and then the dove flew off. *That was strange.*

She glanced back down toward the man in the park and found him looking up at her. He smiled and waved, and she returned the wave. *He appears to know me, or maybe he's just being friendly.* She tilted her head. *There's a familiarity about him.* She looked again. *Is it possible? Has he returned, Lord? I can't tell with certainty from this distance.* Shivering, she stepped back inside, closed the french doors and the drapes. "Now what, Lord? How do I go about the business of living again?"

Checking her watch, she realized it was nearing six o'clock, time for the breakfast meal at Christmas Hotel. *I can't face people yet. I don't think I slept much last night. I'll drive to the truck stop and grab a light breakfast.*

In the bathroom she scrutinized her face in the mirror, and her red-rimmed blue eyes — her mom's and twin brother's blue eyes — stared back at her. *I look as though I've aged five years in the past six months.* The bruising was finally gone, leaving only a few small scars from the cuts six months earlier. She ran warm water and washed her eyes and face. After brushing her teeth, she picked up the hairbrush to untangle the waves of her long hair. Her thoughts recalled the day she first met Andrew six years ago, and she smiled for the first time in weeks.

Chapter Two

Staff Sergeant Andrew McConnaughey

*"Delight thyself also in the LORD: and he shall
give thee the desires of thine heart."*
Psalm 37:4

The Past, six years ago
Monday, early afternoon
December 16, 1968

Carrie Emeline rushed into the front door at Christmas Hotel. "I'm home for Christmas," she announced smiling from ear-to-ear. Her parents and younger brother Chris hastened out from behind the front desk to hug her.

"I thought you weren't coming home until tomorrow."

"Well, Mom, the snow is piling up in Louisville, so the school buses couldn't run. It was our last day of school until January second, so I'm off from teaching until then. I thought it best to get an earlier start."

"You took the interstate with snow piling up?" asked her father, with that familiar frown that drew his brows together; a habit he picked up from his wife over the years.

Carrie Emeline chuckled and shook her head. "I was careful, Daddy. I've been driving for ten years, and I know how to drive in the snow. After all, you taught me," and she winked at Chris. "I suppose you'll be teaching little brother in three years."

"Actually, Carrie Emeline, I've been learning to drive this past summer ... at least on a tractor. I spent the month of July working on the McLemore farm, and Robert taught me. We didn't just drive the tractor on the farm; he sometimes let me drive the tractor on the road to Gold City to get a Coke." At that piece of information, Chris looked sheepishly at his father. Chris was tall for his age and now stood eye-to-eye with Dad.

"Well, I suppose it's okay," Dad said, ruffling his son's hair. "I know those McLemore boys began driving those tractors with their daddy by the age of four. I'm sure Robert watched over you."

They all turned as a blast of cold air hit them when the front door opened. In walked an army soldier with a large pack thrown over one shoulder. As soon as he stepped over the threshold, his cap was immediately in his hand.

Carrie Emeline checked out the tall figure with the muscular build and the military-short blond hair. He stomped the snow from his boots and brushed the snow off his shoulders onto the large mat. When he looked up, his blue eyes landed on Carrie Emeline. He smiled with a slow crooked grin, and she blushed.

He slowly turned away from her and addressed her father. "I'm Staff Sergeant Andrew McConnaughey," he announced in a commanding voice while shaking Christopher's hand. "A buddy of mine stayed here with his family several years ago. He told me all about Christmas Hotel and how special it is. I'm on leave, and I thought that this is where I'd like to spend my leave. Would you have a room available for the next twenty days?"

Christopher nodded. "Yes, we have a room for you, and we'd all like to welcome you to Christmas Hotel. My name is Christopher Wright, and this lovely lady is my wife Jerilyn." He looked on her with fondness, while hugging her to his side. "Also, on behalf of my family, we thank you for your service to America."

Sergeant McConnaughey nodded to her dad. "Welcome to Christmas Hotel," Mom smiled, as she shook the sergeant's hand.

Chris stepped forward. "I'm one of their two

sons, and you can call me Chris."

Sergeant McConnaughey shook Chris's hand. "It's nice to meet you, Chris."

Dad now hugged Carrie Emeline to his side. "This young lady is one of our three daughters: Miss Carrie Emeline Wright."

Sergeant McConnaughey took Carrie Emeline's hand, but instead of shaking it he drew her hand to his lips and tenderly kissed it. "It's a pleasure to meet you *Miss* Carrie Emeline."

Carrie Emeline noticed his blue eyes as they twinkled, and his lips curled into a crooked grin when he accented Miss.

She laughed and blushed again from the attention. "It's my pleasure to meet you, also, Sergeant McConnaughey." During the introductions, she had already noted he wore no wedding band.

Dad cleared his throat, interrupting the meeting of the sergeant and his daughter. "If you'll step over to the front desk, we'll get you checked in."

Sergeant McConnaughey set his pack on the floor and began filling out the short form.

"We'd love to have you join us at our family table in the dining room at six o'clock for the evening meal, Sergeant McConnaughey," said Jerilyn. "It will be our way of welcoming you to

Christmas Hotel. The dining room is right through those doors," and she pointed in the direction. "Please feel free to explore the hotel at your leisure. I hope you'll enjoy your stay at Christmas Hotel."

"I'm sure I will, ma'am," but he glanced back at Carrie Emeline when he spoke. "I'll also take you up on the offer to sit at your family table for dinner. I'm honored."

"Well, Sergeant McConnaughey, my family and I are honored that you chose Christmas Hotel for your leave from the army," Dad nodded while handing the sergeant the key to room number eight. "You'll like this room. It's one of the few rooms with a balcony that overlooks the town square."

Chris picked up the sergeant's pack on the floor and addressed the sergeant. "If you'll follow me, I'll lead you to your room."

As Sergeant McConnaughey turned toward Chris, he glanced again at Carrie Emeline and smiled his crooked smile. He nodded his head to her, said "Miss" and followed Chris up the cherry staircase in the lobby of Christmas Hotel.

Chapter Three

Getting Acquainted

"Thou wilt shew me the path of life: in thy presence is fulness of joy; at thy right hand there are pleasures for evermore."
Psalm 16: 11

The Past
Monday afternoon
December 16, 1968

When walking into his room, Andrew McConnaughey had noticed nothing but the bed — which beckoned to him after the long journey from Germany — the open drapes at the windows, and the door to the balcony. He set down his pack, closed the drapes, undressed, hung up his uniform, and stretched out on the bed. It didn't take long to fall asleep.

An hour later, he sat up and stretched his arms in the darkened room. Taking a moment to allow his eyes time to adapt, he rose and headed straight to the bathroom. After adjusting the shower head, he stepped in and allowed the hot water to refresh him. He dried off with one of the

Christmas Hotel luxurious towels on the warming rack. Each towel was monogrammed with CH. Two monogrammed bath robes hung on the hooks. He chose the man-size robe and noted the soft, plush feel. "A lot different than the army barracks in Germany," he said aloud.

After brushing his teeth, he methodically laid out clean blue jeans, a button-down shirt, socks, gym shoes, underclothes, along with his well-worn Bible. After dressing he breathed a sigh of pure pleasure. *It certainly feels good to be a civilian, even if for only twenty days.*

Walking to the windows and french doors, he opened the drapes and stepped out on the balcony. The air was definitely chilly, but it felt refreshing to breathe the clean air of this little town. He hadn't had time to check out the sites. When he arrived on the bus, he had stopped in at the diner in the bus stop. A pretty woman took his order: a cheeseburger, french fries and a Coke. On her nametag he read the name Carol Ann. He finished his meal and paid his bill, which Carol Ann rang up at the cash register, all the while using her right foot to slowly rock a baby in a large wooden cradle. The baby girl cooed and laughed as she stared, wide-eyed and reached with chubby arms toward the mobile above her head with horses revolving around the carousel.

Andrew was not an expert on baby ages, but he guessed her around four or five months old. He could tell she was still too young to crawl or sit up.

After leaving the balcony, he closed the french doors and sat down in a chair in front of the window. Opening his Bible, he reached up and switched on the end table light. Then he bowed his head and spoke a short prayer. After thirty minutes of reading and prayer he checked his watch. *Five o'clock. I still have an hour before the evening meal. I have time to explore part of the hotel and maybe walk around the town square.*

He threw his civilian jacket over his shoulder, switched off the light, grabbed his room key, and locked the door. A young couple holding hands passed him in the hallway. He nodded to them, and they nodded to him, but quickly turned their attention back to each other. He smiled, knowingly.

Andrew descended the beautiful cherry horseshoe-shaped staircase, taking in the beauty of the lobby for the first time. A huge two-story Christmas tree graced the center of the lobby with life-size figures of the Nativity Scene. A massive fireplace took up one wall with many stockings hanging from the mantel. He recognized the names of Christopher, Jerilyn, Carrie Emeline and Chris, and assumed all the others were family. He remembered Christopher saying Carrie Emeline was one of his three daughters, and Chris said he was one of two sons. Andrew guessed the small stockings belonged to grandchildren. From the lobby he looked to the top of the Christmas tree, and an angel atop the tree appeared to be smiling down at him.

Turning toward the front desk he saw that Christopher, Jerilyn, and Chris were busy checking in more guests, so he wandered into a small room that was obviously a chapel. The focal point of the room was straight ahead, on the wall behind the pulpit, where a large, empty wooden cross hung, symbolizing the risen Christ. One main aisle split the room, with six pews on each side. Andrew walked to the front row and sat, bowing his head.

When he finished his prayer, he stood, looked over his shoulder and found Carrie Emeline seated on the back row. She smiled, and he returned the smile. "Are you stalking me, Miss Carrie Emeline?" he asked with an impish, crooked grin.

Carrie Emeline didn't miss a beat. "You remind me of one of my third graders. They ask me crazy questions, too."

"Crazy questions? So I'm on the level of a

third grader?"

"You said it, not me," she fired back.

"Do you mind if I sit with you?"

"If you sit down, people may think *you* are stalking *me*," she retorted with a slight lift of one eyebrow. "Maybe we should sit in the lobby area where it's neutral territory for both of us. Also, some of the guests may want to visit the chapel and pray."

Andrew followed Carrie Emeline into the hotel's lobby, where they settled in two of the plush chairs. "So you're a teacher of third graders?"

"Yes, I am. It's a great age to teach. They've learned the basic skills, so I can now assist in their mental growth. I have nineteen in my class this year."

"Nineteen, you say. I could not imagine trying to teach so many at the same time."

"Oh, really. Didn't you say you're a sergeant?"

"Yes, I guess I did," he admitted, with that crooked grin.

"So, I would assume you're teaching grown men every day. How many men are in *your* class Sergeant McConnaughey?"

"*Touché*, Miss Wright. By the way, as you can see I'm in civilian clothes for my leave of absence. Would you please call me Andrew?"

"Only if you'll call me Carrie Emeline." She offered her hand. Andrew took it, and this time they shook.

"It's a pleasure to meet you, Carrie Emeline. I think I'm going to enjoy this leave very much." He released her hand, stroked his chin, and that amazing twinkle appeared in his eyes. *Control your feelings, Carrie Emeline. You just met him.*

The grandfather clock in the lobby chimed six o'clock. "I believe its dinnertime, and you're going to enjoy the food at Christmas Hotel. We have some of the best chefs in Simpson County, Kentucky," she said, as she rose to her feet.

Andrew rose at the same time and offered Carrie Emeline his arm. "Please allow me to escort you to dinner, Carrie Emeline."

She smiled up at him and took his offered arm. "I'd be pleased, Andrew."

After everyone was seated at the table, Christopher turned to Andrew. "You know, I was in the United States Army, too, but in its air corps division. Back in 1931, I enlisted for four years, immediately following high school graduation. I was stationed in the Philippines at Clark Field. However, I was only in the army between the two world wars, so I didn't see action. I was also the ship's chaplain."

Andrew nodded. "So far, I haven't seen action

either. My orders say I'll return to Germany after the first week of the New Year. However, that could change at any time. I know more troops are needed in Vietnam."

The waiter arrived for their food orders, temporarily interrupting the conversation. Christopher spoke for his family, addressing Andrew. "We're all having the chef's special for tonight: chicken and dumplings with mashed potatoes and gravy, green beans, and of course southern cornbread, and sweet tea. However, there are plenty of other choices for you."

"Sounds good. I'll have the same."

"Do you have family nearby?" asked Jerilyn.

"No, ma'am. I'm an only child, born to my parents after the age of forty. They began to think they'd be childless. Then I arrived unexpectedly. They nicknamed themselves Zacharias and Elisabeth. Both passed away a few years back, and just ten months apart. I have some cousins, but we grew up many miles apart. I suppose my family is my army buddies. We're all close, but there are two buddies in particular that I'm stationed with in Germany who are like brothers to me. One of them is from Dayton, Ohio, as I am, too."

"Oh!" said Jerilyn in excitement, "that's where I was born and raised!"

"Well, it's definitely a small world, ma'am. Where did you attend high school?"

"I was graduated from Roosevelt High School back in 1939."

"My parents met during their freshman year at Steele High School in Downtown Dayton and were graduated in 1918. I was graduated from Colonel White in '58. It was actually the second year of its existence as a four-year high school. In fact, one of my army buddies graduated from Colonel White ten years after me. It's definitely a small world. Do you go home often, ma'am?"

"No, not really. My best friend growing up in Dayton was Emma Showalter. By the way, she's also currently a teacher at Colonel White. Well, she and I still try to visit here in Franklin or there in Dayton at least every five years. Like you, Andrew, I'm an only child, too, and my parents are also deceased. My home is now Franklin, Kentucky," she smiled, lovingly placing her hand over Christopher's hand. "My children were all born and raised here."

"Emma Showalter ... hmmm, she was my history and geography teacher. Again, what a small world, ma'am."

The food arrived, and Sergeant McConnaughey eagerly dug in. "Wow, you were right. This *is* excellent! I'm going to have to thank my buddy for suggesting Christmas Hotel. I'm also going to need to be careful or I'll gain twenty pounds while I'm here. Where do you recommend I jog or take a daily morning walk?"

Carrie Emeline piped up this time. "A lot of people take a brisk walk several times around the town's square early in the morning before the businesses open. I do when I'm home. Or you'll catch people running around Greenlawn Cemetery."

"Well, Miss Carrie Emeline, how about meeting me around five thirty tomorrow morning before breakfast? We can go for a sprint or a brisk walk. I'd like to see the town, too."

"Okay. I'll meet you in the lobby at five thirty tomorrow morning, Andrew." She caught the satisfied smile shared between her parents.

Chapter Four

Destiny

"Beloved, let us love one another: for love is of God; and every one that loveth is born of God, and knoweth God."

1 John 4:7

The Past

Early Tuesday Morning
December 17, 1968

Andrew waited at the front desk chatting with Chris when Carrie Emeline arrived in her ski jacket, winter sweats, knit hat, and mittens. She overheard the last of their conversation.

"I come in and work the front desk every morning for a couple of hours before school and a couple of hours after school," explained Chris. "During Christmas vacation, Easter vacation, and summer vacation, I work at least one full shift each day. I enjoy being at Christmas Hotel all year around."

Carrie Emeline added, "Chris will take over the management of Christmas Hotel someday.

Christmas Hotel could not have a better person to carry on its legacy." She kissed her brother on the cheek.

Chris's cheeks reddened. "Thanks, sis." Turning to Andrew, she asked, "Are you ready for the jogging tour of the town?"

"I certainly am." He offered his arm, and Carrie Emeline linked her arm around his as he opened the heavy front door.

"See you later, little brother," she called over her shoulder.

"Have fun," was his only verbal response, but the huge grin on Chris's face revealed more.

"You know we're missing that great Christmas Hotel breakfast you told me about," Andrew said as he waggled his eyebrows at her.

"I figured since we were going to walk and jog, we'll lose enough calories that I can introduce you to Kwality Bakery on West Cedar Street. You're going to love their donuts and hot chocolate."

"I'll leave my health and appetite in your fair hands, Carrie Emeline."

"Are you always such a flirt?"

"Only with lovely maidens such as you," he bantered back, displaying the inevitable crooked grin.

Shaking her head, she released his arm and jogged away with him following. They ran side by side around the square and then jogged down East Cedar Street before crossing the railroad tracks. Turning on Scotland Avenue, they came upon Greenlawn Cemetery.

Carrie Emeline didn't stop, and changed her gait into a run. "We're going to run *through* the cemetery?" asked Andrew, a bit surprised.

"It's perfect, with all the trails. You'll love it."

They came upon a tall obelisk with the name Thomas Hoy on one side and Lucy Goodnight Hoy on the other. Running in place, Carrie Emeline pointed toward the monument. "Thomas and Lucy Hoy are the two who built Christmas Hotel back in 1850. They were a prominent couple here in Franklin. They sold it to a Civil War captain and his wife: Captain Jacob Barnabas Bazell and Mary Eve Winters Bazell. There are their two graves," and she pointed at the headstones. "They died on the same day in nineteen forty-two, shortly after my twin Ken and I were born. Their daughter's grave is beside them."

"*Her* name is Carrie Emeline? She died a long time ago," he remarked, with a perplexed expression.

"Yes, I was named for her. My mother called her a sister from another century. That's an amazing story, which I'll have to tell you another day. I'm beginning to get winded ... and cold."

"You want to stop and rest?"

"Let's head over to Kwality Bakery. We can get our donuts and hot chocolate and sit on a bench inside the town's square. How about slowing to a brisk walk?"

The owner boxed up their donuts, offered plenty of napkins, and handed them their hot chocolates. They settled on the first bench inside the square. A light snow began to fall, adding to what was already on the ground.

"So, you said at dinner last night that you were born and raised in my mom's hometown. Did you join the army right after you graduated high school in '58?" She took a bite of her donut.

Andrew swallowed his bite before speaking. "I signed up during my senior year of high school, as soon as I turned eighteen. My parents were both then sixty, but I had their blessing. I hail from an air force town. You've probably heard of Wright Patterson Air Force Base, named for Orville and Wilbur Wright." He paused while she nodded, "I had always wanted to be in the army. I knew I'd enjoy the ground rather than the sky or the sea. I like the great outdoors, and I don't like confinement. I tried to imagine life on a plane or a ship." He shook his head. "That wasn't for me."

"Are you in for life?"

He presented her with that crooked grin that was now becoming quite charming. "Why do you ask, Miss Carrie Emeline? Do I look old to you?"

She blushed and stammered, "Uh ... no. I ... was just curious."

"You already know that I graduated high school in 1958. I promise I spent the normal twelve years in school, and I didn't fail a grade or two." He touched his short hair. "I realize I do have a few silver hairs in here. I assure you it's not from old age. I'm twenty-eight. How old are *you*, Miss Carrie Emeline?"

"You're not supposed to ask a lady her age," she reprimanded holding her chin in the air. "However, I'm twenty-six, if you *must* know."

He grinned. "So, you're an old maid?"

"I *am not* an old maid!" she countered. "It's 1968, and women no longer *must* get married right out of high school. We're allowed to go to college and have careers." She felt a bit miffed, but she also knew she liked him.

"Have you ever had a steady beau?"

She looked at him strangely. "A steady beau? In what century were you born?" She had to chuckle.

"I like poetry, too. Does that make me weird to you, or just archaic?" This time his tone was sober.

"No. Actually, I like that in a man. It shows a sentimental side. Of course, you know I'm going to ask you to recite something now."

He thought a moment, drank the last drop of his hot chocolate, set down his empty cup, and stood. In a melodramatic voice he began. "'Under a spreading chestnut-tree,'" he gestured with his arms wide. "'The village smithy stands;

The smith, a mighty man is he,

With large and sinewy hands;

And the muscles of his brawny arms

Are strong as iron bands.'"

He felt the muscles in each arm and she laughed.

"'His hair is crisp, and black, and long.'" He grabbed his head. "Huh? What happened to my short blond hair with the silver streaks?"

Carrie Emeline was now laughing so hard that people stopped and stared. She grabbed the hem of his coat and pulled him back onto the bench.

"Wassa madda, lady?" he teased.

"Did anyone ever tell you that you're nuts?"

"Just you ... and everyone that knows me. I forgot the rest of the poem, though. I haven't recited it since Mrs. Strang's fifth grade English class. I guess I didn't commit 'The Village Blacksmith' to one of my life-time memories. You know it's now your turn." He then finished off the last bite of his donut.

She looked at him with one raised eyebrow. "What makes you think I like poetry?"

"Well, you're a teacher, you're gentle, and you're pretty."

She bowed her head. "You're making me blush again."

"It's becoming on you. That's how I knew you were gentle."

"Well ... a little-known poem by an English poet is one of my favorites. It's titled 'Destiny' by Edwin Arnold.

"'Somewhere there waiteth in this world of ours,'" she began, and he joined in and recited with her.

"'For one lone soul another lonely soul.'"

She stared at him in surprise as he continued to recite with her.

"'Each chasing each through all the weary hours,
And meeting strangely at one sudden goal;
Then blend they — like green leaves with golden flowers,
Into one beautiful and perfect whole —
And life's long night is ended, and the way
Lies open onward to eternal day.'"

For a moment they just stared at each other in silence. Carrie Emeline was the first to speak. "I can't believe you know that poem, too," she said softly.

"It was one of my parents' favorite poems. They recited it to each other on their wedding day. On every anniversary they played an album of the most famous waltzes of Johann Strauss, and together they danced the waltz in our parlor and recited this poem."

"That's a beautiful memory you have of your parents."

"Yes, I was one of the kids that got blessed with wonderful parents."

"I was, too," she murmured. "I thank God for my parents. They have been my rock many times in my life."

He jumped up so quickly that Carrie Emeline at first felt she had said something wrong. He tapped her shoulder and took off running.

"Tag, you're it!" he yelled back over his shoulder.

She grabbed their garbage, tossed it in the trash can, and ran after him. "I'll catch you in the next block," she yelled.

"Yeah, right!" He threw back his head and roared with laughter.

Chapter Five

Dating and Beaus

*"This is the day which the LORD hath made; we
will rejoice and be glad in it."*
Psalm 118:24

The Past
Six o'clock, Tuesday Evening
December 17, 1968
Carrie Emeline was sorry she hadn't invited
Andrew to dinner at her parents' home following
their morning jog. She listened to the idle chit-
chat from Chris and her parents as she picked at
the food on her plate.

"I heard from Lily today," Christopher
announced with a huge smile on his face. "She
and John will be coming with the children for
Christmas Eve. They promised to stay a couple of
days."

Jerilyn nodded her head. "I heard from both
Ken and Lydia Grace who also called today. They
will be home on, too; Ken on Christmas Eve and
Lydia Grace this Friday or Saturday It's always

wonderful having the whole family together."

Carrie Emeline felt the light tap on her hand. She looked up and everyone was staring at her. "Are you okay, honey?" asked Jerilyn. "Are you coming down with something? You're so quiet tonight."

"She's okay, Mom," grinned Chris. "She's just all starry-eyed over Andrew. She's been that way since their date this morning."

"It wasn't a date, little brother," she gave him the narrowed-eyes look. "We just went jogging this morning."

"Oh, really? Andrew came back to Christmas Hotel and told me that you two had donuts and hot chocolate. Sounds like a breakfast date to me," he said with pursed lips, brows raised, and his eyes round as the full-moon.

"Chris, you can be exasperating at times. It *wasn't* a date."

"I think the lady doth protest too much," Chris replied impishly with his best cheesy grin.

"Sometimes, you can be a brat, you know." Carrie Emeline said it with a wink, but she quickly changed the subject. She glanced into the parlor at the decorated Christmas tree. "It looks as though you went early this year to the McLemore Farm for the Christmas tree." She felt somewhat disappointed. Cutting down and decorating the tree had always been a family event. However, since she moved to Louisville, she now missed out on many of the special, family events.

"We did, sweetheart," her dad admitted. "With four of our children coming home at different times, your mother and I decided to change our plans this year.

"With only Chris at home now, we chose to revert back to the first Saturday after Thanksgiving. I hope you're not terribly disappointed."

Carrie Emeline smiled at her dad, allowing the wave of nostalgia washing over her to subside. The change made sense, after all. While she, Lily and Ken all still lived in Kentucky, they were scattered about the state — her in Louisville, her sister in Russellville, and Ken in Lexington. Her sister Lydia Grace, a college student, now lived all the way up in Cincinnati, Ohio.

She smiled at her dad. She could never be upset with him. "No, Daddy, I understand. Sometimes change is hard. I love my life in Louisville. I have wonderful students and friends, but I guess I miss the family life."

He reached over and patted her hand. "That's part of growing up, honey. Someday you'll be a wife and mother, and change will come again."

Carrie Emeline looked around at the empty plates of the others, and rose. "If everyone is finished eating, I'll clear the table."

Jerilyn stood, too. "I'll help. Some Christmas music would be nice," and she winked at Christopher.

"Is that my cue to put on a stack of records, or go sit at the piano and play?"

"Whatever you prefer, my dear."

Carrie Emeline smiled at the love her parents clearly demonstrated toward each other. *Maybe someday I'll experience that, too.*

Carrie Emeline gently pushed her mom into the living room. "You go and sing with Daddy. I'll clean up in the kitchen."

When she finished in the kitchen and entered the living room, her dad still played Christmas hymns at the piano, and her mom and brother were singing along.

She stood and watched them sing one hymn before her dad looked in her direction. "Come join us, honey."

"Thanks, Dad, but I think I'll take a walk around the square and walk off some of Mom's wonderful dinner."

Chris looked at her as if she'd grown two heads. "You didn't even eat all your dinner. What do you need to walk off?"

"Well, if you must know, little brother, I enjoy being home and walking around the square. It's so beautiful when it's all decorated at Christmastime. Would you like to walk with me?"

"Nah, 'The Virginian' will be coming on television, and I always watch it with Dad."

"Well, I can't have you missing 'The Virginian' with Dad. What a shame that would be," she said, while playfully tousling his hair. "All kidding aside, I love the fact that you two have special things to do together. Mom and I have always enjoyed shopping together."

Jerilyn walked up to her and hugged her. "Let's go shopping together on Saturday, Carrie Emeline. I haven't finished my Christmas shopping, and if I know my daughter, neither have you. Lydia Grace will be home and will probably want to go, too."

"Sounds like a plan, Mom."

Once Carrie Emeline was out the door, she looked up and down South College Street at the beautiful historic homes all decorated with sparkling lights. She hurried down the few steps and turned back to her home and stared. Everything was just as it was supposed to be. The tree twinkled in the living room. The balcony above the front door was richly decorated, and the columns were wrapped in holly and lights.

Above the 210 for the address, the Wright Family plaque was in its place. *Familiarity is what it is. I like the fact that home is familiar and comfortable. It's where I can always go to love and be loved.*

She strolled down South College Street toward the square where young couples held hands, and parents with children milled around. At the corner, she continued across West Cedar Street to North College Street, stopping in front of the Methodist church. The yard was brightly lit with flood lights displaying the Nativity Scene. She looked down at the Baby Jesus and bowed her head. *I'm lonely, Jesus.* One tear escaped, and she wiped it away. *I can't believe I admitted that, but it's true.*

After a moment, she raised her head and continued to walk. Next, she stopped in front of the Franklin Flower Shop. As usual, they had a beautiful window display of table arrangements, wreaths, and mantel ornaments.

After crossing onto West Kentucky Street, she paused in front of Frank Shannon Jeweler. Necklaces, rings, bracelets, and watches were surrounded by blinking window lights and boughs of holly.

"See anything you like?" The booming male voice surprised her so much she jumped back into the voice's body.

"Oh, Andrew!" she said, when she turned around and saw the face belonging to the voice and body. "You startled me!"

"I see that. Do you always walk at night all alone?"

"I'm not really alone. I'm at home. Look at all the people appreciating the Christmas decorations and getting ideas for Christmas gifts."

"You didn't answer my first question."

"What was that? I forgot, because you scared me to death."

He chuckled. "You look quite normal to me now. The color's returned to your cheeks. You were inspecting this jewelry store window ever so carefully. I asked if you saw anything you liked."

"Well ... I'm female ... of course I see things I like."

With a soft whistle, he looked her up and down. "Yes, I do believe you're a female." Once again he presented her with his crooked grin and waggled his eyebrows.

"Oh, stop teasing me. Of course I like jewelry. What woman doesn't?"

"If you could buy anything in this window, what would it be?"

She turned back to the jewelry on display. "That's really hard. Everything is beautiful."

"In what month were you born?"

"May."

"That's an emerald ... right?"

"Why, yes, it is. Do you know someone born in May?"

"Yes, my mom. She had a beautiful emerald and diamond ring. My dad was born in April, and diamond is the birthstone for April. He gave it to her as an engagement ring and said, 'We're now forever joined.'"

"Aw ... that's so sweet. My mom's engagement ring was a sapphire and diamond. She and my dad really couldn't afford rings when they married, so Mr. and Mrs. Bazell, who previously owned Christmas Hotel, gave them their rings. Mom and Dad still wear those rings. They're older than the Civil War. The rings, not my parents."

"The gems are even older than that."

She thought about that and then laughed. "Okay, technicalities! I get it; the gems are probably as old as planet Earth. Let me rephrase my previous statement. The gems were mounted on the ring before the Civil War. Are you always such a stickler for detail?"

"No, not really. I just like joshing you. You're a good sport."

She smiled up at him. "Would you like to walk around the square with me? I love this time of year."

"I do, too, and I would be honored to walk with you, my lady," he said in a thick British accent, and bent his body into a mock bow. Another couple walking by smiled.

"Okay, Andrew, straighten up. We're being watched."

"Are you too pretty to be looked at?" he jested.

"I just embarrass easily. I don't consider myself pretty."

"You've got to be kidding me. You're not just pretty, you're beautiful! I think you haven't been told that often enough. I suppose you just haven't had the right beau."

"There you go again with the archaic speech. Also, I had a *beau* in high school."

"Only *one* beau?"

"Yes," she answered warily. "Is there something wrong with that?"

"I'm just surprised, is all."

"I'm picky."

They continued down the block and rounded the corner to North Main Street.

"I hope you're not too picky to look at *me* as a beau."

She stopped and stared up at him. "I hardly know you. You're going to be gone soon, anyway."

He took her hand. "Maybe you just talk too

much. Maybe you don't give a guy enough of a chance to court you properly."

She looked down at her small hand in his and tilted her head back up at him. "Okay, if I gave you a chance to court me properly, how would you court me?"

"Well, I'd continue to beat you at walking, running, or jogging every morning."

She smacked his arm with her free hand. "We'll see about that tomorrow, Mister."

"See, I've already wheedled a date with you in the morning. That was easy."

She laughed, and was pleased with the easy banter. "Okay, go on and tell me more."

"I'd have dinner with you every night, and we'd walk after dinner. I'd go to church with you every Sunday."

That really got her attention. "Are you a Christian, Andrew?"

"Yes. I accepted Jesus Christ as my Lord and Savior when I was twelve years old."

"I was ten."

"Maybe that's why you're picky about your beaus, Carrie Emeline."

"You're probably right. I haven't found the right man at the right age that's a Christian."

"I went straight from high school into the army. I haven't met any Christian woman my age and unmarried, while I've been in the army ... until now."

She didn't respond to what he implied, and they kept walking until they were in front of Christmas Hotel.

"What was it like growing up at Christmas Hotel?"

"You've just asked a question that will take a lot of conversations to answer."

"Good. I hope to have a lot of conversations with you."

"Let's suffice it for now to say that it was amazing. Please continue the courting conversation."

He grinned. "You have no problem getting to the point, do you?"

She grinned back and tilted her head in a coquettish manner.

He laughed. "Well, with all those dinners we'll need plenty of exercise. I love to ice skate. Do you ice skate?"

"Yes, I do! There aren't any great ice skating rinks in Franklin. We usually go out to the McLemore farm. They have three ponds that are solid enough in the winter, as long as the temperature has been below freezing for a few weeks. So far this month it's been cold enough. How about jogging in the morning and skating after lunch tomorrow?"

"See, I just coaxed another date, without even trying. This is fun, Carrie Emeline. Let me hurry up and walk you home, so tomorrow can come faster."

She shook her head and grinned. They walked slowly, holding hands on the walk home.

Chapter Six

Secrets

*"Shall not God search this out? for he knoweth
the secrets of the heart."*
Psalm 44:21

The Present Day
Monday
December 02, 1974

Carrie Emeline drove the few miles to the truck stop, the divorce papers very much on her mind. It was cold, and as she closed the car door she wrapped the scarf tighter around her neck and ran to the front door of the diner. The tables were all full when she stepped in, but she spied one lone stool at the counter. She hung up her coat and scarf on a wall hook, and stuffed her knit hat and gloves in the pockets. Hurrying to the stool, she bumped into a waitress.

"Sorry," she apologized. As soon as she sat down, a menu was placed in front of her and a glass of water.

"Can I get you a cup of coffee, honey?" asked the waitress with a genuine smile.

"Yes, please." She rubbed her hands together for warmth. After studying the menu, she was ready when the waitress returned. "I'll have link sausage, two eggs over medium and whole wheat toast with butter and strawberry jelly, please." *I'll probably not be able to eat all that, but it sounds good.*

"Coming right up, Miss." The waitress whirled around, placed the order on a clip hung from a metal wheel in the pass-through window to the kitchen, and spun the wheel. "*Order in!*" she yelled.

While awaiting her food, Carrie Emeline checked out the Christmas decorations. Five stockings aligned one wall behind the counter with the names of the waitresses who worked there. The stockings bulged with extra Christmas tips. A small Christmas tree sat on the counter beside the cash register, decorated with tiny twinkling lights and brightly colored red, green, and gold bulbs. The laughing, happy patrons appeared in high spirits. She saw people she knew, but she didn't feel like talking so she kept her head down. *Coming here was a bad idea. If the people who know me see me, they're going to ask about my family.*

Her food arrived, and she quickly ate, finishing most of what was on her plate. Laying a dollar on the counter for a tip, she paid the check at the cash register. While putting on her coat, she heard her name and turned. It was Sadie Isenhower.

Sadie walked up and hugged her. "Hi, Carrie Emeline. It's good to see you! Larry and our daughters are here, too." She pointed to the corner table, from where Larry and the two girls waved. "Would you like to join us?"

"Well, I was just leaving. Can I get a rain check?"

"Of course. We're in town visiting my parents for a couple of days. Maybe you and hubby can get together with Larry and me for dinner one night — *sans* kids."

"I'll call you. I'm sorry, but I have to go." With that said, she hurried out into the cold. She didn't even take the time to button her coat and put on her scarf, hat, and gloves. She just rushed away to the safety of her car, where she slid behind the wheel, put her head down and cried. *Dear Jesus, that was so rude. How do I tell all my happy friends that I'm about to be divorced? I haven't even told my children, let alone my parents and siblings. How do I have a merry Christmas this year and put on a happy face? Help me, Jesus. I need You.*

When she reentered Christmas Hotel, her brother Chris was the manager on duty, but he was busy checking in guests and didn't see her. She hurried up the staircase and unlocked the door to her room. She turned in time to see a young couple entering their room. It was Chris's idea for the past seven Christmases, that during the Christmas season, mistletoe would be hung above each doorway. A young man spotted it and kissed his wife.

Carrie Emeline opened her door and threw her keys on the desk. She lay curled up on the bed without removing her coat. Tears freely flowed down her face. In the dark she cried out to the Lord. "Dear, Lord, help me, please." A wonderful memory of Andrew and mistletoe crossed her mind, and she wiped her tears and smiled.

Chapter Seven

Mistletoe and Ice Skating

*"Many waters cannot quench love, neither can
the floods drown it:"*
Song of Solomon 8:7

The Past
Wednesday
December 18, 1968
Carrie Emeline arrived at Christmas Hotel at six o'clock to meet Andrew for breakfast. "Are we still going jogging this morning, Carrie Emeline?" he asked.

"Yes, and after we have our morning jog, I'll drive us to the McLemore Farm for some ice skating, since you coaxed that extra date from me last night. Do you have skates?"

"I do, but I didn't bring them with me. They're on base in Germany. A bit too far to jog over and fetch. There's no bridge over that pond, either."

"You're goofy." She shook her head and added a soft jab in his ribcage with her elbow. "What size shoe do you wear?"

"Twelve D."

"My dad and Chris both wear that size. I'll see who's able to loan their skates. We'll check first with Chris. He's at the front desk again this morning."

Chris was providing information to a young couple. Carrie Emeline waited patiently with Andrew for Chris to finish and then stepped up to the desk. "Andrew and I are going skating at the McLemore Farm later today, and he needs a pair of skates. Andrew wears the same size as you. Would you mind if he borrowed yours?"

"Not at all. They're down in the basement at home hanging on my wall hook near yours. Enjoy!"

Andrew nodded to him. "I appreciate it, Chris. I promise to take good care of them, and I won't return them dirty. Let me know if I can return a favor."

"Don't mention it, Andrew. Have a good time!"

After the jog, they walked to Carrie Emeline's home. Andrew stood out front. "Beautiful home, Carrie Emeline. I couldn't see it well last night. It's Italianate ... correct?"

She watched as he checked out the Christmas tree in the window, and then the balcony. "That's correct. It was built in 1860 by William Clement

Montague. He was another prominent citizen from Franklin. Later, my grandparents bought the home when they married. My dad inherited it when his parents were killed in a car accident. He's lived here all his life. I did too, until I went to college. It's still home for me, though. Come on in. Mom and Dad are probably home."

As soon as they entered, Gabe lifted his old, tired bones from the hearth and staggered towards them.

"Wow, big dog," murmured Andrew, barely audible.

"He's friendly. Gabe is my younger sister Lydia Grace's dog. Lydia Grace will be home later this week from the University of Cincinnati. She's studying for her masters in music composition. She's the best pianist, and along with several other instruments, you've ever heard. She's also learning Greek, Russian, and taking a creative writing class. She already speaks fluent French and Spanish. One never knows what that girl will do next!"

Andrew's eyes widened. "She sounds like an extremely well-rounded individual."

"She is. She's quite extraordinary. Everyone loves her." Carrie Emeline knelt down and petted Gabe, and Andrew did the same as her mom joined them from the kitchen.

"Hi, Mom. We're getting my skates and Chris's, and heading out to the McLemore Farm."

"Please tell Booker, Sue, and Robert to join us for Christmas Eve service in the chapel," Mom said while wiping her hands on a dish towel.

"Will do, Mom."

They entered the garage, and Andrew stopped and whistled. "Nice car." Andrew ran his hand over the hood of Carrie Emeline's 1967 red Camaro. "Sleek and definitely a beauty."

She chuckled. "I bought it new last year, but it belongs more to the bank than me."

"Hmmm. Nice gift to yourself."

Traveling the twelve miles into the country was a pleasant drive; and although cold, the sun was shining. However, the weather abruptly changed when they reached their destination. The sky clouded over, and a light snow began to fall as Carrie Emeline pulled into the driveway and stopped. Two hound dogs ran toward them, barking loudly. Carrie Emeline turned to Andrew. "Don't worry, they're very sweet dogs. She stepped out of the car and called to them. "Jake, Bob, it's me." The hounds calmed down and accepted the pats on the head from Carrie Emeline and Andrew.

Mrs. McLemore walked out on the porch to greet her, shivering in only her house dress.

"Come into the house and get warm."

After introducing Andrew, Carrie Emeline asked, "Do you mind if we skate on the pond closest to the house? It's my favorite."

"Not at all. Would you like some hot chocolate first?"

"Thank you for offering, but maybe later. Would that be okay?"

"That's fine. Just come up to the house when you're ready. How are your parents?"

"Wonderful. Mom told me to remind you about the Christmas Eve service in the chapel."

"Tell her Booker, Robert, and I will be there with bells on. Have fun!"

Carrie Emeline and Andrew walked back to the car, opened the trunk, and slung their skates over their shoulders. At the pond they sat on a huge rock to remove their boots and put on the skates.

"By the way, this is also the rock everyone uses in the summer to sit on and fish. Too bad you won't be here in the summer. It's beautiful on the farm. All those trees are leafed out, and Mrs. McLemore has many flowers, around the house and along the driveway, and all in bloom. The cows will be out of the barn during the day, and grazing in that field," She pointed toward the lower field near the road. "Mr. McLemore will have several fields growing his crops on this side of the road and their other farm across the road. Mrs. McLemore's mother, Mama Harris, will be tending her little vegetable garden." She looked over at Andrew. "Have you ever experienced a working farm during the summer?"

"No, but I always wanted to live on a farm. Growing up, I wanted a horse." He laughed. "If I'd grown up in Kentucky horse country instead of an Ohio city, I may have been able to experience that dream. Maybe I'll do that when I retire from the army." He finished lacing his skates and leaned back, his hands behind him on the rock. "This is the life."

"I agree." She finished lacing her skates and stood. "Ready?"

He stood beside her. "Ready as I'll ever be."

They glided around the pond, doing their best to miss the uneven spots. Andrew was the first to hit a bump and fall. Carrie Emeline laughed as she helped pull him back onto his feet. Of course he hooted with laughter when *she* fell, and he picked her up off the ice.

She rubbed her backside, sticking her tongue out at him.

He drew closer to her and took her hand for a trip around the pond. "I hear a Strauss waltz in my head. Can you hear it?"

"Hear the waltz?"

He hummed the music in her ear, and they glided around the pond, carefully missing the uneven spots. After a while, he broke apart from her and headed toward a low hanging tree branch just slightly above his head. From a short distance, Carrie Emeline watched as he did something to the branch. A moment late, he asked her to skate toward him. "Look up, Carrie Emeline."

Hanging over their heads, mistletoe dangled from the branch. He drew her close and searched her face and eyes. With one gloved hand, he caressed her cheek, and she tilted her head into his hand. "I'm enchanted with you, Carrie Emeline. You are the woman I've been waiting for. May I kiss you?"

This time he sounded serious, with no impish crooked grin. She didn't answer, but reached up to him and brought his mouth down to hers. They drew apart and stared at each other with no words, and then they kissed again.

Finally, they broke apart. Carrie Emeline smiled. "Enchanted? You are definitely from another century, Andrew. But I rather like it. You certainly don't follow the crowd."

"No, I don't, my dear."

"By the way, that mistletoe hasn't been

hanging there all by itself. You put it there," and she winked at him.

The crooked grin slowly formed and he waggled his eyebrows. "Guilty as charged. Are you going to report me to your father?"

She laughed and cuddled in his arms. "Only if you report me for liking the kiss. Where and when did you get the mistletoe?"

"Chris placed it above all the doorways at Christmas Hotel. I stole mine."

"I love my little brother. He's going to make a great manager for Christmas Hotel when the time comes."

"I couldn't agree more," and he kissed her again.

Chapter Eight

Intentions

"Therefore my heart is glad, and my glory rejoiceth: my flesh also shall rest in hope."
Psalm 16:9

The Past

Friday morning
December 20, 1968

Carrie Emeline and Andrew had been nearly inseparable all week. She awakened at her South College Street home to the merriment of family already downstairs. Her younger sister, Lydia Grace, had arrived from Cincinnati.

"I missed my family and came home as soon as I finished my last assignment for the year and drove all night," she called up to Carrie Emeline who was still in her nightgown, leaning over the banister to see the reason for the excitement below.

Carrie Emeline dressed, then joined her family. Chris had traded shifts with Mr. Mullins, the assistant manager at Christmas Hotel, to spend the morning with his parents and his two sisters. Everyone was dressed and in the kitchen cooking breakfast when Carrie Emeline joined the family.

"Hi there, sleepy head," Lydia Grace said, with obvious affection toward her older sister.

"Aw, don't pick on her too much," said Chris. "She's spent the whole week entertaining her new boyfriend, and she's probably tired."

Carrie Emeline blushed, but quickly recovered and punched his arm in fondness. "You're just jealous because you don't have a girlfriend."

Chris hugged her. "I'm happy for you, sis. Andrew seems like a great guy."

"He is."

"You two have been spending a great deal of time together," said her dad. "Maybe it's time for me to ask his intentions."

She frowned. "Daddy, that's so old-fashioned."

"Not to your mother and me, honey. We want to make sure that he's having honorable thoughts towards you."

"Well, on second thought, maybe you should have that talk with him. Andrew is a bit old-fashioned, too. Can you believe he likes poetry, and he can dance a waltz?"

Jerilyn placed her arm around Carrie

Emeline. "Your father likes poetry *and* can dance a waltz. It sounds like he'll fit right in with this family ... that is if it comes to a future with him for you. Why don't you invite him to dinner tonight and to church on Sunday?"

"I'll do that."

*****

After eating breakfast in the dining room, and then going for a quick jog, Andrew returned to his room for a shower and to spend time in devotions. He sat in front of the window reading his Bible and praying. "Dear Heavenly Father, I have feelings for Carrie Emeline, and I think she has feelings for me. In fact, I love her. I need to know in my heart if she's the one You have chosen for me. Help me know for sure."

Several hours later his phone rang and he stood to answer it. He smiled, and his heart jumped. Carrie Emeline was calling. "What are you doing?" she asked.

"Just waiting to hear from you. Are you having a nice visit with your sister?"

"Yes. Look, if you don't have plans, my parents have invited you to dinner tonight at our home, and to church on Sunday."

He didn't say anything for several seconds.

"Andrew, it's okay if you're busy. I'll understand."

He heard the hurt in her voice. "It's not that, Carrie Emeline. I'd enjoy spending time with your family, and I really want to go to church with you, as I've said, but I don't want to intrude either, with Christmas coming up and all."

"Andrew, you wouldn't be intruding. At our house, Christmas isn't just family. It's for friends, too."

"If that's the case, I'd be honored to have dinner with your family tonight."

"Dinner is at six o'clock."

"I'll be there."

With that settled, Andrew left his room and went outside into the cold air. Stopping by the Franklin Flower Shop on North College Street, he chose flowers for Carrie Emeline's mother. In his joggings around the square he had memorized all the businesses — except when he was with Carrie Emeline. When he was with her he didn't always think clearly, his heart raced, and it wasn't from jogging.

Promptly at six o'clock he arrived at the Wright home. Carrie Emeline opened the door to his knock, and eyed the flowers. "For me?" she inquired.

"Sorry to dash your hopes. They're for your mother. After all, she invited me."

"Okay. I can't be jealous of my mom." Then

she laughed, "However, my *dad* might be jealous of you. You *are* a flirt, you know."

"I flirt only with you, my lady."

"Ahem," interrupted Chris. "Sorry to intrude on your *argument*, but I just wanted to welcome Andrew."

The two shook hands and then Lydia Grace entered. Carrie Emeline turned to Andrew. "I'd like you to meet my younger sister Lydia Grace, the University of Cincinnati scholar I told you about. Lydia Grace, this is my ... a ... friend, Andrew."

He could tell Carrie Emeline was nervous on how to introduce him and took that as a good sign.

Lydia Grace shook his offered hand. "It's nice to meet you, Andrew, and welcome to our home."

"It's my pleasure to meet you, too, Lydia Grace. Carrie Emeline speaks highly of you."

"I think the world of Carrie Emeline, too."

Jerilyn and Christopher entered from the kitchen, with Jerilyn wiping her hands on a towel and then stuffing it into her apron pocket. "Thank you so much for coming, Andrew." She hugged him, and Christopher echoed her greeting and shook Andrew's hand.

"These flowers are for you, Mrs. Wright."

"Why, thank you, Andrew."

"You're welcome, Mrs. Wright."

It was Christopher's turn to welcome Andrew. "Andrew, I'm proud to have you in our home, and let me say again, thank you for your service to our country. We need more young men like you to volunteer to serve. We wouldn't need a draft if they did."

"Thank you, sir."

Jerilyn held up the bouquet. "I'm going to put these flowers in water. Dinner is in fifteen minutes. I hope you like roast beef, Andrew."

"I love roast beef, Mrs. Wright."

The sisters helped their mother arrange the food on the table that Carrie Emeline had set earlier with the best tablecloth, matching napkins, both linens embroidered with a "W" in each corner, china, matching crystal, with the Wright family crest embossed on both, silverware, and silver candlesticks. A Christmas poinsettia arrangement graced the table as the centerpiece. Jerilyn called the men to the table. Carrie Emeline seated Andrew beside her and Christopher asked everyone to hold hands while he asked the blessing.

"Dear Heavenly Father, we thank Thee for the food Thou hast provided for the nourishment of our bodies. I thank Thee that Lydia Grace made it safely home from Cincinnati, and I thank Thee for our special guest, Sergeant Andrew McConnaughey. It's a special pleasure having another fellow army man at our table. I thank Thee for our daughter Carrie Emeline who made the trip home again this Christmas. I thank Thee for our son Chris, who continues to astound us with his abilities in learning the art of management at Christmas Hotel. We pray this in the name of Thy Son Jesus Christ our Savior, amen."

The others softly added their amens.

Following the meal, the family discreetly retreated to the kitchen while Christopher asked Andrew to join him in the living room for a cup of coffee.

Andrew looked around the lovely room. A highly polished grand piano filled one corner, and the beautifully decorated Christmas tree sat in front of the window. Gabe, the German Shepherd dog lay in front of the fireplace hearth. The old dog slowly raised his head and laid it down again with a deep sigh. Family photos were scattered on the piano, tables, and the walls. What a homey room, definitely suited to this warm, kind family, he thought.

After the two men were settled, Christopher didn't waste time in asking questions of Andrew. "You've been spending a great deal of time with my daughter. Although, I like you, Andrew, I must ask your intentions."

Andrew stared into Christopher's eyes and responded, "I appreciate your concern, sir. I also greatly respect your daughter, sir. She has already come to mean a great deal to me. I look forward to our time together. At this moment, I can't imagine our time together coming to an end. In fact, I don't want it to come to an end."

"So, are you going to attempt a long-distance romance through letters?"

"No, sir. I wouldn't put her through that." Andrew continued to look Christopher square in the eyes. "With your permission, sir, I am going to ask Carrie Emeline to marry me and meet me in Germany. I know it's sudden, but I love her. I think she loves me, too."

Christopher returned Andrew's gaze. "Yes, it *is* sudden, but ... yes, I understand. The same thing happened to me when I met my lovely wife Jerilyn. I knew within a few days that I loved her. Are you a Christian, Andrew? I don't want my daughter unequally yoked."

"I'm a devoted Christian, sir. I was saved as a twelve-year-old in a Bible-believing Christian church in Dayton. I know I've been born again."

"Well then, Andrew, if my daughter wants to marry you, you will both have my blessing. I want only happiness for my children."

"I wish I could guarantee her nothing but happiness, but I *am* in the United States Army. I will make sure she knows the possibilities ... if she says yes to me."

"When will you ask her?"

"I intend to go to church with her and your family on Sunday, and I'm definitely going to continue to pray about this decision. If I feel it's the Lord's direction, I'll escort Carrie Emeline to dinner Monday evening and ask her."

"You're a wise man asking the Lord's council. If it's the Lord's will, God bless your union with my daughter."

One by one everyone entered the living room from the kitchen. Jerilyn glanced at Christopher and he nodded in the affirmative. Andrew smiled. He knew his conversation with Carrie Emeline's dad must have gone well.

"How about some Christmas songs, Lydia Grace?" asked Carrie Emeline. "I want Andrew to know I wasn't kidding when I told him you were an amazing pianist."

Lydia Grace settled at the piano bench. "Okay, you pick first, Carrie Emeline."

"Let's have Andrew pick first," said Carrie Emeline, as she sat down beside Andrew.

"Okay, I choose 'It Came upon a Midnight

Clear.' That's always been one of my favorite Christmas hymns."

"Good choice," said Lydia Grace as she thumbed through the hymnal. Soon she began to play, and they all sang with gusto.

Andrew smiled as he watched the happy faces. He knew what he missed. A loving family.

Chapter Nine

Shopping In Nashville

"As for God, his way is perfect; the word of the LORD is tried: he is a buckler to all them that trust in him."
2 Samuel 22:31

The Past
Saturday
December 21, 1968
"Okay, girls, let's go shopping in Nashville." suggested Jerilyn. "If you two don't mind, I'd prefer to take the van, since you girls drive such small cars. There's a light snow coming down, and Interstate 65 may be a bit slick."

Carrie Emeline glanced outside to where the family's 1968 Ford Econoline Van sat parked at the curb. Her father bought it a year ago after her mother wrecked her small compact car while driving in a rain storm. Fortunately her mother wasn't hurt, but the little car was totaled. The accident scared her father more than anything. He bought her the larger vehicle for safety reasons.

Carrie Emeline chose to tease her mom a little. "So you don't like the idea of traveling in a sporty Camaro or a Corvair?" asked Carrie Emeline with a chuckle.

"To be honest and blunt with you ... no. I don't think either of your vehicles should be driven in the snow. "

Lydia Grace rolled her eyes and laughed. "Okay, Mom, we'll ride in your gigantic monstrosity of a van."

Carrie Emeline raised an eyebrow and nodded, "We can take the hint, Mom."

Since 1942, when Harveys Department Store first opened, her mother had made shopping there at Christmastime a family tradition. When Carrie Emeline was a child, she'd loved riding the carousel horses, and that was always included as part of the family outing. It was the first store she remembered having escalators and a "real" Santa Claus.

"What do you think about this pale blue shirt and royal blue sweater vest for your dad?" Mom asked as she held it up. She picked up a tie striped with both colors and held it in front of the shirt. "I like this tie, too."

"Perfect," the girls said in unison.

Lydia Grace turned to Carrie Emeline. "How

about you and I go in together for a new pair of pants for Dad to go with Mom's gift for him?"

"Sounds good to me. What should we get Chris?"

Mom was quick with a suggestion. "Your brother's been hinting for a particular book on photography. We can head over to the bookstore area and see if Harveys has it. That would be a good gift from you girls."

Carrie Emeline laid the sweater down she'd been considering for Chris. "Okay, Mom, and thanks for the suggestion. My budget isn't very big, so going in with Lydia Grace is perfect for this year. Do you agree, Lydia Grace?"

"Whew! Thank you! I didn't know how I was going to handle this Christmas. Our family is growing so large, that maybe next year we should just draw names. Carrie Emeline, Chris, and I now have five nieces and nephews, and who knows when more will arrive."

Mom draped the shirt, sweater, and tie over one arm that she would purchase for her husband. "That's a great idea, Lydia Grace. We can draw the names every Thanksgiving, beginning next year."

The women finished much of their shopping and headed to Harveys Luncheonette. After checking the menu and giving the order to the waitress, Jerilyn turned to Carrie Emeline. "What are you giving Andrew for Christmas?"

"That was to the point, Mom, and not very subtle. I think you're really asking, 'How serious are you and Andrew?' Am I correct?"

"Well ... now that you mention it—" she said, staring directly into her daughter's eyes.

"Now that you've cornered me, I really don't know." Carrie Emeline hung her head, took a deep breath, and blew it out. She then looked back up to face her mom. "I'm torn, because I haven't known him long. I know Andrew cares for me, but I don't know if he's *in love* with me. I *think* I'm in love with him, but I just can't be, not after barely a week. Is that possible?"

Mom smiled. "I'm probably the wrong person to ask. You know that I've told you about the love I had for your biological father. We were inseparable all through high school. I considered him my soulmate, and I sincerely believe he felt the same about me. Those first two years of our marriage, we didn't spend much time together though; he in the war and me at home. A military marriage can be lonely. I missed him dreadfully. However, I had loving parents, and the best friend a girl could have in Emma. They kept me company."

Mom paused for a moment of reflection.

Then, "When Kenneth was killed at Pearl Harbor, and I met Christopher, I began having feelings for Christopher soon after. I, too, wondered if that was possible — or even more so, was it morally right? I'd known Kenneth four years before we married. How could I possibly love two men in the same month? But I prayed about the situation and realized that God used Kenneth for my past, and my future was with Christopher, and of course I was pregnant with you and your brother. Through much prayer, both Christopher and I knew God brought us together. With Kenneth, our love was a young love. With Christopher, love has been a more mature love ... and a much deeper love than I could have imagined. Christopher is truly my soulmate. I was blessed to have had two men to love as soulmates."

She looked her daughter in the eye. "Carrie Emeline, you need to pray too, and trust in the Lord's perfect decision for you and Andrew. Andrew is a good Christian man. You'll know if your love is meant to be."

Carrie Emeline nodded. "Thanks, Mom. I promise I'll do that."

Mom looked out the window. "Oh my. It's really snowing hard, now. We need to finish eating and drive home before the roads get worse. We don't want your dad to worry."

Lydia Grace grinned, wiggled her eyebrows, and winked at her sister. "Right, Mom. After all, we wouldn't want Dad to think you wrecked another car!"

Mom just wrinkled her nose and shook her head at her spunky daughter.

Chapter Ten

Igloos, Snowmen, and Snowball Fights

*"He that handleth a matter wisely shall
find good: and whoso trusteth in the
LORD, happy is he."*
Proverbs 16:20

The Past
Sunday Morning
December 22, 1968
As previously planned, Andrew met the Wright
family at six o'clock in the Christmas Hotel dining
room Sunday morning for breakfast. He hadn't
packed a civilian Sunday suit, so his army dress
uniform would have to do. He had pressed it the
night before, and shined his shoes.

"You should try an omelet," suggested Carrie
Emeline. "The Christmas Hotel chefs only
prepare their amazing omelets on Saturdays,
Sundays, and holidays. You can have any
ingredients you like. 'Have it your way', as they
say. See how full the dining room is?"

Andrew scanned the room.

Carrie Emeline laughed. "These people are here for the omelets and a social get-together before church. We are always packed on these days. As you get to know the townspeople, you'll see many of them here." Carrie Emeline's eyes went from bright to dark.

She just realized I won't be here long enough to know the townspeople. He covered her hand with his. "I'll come back, Carrie Emeline. I do want to meet as many in your special town as I can."

She stared at him, swallowed, and smiled. "Thank you, Andrew."

While eating his South Western Omelet, all Andrew could say was "Wow", or "Wonderful", or "This is good," while the others chuckled. "How am I going to ever eat army food again? Christmas Hotel and the hospitality you've shown me at your home have spoiled me. I need to get on some scales to see how much weight I've gained." He patted his stomach. "This uniform is a little tight."

Carrie Emeline rolled her eyes. "I don't see that you've gained an ounce. You men have a much better metabolism than we women. I wouldn't worry, Andrew, and you'll work up a good sweat this afternoon. With all the falling snow, we're going to spend the afternoon at one of our favorite family traditions: building snowmen and igloos!" She glanced at Chris. "If I know my little brother, there might be a snowball fight thrown in there, too."

Chris laughed. "No might about it, sis!"

After breakfast, the group headed across the square to the First Methodist Church of Franklin. Outside the church stood the life-sized Nativity Scene that Andrew saw each morning on his jogs with Carrie Emeline. Laughing, happy families greeted the Wrights, with Jerilyn and her daughters hugging the women, and the men shaking hands with Christopher, Chris, and Andrew, as Christopher introduced Andrew to them.

Just inside the foyer, Pastor Palmer and his wife Mary greeted each and every member and visitor. Christopher nodded and shook their hands. "Good morning, Pastor Palmer ... Mrs. Palmer. I'd like you to meet Staff Sergeant Andrew McConnaughey. He's spending his leave at Christmas Hotel, and he's become a good friend of the Wright family."

"A hearty welcome to you, Sergeant McConnaughey! My wife and I thank you for coming to our worship service."

Andrew shook hands with Pastor and Mrs. Palmer. "The pleasure is all mine."

The Wright family settled in "their" pew in the second row center with Andrew. The choir sang one Christmas hymn after another, and one of the men read a narration, throughout the wonderful Christmas cantata.

Pastor Palmer delivered a short sermon titled Jesus Christ: God's gift to a broken world.

Carrie Emeline noticed that Andrew was especially intent throughout the sermon. Following the Lord's message, Pastor Palmer asked if anyone would like to come to the altar to pray for salvation, or rededication of his or her life, church membership or anything else. The altar was open for prayer.

Several of the congregation headed to the altar and knelt to pray. Andrew excused himself and sank to his knees at the altar. Carrie Emeline followed and knelt a few feet away. They finished their prayer at the same time, and Andrew rose, took her hand and smiled as he helped her to her feet. Carrie Emeline returned the smile, and together they walked hand-in-hand back to the pew. Carrie Emeline caught the smile and nod of approval from her mom.

After church, Andrew rushed back to his room at Christmas Hotel to hang up his uniform and change into jeans, a hooded United States Army sweatshirt, and boots. When he arrived at the

Wright family home, everyone was already in the backyard shoveling the snow into piles for the igloos, except for Jerilyn, who said, "You all have fun. I'll stay warm and cook lunch for everyone."

Andrew stared at all the snow piles. "I've never built an igloo. It must be difficult."

"Nah," said Chris. "Dad taught all of us as young children. They're pretty warm inside, too. You'll have a great time."

After completing three igloos with adjoining tunnels, they poured buckets of water over the igloos to form ice. While waiting for the ice to set, they began building Mr. and Mrs. Snowman in the front yard.

"Okay, it's the guys against the girls on Mr. and Mrs. Snowman," said Chris. "Mr. Snowman will be better dressed, and have more decorations than Mrs. Snowman when we're finished."

"You're on!" yelled Lydia Grace, accepting the challenge. The two sisters ran into the house, and Lydia Grace rounded up a scarf, an apron, and a shawl. Carrie Emeline hurried upstairs to her mother's sewing room, and chose two large buttons from the button jar. She remembered her mother changing out the old large black buttons on her winter coat, so those are the buttons she plucked from the jar.

"I've got two black buttons that will be perfect

for the eyes!" she yelled to her sister.

Jerilyn was chopping carrots, so she aided her daughters with a large carrot for the nose. "Here's a carrot, for the girl's team. You two are outnumbered anyway. Grab some cherries out of the fridge to line the mouth. You can also use my old brimmed hat. I never wear it anymore. It's from the 1940s."

The girls raced back with their articles of dress. They pushed the black buttons into the head for the eyes, added the carrot nose and cherry mouth, placed their mom's hat on the head, wrapped the shawl around the body, the scarf around the neck, and tied on the apron.

The men returned with a straw hat, two pieces of charcoal for the eyes, and Christopher's scarf.

"Where's the corncob pipe?" Carrie Emeline asked Chris. "It's always been your favorite item for Mr. Snowman."

"I knocked on Mr. Davidson's door, but he wasn't home. I ran to the square and no one was sitting on the benches today; too cold I guess. I suppose the girls win with more decorations. However, the guys will win this." At that, he threw the two snowballs from his pockets and hit Carrie Emeline and Lydia Grace.

"Okay, little brother," said Lydia Grace," we'll get you back."

The girls quickly packed snowballs and fired at Chris and Andrew. Christopher backed away holding his hands up in the stop position. "I'm joining your mother in the kitchen. Try not to kill each other in this war."

After about ten minutes the four of them were exhausted. "Let's try out the igloos," suggested Carrie Emeline.

She and Andrew crawled in one and Lydia Grace and Chris in another.

"Your mother and I are getting into the third igloo," yelled Christopher from the back door, and the kitchen door slammed.

"It *is* warm in here," noted Andrew.

"When Lydia Grace was only eight years old, an igloo like this, a stray dog, four children, and an angel saved her life," Carrie Emeline whispered to Andrew.

"Really?" said Andrew. "I suppose that's another long story you'll tell me later."

"Yes, it is."

"It sure is cozy, Carrie Emeline, but dark. I wonder if I can find your face to steal a kiss."

"Well, let's give it a try."

"I heard that!" shouted Christopher.

"Time for dinner," announced Jerilyn.

They all scrambled out of the igloos and brushed themselves off.

"Race you all to the house," yelled Chris, and everyone took off running.

Andrew placed his arm around Carrie Emeline. "There's never a dull moment with your family, Carrie Emeline, and lots of love, too."

"Yes, you're right. I wouldn't want it any other way."

"Me either," and they joined the family at the kitchen table.

Chapter Eleven

Memories

"How long wilt thou forget me, O LORD? for ever? how long wilt thou hide thy face from me?"
Psalm 13:1

The Present Day
Monday
December 02, 1974
Carrie Emeline slowly sat up on the bed and turned on the light. Yes, the memories of Andrew had been wonderful, but she couldn't live in the past. She had her future and her children's future to consider. Standing, she removed her coat and hung it on the coat and hat tree. As if in a daze, she walked to the windows, opened the drapes and the french doors, and stepped out on the balcony. The brisk air hit her in the face, but it was invigorating. Two young couples jogged around the square, causing a smile, in spite of the divorce papers lying on the bedside stand.

Stepping back into her room, she re-latched the doors and entered her bathroom. In the mirror, swollen red rimmed eyes still peered back at her.

Will my face ever look right again, and when did the bags under my eyes appear? Running cold water, she splashed it on her face. She grabbed the hand towel and patted her face dry. *I've got to quit crying. I can't leave Drew and Angela with my parents much longer. Mom and Dad must wonder what's wrong. I'm sure the children are confused. I know I'm a wreck, and Drew and Angela don't need to see me like this. I'd only scare them. I've got to get out of this revolting mental state. I always thought I was a strong woman. I realize I'm not. I'm scared, Lord Jesus. I know I need to lean on You.*

Sitting down at her vanity, she picked up her hair brush and brushed her tangled mane of hair. *Maybe I need to go back and read all those old diaries from the young lady for whom I was named: Carrie Emeline Bazell. Her final diary told of great anguish, but she was able to overcome the despair with Your help, Jesus. That final diary helped my mom. I've always been able to trust in You, Jesus. Please help me. Please don't hide from me.*

Over on the marble top dresser sat her jewelry box. Clasping her fidgety hands together, she walked to the ornate box and opened the lid.

A *pas de deux* featuring a danseur and a ballerina *en pointe* spun around to music from the ballet *Romeo et Juliette*. Andrew had bought her the jewelry box when they attended *Romeo et Juliette* at Stuttgart Ballet at the Staatsoper Stuttgart House in Stuttgart, Germany. The jewelry box held a diamond and emerald engagement ring. She removed her current ring from the ring finger of her left hand and replaced it with the diamond and emerald engagement ring. Holding the ring next to her heart, she closed her eyes and remembered.

Chapter Twelve

The Proposal

"Forsake her not, and she shall preserve thee: love her, and she shall keep thee."
Proverbs 4:6

The Past
Monday Morning
December 23, 1968

Carrie Emeline joined Andrew for a light breakfast in the Christmas Hotel dining room. After breakfast, they bundled up for their morning jog. Thankfully, the sidewalks had been shoveled and salted, but the snow continued to fall. Playfully, Carrie Emeline made a snowball and threw it at the back of Andrew's head when he'd jogged ahead of her. He turned around, and she noted his surprise. He packed a snowball of his own, and threw it back at her, laughing at her shrieks of laughter.

Carrie Emeline stopped to catch her breath, placing one hand on each knee. When she looked up, she saw others on the square stopped, laughing, and pointing at the two of them. Straightening up, she said, "I think we've become the entertainment this morning."

"Maybe we should go somewhere quieter and more private. How about ice skating at the McLemore Farm? I enjoyed our time there the other day."

"I did too, Andrew. Let's go to my house for the skates. Chris is at work, but he won't mind if you borrow them again."

On the ride out to the McLemore's, Carrie Emeline and Andrew discussed favorite book characters, and why. "My favorite book, which was published early in this decade is *To Kill a Mockingbird*," said Carrie Emeline. "I can identify with Scout, the little girl in the story. From an early age, my father was a lot like Atticus, Scout's Father. Like my dad, Scout's dad taught her to see what was in the heart of another person. She grew from her compassionate father's teachings, as I have grown from my father's."

"I enjoyed that book, too. However, I've always been fascinated with time travel. I'd have to choose the character H. G. Wells simply called The Time Traveller from his 1895 novel, *The Time Machine*. I would like to be The Time Traveller for a day and experience the past."

"Would you go into the future, too?"

"No. I don't think I'd want to know the future. I don't think God means for us to know the future. It would probably scare us."

She pondered that and nodded her head in the affirmative. "I agree. I'd love to visit the past, but not the future for the same reason. If we knew the future, it might be too depressing to enjoy the present day. We're here, so I'm ready to enjoy this particular day!"

"I'm with you, Carrie Emeline!"

Once they reached the pond, they quickly laced up their skates and glided out onto the ice. They now knew the whereabouts of all the cracks and bumps, but a thin film of snow kept blowing across the frozen pond. The cows walked up to drink, but Robert was out herding them toward another pond. "You two continue your skating!" he yelled over the wind. "We've got two more ponds where I've broken the ice so the cows can drink. We'll keep this pond frozen for skating."

"Thanks, Robert!" Carrie Emeline yelled back.

After about an hour of skating and goofing around with one another, Carrie Emeline began to shiver. "I think the temperature's dropped another fifteen degrees."

"I'll agree with that, but I know how to get warmer." He skated under the branch where he had previously tied the mistletoe and looked up, and then back at Carrie Emeline, smiling that adorable crooked grin. He wiggled his fingers for her to come to him, and she did. They kissed under the mistletoe.

"You know if Robert returns, we're going to be *his* entertainment," she said, pushing slightly away from him.

"How old is Robert?"

"He's sixteen."

"I was sixteen once. I'm pretty sure he's kissed a girl," and Andrew drew her close and kissed her again.

On the way back to Franklin he drove. "Tonight, I'd like to take you somewhere else other than Christmas Hotel for dinner and a movie, but I discovered Franklin's Roxy Theater no longer shows movies. What do you suggest?"

"There are nice places to have dinner in Bowling Green, which is only about thirty miles from here. I happen to know that the State Theater is playing old movies this month. Would you like to see *Casablanca*?"

"Sounds like a winner."

"Okay, I'll meet you in the Christmas Hotel lobby at six o'clock tonight. We can have dinner, and then go to the eight o'clock showing of *Casablanca*." He stopped her Camaro in front of

tonight."

He shook his head and smiled. "Hmmm ... I think I'll be fighting the men off when they see you." He helped her into her coat.

She took his arm, "Shall we go, soldier?"

"Yes, my lady. I'm all yours."

Carrie Emeline sat crying at the end of the movie and dabbing at her eyes with a tissue. "It's so sad. It's a love that could never be."

"They did have their moment of love. Isn't that what's important? Alfred Lord Tennyson said it best.

> "'I hold it true, whate'er befall;
> I feel it, when I sorrow most;
> Tis better to have loved and lost
> Than never to have loved at all.'"

Andrew repeated, "Tis better to have loved and lost than never to have loved at all.' Do you agree, Carrie Emeline?" he asked, as they walked to the car.

She was silent for such a long time. He wasn't sure she heard him. He didn't ask a second time, but he broke the silence. "May I drive us home? I think I know the way back."

"Please do," she said barely above a whisper

and handed him the keys. He opened her door and helped her into the passenger seat.

After he started the car, and they were on the road, she answered his question. "Yes, I believe it's important to love. I know that loss is hard, because my mother endured it with my biological father. However, she's always said that she was happy she had the opportunity to love him. After all, out of that love, my twin Ken and I were conceived."

"Tell me about your mom and your biological dad."

By the time they arrived back in Franklin, Carrie Emeline had finished the story.

"Your mom endured a lot to get to where she is now."

"She's a strong woman. She loves the Lord, and her faith is strong. My dad is a strong man, too. Sometime I'll tell you about his first wife: Lily's biological mother."

"I'd like to hear that story, also."

He parked the car in front of her house. "Will you take a stroll with me around the square?"

She grinned. "Okay."

"What's the grin for?"

"People don't say stroll anymore."

"That's okay. I'm archaic ... remember?" and he presented her with the crooked smile she adored.

He helped her out of the car and they walked to the bench that faced Christmas Hotel. "Please have a seat. I have something to say to you, Carrie Emeline."

After she sat down, he continued. "I'm in love with you. I prayed about this at church yesterday." He knelt in front of her on one knee. "This is the emerald and diamond ring my father gave my mother upon their engagement. I would be honored if you'd marry me, Carrie Emeline, and accept this ring as your engagement ring."

She gasped, and placed one hand over her heart. "Oh, Andrew," and she began to cry. Wiping the tears, she touched his cheek with her hand. "I would be honored to be your wife. I love you, too."

He took the emerald and diamond ring from the case and placed it on her shaking finger. "My birthday is April fourteenth, and since you were born in May, we were made for each other, just like my mom and dad."

She stared at it and continued to cry. Choking back a sob, she said, "Those two stones. Your dad's month of April, a diamond birthstone, and your mother's May, an emerald birthstone, now have their birthdays joined together again, with us."

He rose and pulled her to her feet. He kissed her under the holly-wrapped lamppost with the red bow tied to the top.

Chapter Thirteen

The Wedding

"Wherefore they are no more twain, but one flesh. What therefore God hath joined together, let not man put asunder."
Matthew 19:6

The Past

December 24 to 28, 1968

Carrie Emeline didn't want the wedding on Lydia Grace's birthday, which was Christmas Eve, nor on Christmas Day, nor on New Year's Eve which was Christopher and Jerilyn's wedding anniversary. However, they wanted to be married well before January sixth 1969 when Carrie Emeline returned to Louisville to teach and Andrew flew to Germany. Therefore, they chose Saturday, December twenty-eighth when most of Carrie Emeline's friends and family were still in Franklin and could attend.

On Tuesday, Christmas Eve, before the wedding, Carrie Emeline realized she had only four days to prepare — but she had a large family to help. Both Lily and her mother offered a dress, spreading out each dress on Carrie Emeline's bed for her to choose.

After studying each dress, Carrie Emeline finally spoke. "Lily, yours is beautiful, and I know you spent months at the bridal shop for fittings to make this dress perfect ... and it is. It's probably one of the most beautiful wedding dresses I've ever seen, and you were a beautiful bride. However, I think it should be saved for Teresa, Mary Beth, or Ellie if they choose to wear their mom's dress. I want to wear something older looking."

She smiled at her mother. "Mom, I love yours, too. However, it's blue. I want to marry in a white gown, but I do want a vintage dress, because Andrew is definitely old-fashioned in his thoughts and ways. I just don't know what to do."

"I have a suggestion," offered Jerilyn. "There's a vintage bridal shop in Nashville which might fit what you're wanting. We can go today and look."

Carrie Emeline's spirits brightened. "That's a great idea, Mom. Do you think they'll be open on Christmas Eve?"

"We can call first."

"I'll have John watch the children and go with you," said Lily. "I'm sure Lydia Grace will want to go, too."

The shop was open, so the four women piled into Jerilyn's van and headed to Nashville. A matronly woman, who introduced herself as Abigail Carlisle, listened to what Carrie Emeline hoped to find in a wedding dress. She explained about her old-fashioned soldier-fiancé, and Abigail helped them in a selection.

Three gowns now appeared in front of Carrie Emeline. They were all beautiful, but Carrie Emeline was drawn to one in particular: a floor length white silk with a high neck lace collar and lace at the end of the sleeves. White pearl buttons began at the back of the collar and continued down the back to below the waist. The dress fit snug around the breast and waist, and then fanned into an A-line skirt. The dress was everything Carrie Emeline had pictured. She tried it on, and it was as though it was made for her. *It was perfect.*

"From what era was this dress sewn?" she asked.

"Nineteen fifteen," Mrs. Carlisle said without hesitation. "It was well preserved by the owner ... my aunt. There's a veil that goes with it, too." She walked away and returned with a long rectangular box filled with white tissue paper, and removed the white lace veil with the attached gold tiara. As she placed it on Carrie Emeline's head, a hush fell over the room.

Carrie Emeline stared into the floor-length mirror, and a vintage woman stared back. She turned around and looked back at the veil cascading down the back of the dress to the floor, with at least a three foot trail beyond the hem of the dress. Tiny little pearls were sewn into the veil.

Carrie Emeline was almost afraid to ask. "How much is the dress and the veil?"

The woman studied Carrie Emeline. "My aunt always said, 'Choose wisely for the woman that wears my dress.' I choose you to wear this dress and veil for your old-fashioned soldier-fiancé. Aunt Rose had no daughters to wear the dress. Her husband was an American soldier who died in France in the Great War. Aunt Rose is now deceased, too. I think she would be pleased to have you wear her dress. There is no price tag on this dress. I was to give it to a worthy young woman, and I deem you that woman."

"Thank you, Mrs. Carlisle." Carrie Emeline hugged her, tears welling in her eyes. "I wish I could thank your aunt, too. I will cherish this dress and pass it down to a daughter of my own, if it's God's will."

"God bless you and your marriage to your

soldier. God go with you."

"Thank you, Mrs. Carlisle."

*****

The day of her wedding, Carrie Emeline mentioned the borrowed, blue, and new, to her mother and sisters as they dressed in room #7, the Wright family room at Christmas Hotel. "I have my dress as the old. I can't count my new gold wedding band Andrew purchased at Mallory's Jewelers on the square as the new, because I won't be walking down the aisle with the gold band. I know ... I can count my new white heels for something new, as I walk down the aisle. I need something blue and borrowed."

"I have the blue!" piped up Lily. She handed the blue garter to Carrie Emeline. "After all, Andrew will need to remove this after the wedding," and her eyes twinkled in merriment. "I thought as the matron of honor it was my duty to purchase the garter!"

Jerilyn stepped forward waving a white lace handkerchief. "I have the borrowed. This handkerchief belonged to my mother ... your grandmother. I want you to carry it down the aisle." She handed it to Carrie Emeline.

Carrie Emeline wiped a tear. "Thank you all so much. I love you."

Mother and her three daughters all hugged.

"We love you, too," Jerilyn murmured, and the others all echoed their sentiments.

Lydia Grace hurried down the stairs to begin playing the music as the guests arrived. Andrew had chosen Chris to be his best man. Christopher played two roles: walking Carrie Emeline down the aisle and also marrying the couple.

Carrie Emeline looked down the stairs and smiled at her father who waited for her in the chapel doorway. As soon as Lydia Grace began the wedding march, Carrie Emeline descended the stairs.

Quickly wiping a tear, he took his daughter's hand and smiled at her. "Are you ready, honey?"

Carrie Emeline returned the smile. Although Christopher was not her biological father, she could not have asked for a better father. He had always been there for her, and he treated all five of his children equally. When she was in second grade and an older girl pushed her down on the playground, it was her father who discussed the situation with the girls' parents. When she was in the ninth grade, he helped her with her Algebra homework, patiently teaching her the formulas until she understood. Now here he was giving his second of three daughters in marriage. She saw his tear, but she didn't let on to him. She looked up at him. "I'm ready, Daddy. I love you."

"I love you too, Carrie Emeline. I will always be available for you, if you ever need me for anything."

"I know, Daddy. Thank you."

Lily's son Brian walked the aisle as the ring bearer, while Lily's three daughters, Teresa, Mary Beth, and Ellie spread rose petals in the aisle.

The congregation of family and friends all stood as Christopher guided Carrie Emeline down the aisle. Carrie Emeline never took her eyes off Andrew as she slowly walked the aisle, stepping to the wedding march. He smiled at her with the crooked grin she adored. *Thank You, Lord, for giving me this wonderful man to love and spend my life.*

Christopher placed his daughter's hand in the hand of her betrothed and positioned himself in the pulpit and began the ceremony. "We are gathered here today in sight of God, and the presence of friends and loved ones, to celebrate one of life's greatest moments. Marriage is a most honorable estate, created and instituted by God. Andrew and Carrie Emeline, please face each other and join hands."

He paused while the couple joined hands. "At this part of the ceremony, Andrew and Carrie Emeline will recite a poem together."

Gazing into each other's eyes they began.

"Somewhere there waiteth in this world of ours
For one lone soul another lonely soul
Each choosing each through all the weary hours
And meeting strangely at one sudden goal.
Then blend they, like green leaves with golden
flowers,
Into one beautiful and perfect whole;
And life's long night is ended, and the way
Lies open onward to eternal day."

"Andrew Michael McConnaughey, do you take Carrie Emeline Wright to be your wedded wife, to live together in marriage? Do you promise to love her, comfort her, honor and keep her for better or worse, for richer or poorer, in sickness and health, and forsaking all others, be faithful only to her, for as long as you both shall live?"

"I do."

Christopher turned and addressed Lily, and then Chris. "Please hand me the rings." Christopher held up the two rings. "The circles of these rings are the symbol of eternity, with no beginning or end; a never-ending circle of eternal love." He handed the smaller gold band to Andrew.

"You may place the ring on her finger."

Andrew placed the gold band on Carrie Emeline's finger. He then reached in his pocket to retrieve the emerald and diamond engagement ring and smiled at her when he placed it behind the gold band.

"Carrie Emeline Wright, do you take Andrew Michael McConnaughey to be your wedded husband to live together in marriage? Do you promise to love him, comfort him, honor and keep him for better or worse, for richer or poorer, in sickness and health and forsaking all others, be faithful only to him so long as you both shall live?"

"I do."

He handed the larger gold band to Carrie Emeline. "You may place the ring on Andrew's finger."

Carrie Emeline's eyes teared as she pushed the ring onto Andrew's finger.

"Andrew and Carrie Emeline, in so much as the two of you have agreed to live together in God's holy matrimony, and have promised your love for each other by these vows, the giving of these rings, and the joining of your hands, by the power vested in me I now pronounce you husband and wife. Andrew, you may kiss your bride."

Andrew lifted Carrie Emeline's veil just as a tear slid down her cheek. With his thumb, he wiped away the tear and kissed her ever so tenderly. He looked into her eyes. "I love you, Carrie Emeline," he whispered.

"I love you, too, Andrew," she sniffed and whispered back.

"I present to you Sergeant and Mrs. Andrew Michael McConnaughey."

The guests applauded and threw rice as Andrew and Carrie Emeline hurried down the aisle in the chapel at Christmas Hotel.

Chapter Fourteen

Goodbyes

*"Finally, brethren, farewell. Be perfect, be of
good comfort, be of one mind, live in peace; and
the God of love and peace shall be with you."*
2 Corinthians 13:11

The Past
January to June, 1969
Carrie Emeline and Andrew spent five days
honeymooning at Christmas Hotel, but then it
was time to say goodbye to family and friends and
drive to Carrie Emeline's home in Louisville. They
packed her Camaro with the wedding gifts and
their personal belongings. Carrie Emeline hugged
her parents, emotions running wild.

"I love you, Mom and Dad. This visit has been
amazing. You two are the best parents a girl could
have. I'm so happy that I met Andrew at
Christmas Hotel." She turned to her father.
"Thank you for your blessing on our marriage,
Daddy, and thank you for marrying us." She then
turned to her mom. "Thank you, Mom for helping

me to choose the perfect dress."

Carrie Emeline began to cry, and Andrew placed his left arm around his wife, shook the hands of his new in-laws, and said, "It's been a pleasure meeting all of Carrie Emeline's family. I want you to know that I love your daughter very much. I promise to be a devoted husband to her."

"I know you will," said Christopher. God go with both of you."

Three days later it was time for the newlyweds to say goodbye to each other. After a wonderful Sunday morning worship service at Carrie Emeline's church in Louisville, the pastor and the congregation prayed for Andrew's safe return home, and Carrie Emeline and Andrew departed the church. Andrew had packed his belongings in Carrie Emeline's Camaro early in the morning, so they could head straight from the church to the airport. Carrie Emeline wasn't the only one saying goodbye to her husband. Other women and some with children were seeing their own men off. Many tears were shed that day in Louisville's airport.

"I'll be counting the days until I see you in early June, Carrie Emeline. I wish I'd been able to meet the children in your classroom and your teacher friends. I love you."

"Oh, I love you too, Andrew. Four weeks ago we were single and didn't know each other. God is sure amazing."

"That He is, my lady," and he kissed her. "They just called my row. I've got to go."

"Andrew, I'll count the days until school is out, and I'll see you again. I'll get my passport and shots this week. I don't want anything holding me up from joining you in Germany."

"If you have any problems, call the army base at Fort Knox. They'll be able to help you. I'll send details for your flight. You may have a layover in Baltimore, as I will have today. Farewell, my love."

"Farewell, my wonderful, antediluvian husband."

They shared one last kiss when his row was called again. He threw his duffel bag over his shoulder, hurried to the exit, handed his ticket to the stewardess, and turned one final time to see Carrie Emeline waving and throwing kisses, tears streaming down her cheeks.

*****

The weeks dragged, but soon it was time for Carrie Emeline to say goodbye to her class for summer vacation. She was already packed for her flight to Germany. "Will we see you again, Mrs. McConnaughey?" Some of them still called her

Miss Wright, before remembering she had married over their Christmas vacation.

"Well, I'm not sure. Remember, you'll be in the fourth grade next year with a new teacher. I'll be in Germany at least for the summer. As you know, my husband is in the army. His orders might keep him in Germany. If that happens, I'll stay in Germany with him."

The questions were intelligent for third graders. "Do you speak German, Mrs. McConnaughey?"

"I must admit, not very well. I'm being tutored by a friend who's the German teacher over at Seneca High School. I think I know enough phrases to get by in the beginning. I also have an English-to-German book for translations. My husband had four years of German in high school, so he hasn't had problems. It seems to come naturally for him."

"Will you be able to live in the same house with Mr. McConnaughey?"

"Yes. He's already secured quarters on the base for us."

"Can ... I mean *may* we write to you?"

"Oh, most definitely! I'd love to receive letters from you. In fact, I'll write the address on the blackboard now, and you can copy it down. This is the address I use when I mail letters to my husband. It's too expensive for long-distant calls, so we write lots of letters." She wrote the address in large block letters on the board, and the children copied it in their yellow primary paper tablets.

"If you always send letters, when was the last time you talked to him?"

"The last day I saw him and heard his voice was when he flew away on the plane to Germany. That day was January the fifth, the day before we all returned to school from Christmas break. I can't wait to hear his voice again." She was about to tear up when the bell rang. School was officially out for the summer.

The children filed by her desk and hugged her, and some cried. "We'll miss you, Mrs. McConnaughey," each child said to her.

"I'll miss you all, too." When the last child exited the room, she closed the door and let the tears spill.

Chapter Fifteen

Interruption from Memories

"He will swallow up death in victory; and the LORD God will wipe away tears from off all faces; and the rebuke of his people shall he take away from off all the earth: for the LORD hath spoken it."
Isaiah 25:8

The Present Day
Monday
December 02, 1974
It's sometimes hard to believe, but those wonderful children are now juniors in high school. Where did the six years go? I've certainly enjoyed their visits with me, when they've returned to see me at the elementary school. They laugh when they sit in their old desk that's now too small for them. It's been a joy to hear about their current lives. Many have thanked me for the difference I made in their lives. I wonder what they'd think if they saw me today, wallowing in my grief.

The knock at her door interrupted her thoughts. It was her mother with a stern expression on her face. "I think it's time we talked, Carrie Emeline," she said in a firm tone. She marched in and took a seat on one of the two brocade chairs in front of the window and motioned for Carrie Emeline to sit.

Carrie Emeline realized she still wore Andrew's ring and tried to hide her hand, but sunlight glinted off the gemstones, and her mother's gaze shifted to Carrie Emeline's hand before she covered the ring.

Carrie Emeline was immediately on the defense. "I was just reminiscing, Mom. There's nothing wrong with that."

Her mom didn't respond, but only stared into her daughter's eyes. Carrie Emeline lowered her head. "You're making me feel like a little girl, Mom."

"That's not my intention, honey. I love you, and your father and I are worried about you. Chris told us you've been holed up in this room since late last night. You haven't even been to see Drew and Angela since Thanksgiving, and we've taken care of them since then."

"Have they worn out their welcome?"

"That was harsh, Carrie Emeline. Drew and Angela, or any of my family, could never wear out a welcome. We love Drew and Angela ... and we love you. I knew something was wrong when you

didn't pick them up to return to school today."
Her mom paused and said with compassion, "Has
something happened with your marriage?"

At that, the tears began again. "Oh, Mom, I've
made a terrible mistake," she wailed.

Jerilyn stood and knelt on the floor in front of
Carrie Emeline and held her, while Carrie
Emeline continued to cry. Jerilyn spoke soothing
words and patted her back, as she did when
Carrie Emeline was a child and was hurt. Jerilyn
said no more, but waited on Carrie Emeline to get
control of her emotions. Her child was hurt and
as a mother, she regretted she could no longer
wipe away the tears. *You can wipe away the
tears, Lord Jesus. Please help Carrie Emeline.*

Carrie Emeline's eyes pleaded. "Mom, I love
you and Daddy, but I'm not ready to speak about
it. Please take care of Drew and Angela a little
while longer. I know they are missing school, but
I'll catch them up before I send them back to
school."

Jerilyn sighed. "Of course, dear. Please know
that your father and I are available any time to
listen. We love you."

"I know Mom. I love you both, too. Thank
you."

Chapter Sixteen

A German Reunion

"So ought men to love their wives as their own bodies. He that loveth his wife loveth himself."
Ephesians 5:28

The Past

June 02 and June 03, 1969

The plane touched down at Coleman Barracks/Coleman Army Airfield in the Sandhofen district of Mannheim, Germany, a United States Army military installation. Carrie Emeline had taken two flights, leaving Sunday after church with a layover in Baltimore, same as Andrew had back in January. The whole church congregation prayed for her and Andrew that morning after the service. With all the hugs and well-wishes, she was nearly late for the airport. Her parents had joined her at church that morning in Louisville and drove her to the airport. She sat down in her seat on the plane, buckled her belt, and relaxed. *I'm on my way, Andrew.*

She was finally in Germany. Carrie Emeline scrutinized people on the ground from the plane's window to try and spot Andrew as the plane taxied to the gate. The plane stopped, and she tapped her foot in anticipation for the jet bridge to be attached. Finally, they were allowed to disembark. Grabbing her overnight case from the overhead compartment, she wanted to rush, but she also didn't want to be rude and push as she kept trying to look over and around the people in front of her. There were as many speaking German as English.

Soon, soon. I'm coming, Andrew! She crossed the boundary between the plane and jet bridge, and as she walked the crowd parted enough so she saw Andrew waiting for her; smiling and waving. Carrie Emeline broke into a full run down the bridge, dropped her overnight case, and jumped into Andrew's arms. He spun her around, showering her with kisses while the smiling crowd applauded, and fellow soldiers clapped and whistled.

"Well, here we are, the entertainment again, Andrew," she said, laughing.

"I don't care." He planted a passionate kiss on her lips. While waiting for her luggage, he kissed her all over her face, both of them grinning, and laughing.

She giggled and broke away from him. "We have to watch for my luggage, Andrew. There!" Carrie Emeline pointed to her two navy blue suitcases and Andrew pulled them off the carousel. They hurried to the street where he had parked an army jeep, which he was permitted to use.

Andrew drove straight to their new home on the base. At every stop sign, he kissed her. After setting down her luggage and unlocking the front door, he picked Carrie Emeline up and carried her over the threshold. When he tried to close the door, she reminded him that the luggage was still outside. He set her down, and she smoothed out her traveling suit: a pale blue pencil skirt with a short matching jacket, and a white silk blouse.

He set the luggage on the floor, removed his hat, and closed the door. "You are so beautiful," he said with huskiness in his voice, and he gathered her in his arms.

"You're not so bad yourself, soldier. You even wore your dress uniform to meet me."

"I've missed you so much, Carrie Emeline."

She spied the neatly made bed in the other room and took his hand. "Right now we're not going to think about the army," and she led him into the bedroom and closed the door.

*****

The next day, Carrie Emeline was introduced to two of Andrew's friends when they dropped by the house. "Carrie Emeline, I'd like you to meet my two best army buddies: Specialist Four Gerald Staats, he goes by Jerry to his friends, and Sergeant E-5 Marcus Taylor." Andrew laughed. "Marcus goes by Marcus to his friends."

She offered her hand in greeting to both men. Jerry appeared very young, maybe around nineteen and Marcus looked about her age. In the next sentence, she had her answer regarding Jerry's age.

"We've got my buddy Jerry to thank that we met. He knew about Christmas Hotel from Mrs. Showalter, who was one of his teachers at his high school in his home town, Dayton, Ohio. I remember that first dinner with you at Christmas Hotel. Your mom said she was from Dayton, and her best friend was Emma Showalter, who taught at Colonel White. If you'll remember, I said I was from Dayton, and that Mrs. Showalter was a teacher of mine, too."

"Emma Showalter ... my mom's best friend from high school told you about Christmas Hotel, Jerry?"

"Yes, ma'am."

"Wow, what a small world. I can't wait to write my mom and tell her I met Andrew's buddy from Dayton, *and* he was also a student of Mrs. Showalter." She had been correct about Jerry's young age. She remembered Andrew saying he had a buddy from Dayton, Ohio, who graduated ten years after him. That would make Jerry nineteen or twenty. He looked so young compared to Andrew, or even Marcus.

"My buddies helped me think up adventurous outings to enjoy with you evenings and weekends. I was granted permission to spend this first full day with you, and then it's back to work tomorrow. Today I'm taking you for a walk along the Rhine River." He looked at his buddies and smiled. "Alone, guys, so I'll pull rank and say, *auf Wiedersehen!*"

At the Rhine River, Carrie Emeline took Andrew's offered arm. It was a pleasant, sunny and warm summer day for a stroll along the Rhine. Cargo ships and sail boats moved along the river as Andrew and Carrie Emeline strolled down the winding river paths under shade trees, just relishing in each other's company.

"I'll be your tour guide and point out some of the sites. Over here, near the banks of the Rhine is a stretch of wilderness called Rheinauen. Literally Rhine Meadows in English."

As they entered into the Rheinauen, Andrew

continued his narration, "This is a nature protection area and home to many rare birds. If a couple is not already in love, this is recognized as a great place to fall in love." He smiled down at her and kissed her.

"Maybe to continue in love, too." They watched other couples along the path, holding hands and kissing every now and then. Most of the men were is army uniforms. "It appears this is a place for a soldier to bring his girl. Is this like a lovers' lane at home?"

He chuckled. "Definitely a lovers' lane, but without the car."

She laughed. "At least we're not the entertainment here. We blend in with the others."

He looked at his watch. "Let's go to an early dinner. It was recommended that I take you to an old German restaurant in downtown Mannheim where they have excellent, authentic German food. After tonight, and until I'm paid again next month, we'll have to eat beans and hot dogs. We'll be out of money."

"I don't care, darling. I'm with you, and that's all that matters."

Carrie Emeline scrutinized the façade of the restaurant. An old half-timbered house had been converted into the restaurant. Andrew held the door, and they both stepped over the threshold.

Framed copies of paintings of German sites lined the lobby walls. On two long shelves above the prints, German beer steins of different size and shape lined up like toy soldiers. Suspended from the ceiling, eighteenth and nineteenth century model fishing boats and model sailing vessels rounded out the décor. They were greeted by two men, both in authentic German knee-length leather pants and a long sleeve shirt. Fortunately, one spoke English. The host obviously noted the American army uniform and addressed them in English and smiled. "Good evening and welcome to our humble restaurant. I am Ernst Werner and this is my brother Hans, and we are the owners."

Hans nodded, and Ernst handed two menus to a woman who was dressed in a German ruffled apron dress. "Please seat them in one of the tables with a view of the courtyard." Ernst turned back to Andrew. "Please enjoy your meal, and if you have any questions, just ask for Ernst. Most of the staff speaks English."

"Thank you, Ernst." Andrew nodded to Ernst and Hans, took Carrie Emeline's hand, and they followed the young lady to a table overlooking the lovely courtyard.

She handed them the menus and smiled. "My name is Greta, and Ilse will serve you. I will bring you water and bread. Enjoy the garden view."

A vase of flowers graced the center of their table. Carrie Emeline leaned over to smell the flowers, closed her eyes, and smiled. "Hmmm ... heavenly." The attached plaque revealed the flowers as cornflower, German chamomile, edelweiss, and European spindle. Out in the brick paver courtyard, pots of different shapes and sizes with other colorful German flowers were scattered. The second floor windows around the courtyard held baskets of more colorful flowers. "We'll have to walk out in the courtyard after dinner. I see little plaques that probably identify the names of the flowers.

"This restaurant is amazing, Andrew, and that was a wonderful welcome from the Werner brothers and Greta. Are all the German restaurants like this one?"

"I wish I could answer that question. I don't get off the base much. I do my job, go to my room to read, and then to bed. My days are boring." He placed his hand over her hand. "That is until now. I'm so happy you're here with me. I certainly have missed you."

"I've missed you, too."

Greta returned with the water and a basket of warm rye and pumpernickel breads. Andrew and Carrie Emeline studied the menu. Ilse arrived dressed like Greta, and Carrie Emeline was ready to order. "I will have the schweineschnitzel with the warm potato salad."

"Good choice, ma'am. And you, sir?"

"I'll have the sauerbraten with rotkohl."

"And a good choice for you, too." Ilse smiled, took the menus and walked away.

Carrie Emeline looked at him with her puzzled expression of eyebrows knit together. "I know what all the food is except the rotkohl. What is rotkohl?"

"Red cabbage, my dear. We both have much to learn about Germany."

"Yes, we do."

After dinner, they walked around the courtyard, admired the flowers, and then drove home. Carrie Emeline snuggled close to Andrew on the sofa in their tiny dwelling holding hands. "I love it here with you, Andrew. I wish we could freeze time and spend years together in Germany. I could even teach school in Germany, such as English to the German students. I'd also know that you were safe, and I'd not have to worry about you."

"I love you, Carrie Emeline, but you understood when we married that I'm a lifer. My orders could change at any time. I don't want to scare you, but I know that more troops are needed in Vietnam. I just don't want you to get too comfortable. Let's enjoy the time we have together — each moment."

Snuggling closer, she thought about his words. "You're right. Let's make the most of every moment we have together."

Chapter Seventeen

Blessings and Goodbyes

*"A merry heart maketh a cheerful countenance:
but by sorrow of the heart the spirit is broken."*
Proverbs 15:13

The Past

June to August, 1969

Throughout the months of June and July they did a great deal of sightseeing when Andrew wasn't on duty. They visited some of the many German castles, the Jesuit Church with some of the most amazing baroque art, and the Staatsoper Stuttgart House. Carrie Emeline loved opera and ballet, and Andrew's buddy Jerry always wanted to see the opera house that contained his last name. Therefore, Jerry and Marcus acquired dates, and the three couples attended on a Friday night in July, when the three of them were off duty on a Saturday.

They borrowed a military vehicle large enough to hold the three couples and drove the eighty miles to Stuttgart, but instead of the opera they

117

expected to see, the ballet *Romeo et Juliette* was performed. Carrie Emeline was in awe. Naturally, she cried at the end, as she did after Casablanca.

"I can't help it. I'm sentimental."

Andrew hugged her to his side. "I wouldn't have you any other way. I love you just the way you are."

On the way out of the opera house, a boutique beckoned to Carrie Emeline. The ornate jewelry box caught her eye, and when she opened it, the couple danced a *pas de deux* to music from *Romeo et Juliette*. "You like it," Andrew asked softly, "don't you?"

"Oh, Andrew, it's too expensive. We can't."

"Yes, we can. We'll just eat more beans and hot dogs."

The music box went home with them, nestled on Carrie Emeline's lap.

*****

At the end of the month, Andrew came home with a stunned look on his face.

"What's wrong, Andrew?" Carrie Emeline asked in a strained voice knowing something was terribly wrong. She was frightened to hear his answer to her question.

"My orders have changed. I'm being reassigned to Vietnam."

She cupped his face in her hands. "How long

do we have?"

"I leave in three weeks."

"As we said, we'll need to make the most of our time together." However, her voice quivered when she spoke the words.

Over the next three weeks, they spent every minute together when Andrew wasn't on duty. Two weeks prior to leaving, he said, "I want you to go back to Kentucky when I leave. I don't want you to stay in Germany."

"Andrew, I saw the doctor today. We're going to have a baby." Staring into his eyes, she wanted to see his first reaction.

"That's wonderful, sweetheart!" He paused. "What's the estimated date?"

"March twenty-fifth."

"I wish I could be with you. I'll get a two week Rest and Recuperation from Vietnam in early March. Most of the guys go to Hawaii. It's a halfway point for family in the continental United States, and of course it's on American soil. However, you may not be able to travel there, being so close to your due date."

"Andrew, if there's any way possible, I will meet you for that R&R. Wouldn't it be wonderful if your son or daughter was born while we were together in Hawaii?"

On Sunday, August tenth, they sat in their last

church service together. Afterwards, Carrie Emeline asked, "Don't Jerry and Marcus ever attend church?"

Andrew shook his head. "I've explained the plan of salvation to both of them, but so far they haven't shown any interest. Jerry said he attended a little Presbyterian church in Carlisle, Ohio with his mother and sister when he was a small boy. His father never went with the family. Jerry regretted he really didn't know about salvation. He also admitted his mother hadn't taken them to church that often, and he mostly remembered sleeping on his mother's shoulder; he on one shoulder and his sister on the other."

"What about Marcus?"

"Marcus said flat out that he wasn't interested, and I quote, 'Don't bother me with all that religious crap'. However, they're both going to Vietnam with me. Many soldiers get saved in battle. We can only pray for them."

Later that day they discussed baby names. Carrie Emeline didn't hesitate. "If we have a boy, I want him named Andrew Michael McConnaughey after his wonderful father."

"Let's not call him Junior. I always feel sorry for kids called Junior. It's like they really had no name."

"I agree. Drew would be a good nickname.

What about a girl?"

"I've always liked the name Olivia."

"I do, too. Oh, Andrew, I'll miss you. These last two months have been wonderful." She began to cry.

He wrapped his arms around her, kissed her on her forehead, and he began to recite, "'Somewhere there waiteth in this world of ours,'" and she joined in and recited with him, wiping her eyes with one hand.

"For one lone soul another lonely soul,
Each chasing each through all the weary hours,
And meeting strangely at one sudden goal;
Then blend they — like green leaves with golden flowers,
Into one beautiful and perfect whole —
And life's long night is ended, and the way
Lies open onward to eternal day.'"

The next day Andrew saw Carrie Emeline off on the plane back to Baltimore, where she was to catch the second flight on to Louisville. "You take care of our little one," and he rubbed her tummy.

"I'll write you every day, and I'll do my very best to meet you in Hawaii. Take care of yourself, Andrew, and keep your head down. I love you so much."

"I love you, too, Carrie Emeline."

They kissed, and didn't care that they might be entertainment again.

The next morning, Andrew and his two best buddies flew to their new base in South Vietnam.

Chapter Eighteen

The Valentine's Day Flowers

"This is the day which the LORD hath made; we will rejoice and be glad in it."
Psalm 118:24

The Past

August, 1969 to February, 1970

When Carrie Emeline returned home from Germany, she first thanked her neighbor for taking care of and watching over her home. The house felt so empty without Andrew with her. Although she had lived there two years without him, and only a few days with him, his presence was now everywhere. Throughout all the rooms framed pictures of the two of them adorned tables, walls, and on the fireplace mantel.

She initially signed up at the elementary school as a substitute teacher, but in October one of the teachers had a baby, so she would have charge of the teacher's class up until Christmas vacation. It was wonderful; it was a fourth grade class and many of her former third grade students were in this class.

Every evening she wrote long and loving letters to Andrew, keeping him abreast of everything in her daily life. However, she knew that the letters from him were guarded. He didn't describe the battle sites, just the events that happened at the base. She knew he didn't want to alarm her.

On Saturday, February fourteenth, Valentine's Day, she received a beautiful bouquet of one dozen white carnations and a corsage of baby orchids. The delivery driver for the florist apologized that it wasn't the dozen long-stemmed roses that Andrew had requested. The roses were out of season and unavailable to him.

"Oh, I don't mind. It's still a gift from Andrew. Thank you so much!" and she tipped him well.

In her cabinet were several vases, but none that were special. She placed the corsage and carnations in the refrigerator and hurried out to buy a more suitable vase. She returned and lovingly arranged the white carnations in the vase, added water, and snapped two pictures with her Polaroid camera to send a copy to her parents. The next morning, she pinned the corsage to her dress for church. She told each friend she greeted, "The corsage is from Andrew. Isn't it beautiful?"

His next letter arrived a few days later.

08 February, 1970
Dear Carrie Emeline,

By the time you receive this letter, you will have received the dozen long-stemmed red roses for Valentine's Day. At least, I hope they arrived on time. This has to be a short letter. We're heading out in the field on a twenty-one day mission, just as soon as I post this letter. I will write a much longer letter, as soon as I return to the base.

I hope our baby is doing well. I can't wait for the day I see him or her. If you are able to meet me for my R&R that would certainly be a dream come true for me, especially if he or she is born in Hawaii. I wouldn't have to wait until our baby is six months old to meet him or her.

I've enjoyed the pictures you sent me, and I can see how your body has changed. I wish I could have been with you these past months. I would have enjoyed feeling that first kick in your belly with you. I will with our future children. I've decided I'm not going to sign on for another tour of duty in Vietnam. I want to

spend time with you and all our children of which God blesses us. I love you more than anything.
All my love,
Andrew

Holding the letter to her breast, she said aloud, "I love you, too Andrew, and with all my heart. You are the best husband a woman could have, and you'll be an amazing father."

She sat at her desk and picked up pen and stationery.

Dear Andrew....

Chapter Nineteen

The Visitors

"Fear thou not; for I am with thee: be not dismayed; for I am thy God: I will strengthen thee; yea, I will help thee; yea, I will uphold thee with the right hand of my righteousness."
Isaiah 41:10

The Past
Friday
February 27, 1970
The morning began like most days; a healthy breakfast along with a pre-natal vitamin. Carrie Emeline had just finished another long-term assignment. The earlier teacher returned from pregnancy leave after Christmas vacation, and Carrie Emeline had been assigned another classroom in January. This new assignment was a third grade class, and this teacher's absence was due to another baby born.

"It must be something in the water," Carrie Emeline chuckled. She drove to school that morning, taught the class, and then bought groceries for the weekend on the way home. Her parents were coming to town today. They planned to spend the weekend, and she was excited. Every night after school, this past week, she cleaned a different room in the house, planned the meals, so she was ready for her parents' visit. While putting the groceries in the refrigerator and the pantry, she checked her watch. Her parents were due in the next thirty minutes.

The doorbell rang. "They must be early," she spoke aloud. In her excitement, she tripped on a throw rug in the kitchen. She didn't fall, but made a mental note to get rid of the throw rug. *After all, I've got a baby due in a month. I can't take a chance of falling.* On the way to the door, she stopped a second for a quick whiff of Andrew's now fading Valentine's Day flowers.

She opened the door to two army officers in Class A dress uniforms. Dazed, she stared at them, and then saw their United States Army vehicle parked at the curb. Turning her gaze back on them she managed to stammer," May ... I help ... you?"

She saw both men view her large round belly, on which she protectively placed her hand. "Are you Mrs. Andrew McConnaughey?" asked one of the officers.

"Yes. Is Andrew ... all right?"

"May we come in?"

She opened the door. "Is anyone home with you?" one of the officers asked.

"My parents are due shortly. They're coming to help me pack to meet my husband in Hawaii on March ninth for his R&R. Andrew and I have been looking forward to the time together. I've already got my plane tickets. My parents have hired a nurse to travel with me. Andrew didn't want me to be alone. May I get you a cup of coffee, water or anything?" She knew she was rambling and killing time. *Oh, please, God, let Andrew be okay.*

Her face began to sweat. She pulled a handkerchief from her pocket and dabbed around her hairline. Her legs trembled and she was weak in the knees. Breathing deeply several times, she willed herself not to faint.

"Please, ma'am, let us help you to a seat." They each took one of her arms, and led her to the sofa. As soon as she was seated, her parents entered and rushed to her side.

Dad entered first and locked eyes on his daughter. "We saw the car." Her parents looked from one officer to the other.

"Please have a seat with your daughter."

Her mother and father dutifully sat on each side of Carrie Emeline on the sofa. Carrie Emeline began to cry, as did her mother.

"Allow us to introduce ourselves. I'm Major Michael Rouse from Fort Knox, Kentucky."

"I'm Captain James Hardin, also from Fort Knox, Kentucky, and I'm the Fort Knox chaplain."

Christopher placed an arm around his daughter.

"I'm sorry, but I'm required to read this," Major Michael Rouse spoke in a soft, consoling tone. "Mrs. McConnaughey, we are here to inform you that your husband, Sergeant Andrew McConnaughey and his unit were on a search and clear operation approximately twenty-seven miles south of Quang Ngai City in Quang Ngai Province, Republic of Vietnam. Sergeant McConnaughey was mortally wounded when his unit came upon intense enemy small arms fire at ten-ten hours on twenty-sixth February, 1970."

He stopped speaking when Carrie Emeline began sobbing uncontrollably, and her body shook violently. Christopher wrapped his arms around his daughter and hugged her to him. Jerilyn stroked her back.

After a moment Major Rouse continued. "Sergeant McConnaughey was then evacuated by helicopter to the Chu Lai Military Base Hospital and pronounced dead on twenty-sixth February, 1970, at twelve-forty hours. On the behalf of

Melvin Laird, United States Secretary of Defense, I extend to you and your family my deepest sympathy in your great loss. I leave you this document, Mrs. McConnaughey." He handed the paper to Carrie Emeline. She accepted it with a trembling hand, and tears streaming down her face.

The Fort Knox Chaplain spoke next. "A survivor assistant officer from Fort Knox will be here tomorrow to aid in the details in arranging the funeral and bringing your husband home. He will be able to answer all your questions." Then he addressed Christopher and Jerilyn. "Will you be able to stay with your daughter?"

Dad's voice was hoarse when he spoke. "We'll be here for our daughter. I'm a pastor, too, and I was once a chaplain in the army air corps. I don't envy your duty, but it's better than the telegram used in World War Two and the Korean War." Christopher stood. "I thank you for your personal presence on behalf of my family. God bless you both." At that he showed them out, then returned to the sofa to hold his grieving daughter and wife.

Chapter Twenty

The Survivor Assistant

"To appoint unto them that mourn in Zion, to give unto them beauty for ashes, the oil of joy for mourning, the garment of praise for the spirit of heaviness; that they might be called trees of righteousness, the planting of the LORD, that he might be glorified."
Isaiah 61:3

The Past

March 03, 1970

The next few days passed in a blur for Carrie Emeline. Her parents stayed in Louisville with her, and her siblings all called with comforting words. The survivor assistant officer, Captain Robert Hensley, made all the arrangements. He was detailed, calm, compassionate, and extremely efficient. "Where do you want your husband's body delivered?"

"Franklin, Kentucky. That's where we met and fell in love." Carrie Emeline began to cry and dabbed at her eyes. "I'm sorry. Please go on,

Captain Hensley."

"There's no need to apologize, Mrs. McConnaughey," he replied in a comforting voice. "I need to inform you that your husband's body will arrive in a sealed casket. Because of this, you will not be able to open the casket to touch him. I've been informed that the top will be glass, so that you can view him. His face is not damaged."

Carrie Emeline began to cry uncontrollably. "Please ... just give me ... a minute," she managed to say. Her dad walked into the room, sat beside her, and held her as she softly cried.

"Take all the time you need, Mrs. McConnaughey. In fact, I can come back tomorrow, if you like."

She sat up and turned back to Captain Hensley. "No, please. I want to finish. I won't be here in the morning. I'm going home to Franklin with my parents tonight. I will be gone until after the funeral. Will you still be my survivor assistant officer, even if I'm in Franklin?"

"Franklin's in Simpson County, correct?"

"Yes, sir."

He smiled. "Yes, Mrs. McConnaughey, Simpson County is still in my jurisdiction. I'll be there for you. The army will put me up in a local hotel until your husband's funeral."

"That's not necessary. My parents own

Christmas Hotel in Franklin. We'll make sure you have a room."

"Christmas Hotel, huh? I've heard wonderful things about Christmas Hotel. I've always wanted to visit. I never envisioned under these circumstances, though. I'll make the arrangements to have your husband's body transported to Franklin. Do you want him taken to a funeral home ... or maybe a church?"

She turned to her father. "It would be more special and appropriate to have Andrew at the Christmas Hotel chapel, since we met at Christmas Hotel. However, because it's so small there won't be room for all the guests I imagine will be visiting. I really don't want him to go to the funeral parlor. They won't be making him up anyway. What about at Pastor Palmer's Church? There would be room for the guests, and if you don't want to officiate, Daddy, then maybe Pastor Palmer will be available."

"I agree with transporting him to Pastor Palmer's church. That would probably be best, Carrie Emeline," her father replied. "I'll contact Pastor Palmer and make the arrangements."

Captain Hensley nodded. "If that's what you wish, upon Pastor Palmer's approval that's where we will send Sergeant McConnaughey. Will you want interment in Franklin, too?"

"Yes, I want him buried around others in our family at Greenlawn Cemetery. Andrew's parents are deceased, and he has no siblings. He belongs in Franklin, Kentucky near my family...."At that, she began to cry again. She apologized again.

"Mrs. McConnaughey, I have all the information I need for now. I will be in Franklin within two days. I have paperwork to prepare. I'll just need to know the answer from Pastor Palmer by tomorrow, if possible."

"I'll make sure you have Pastor Palmer's answer by tomorrow," said Christopher.

With a strained voice Carrie Emeline asked, "When will Andrew's body arrive?"

"He's scheduled to arrive on March seventh. If you want a visitation, you should be able to arrange it on March eighth and the funeral on March ninth."

"March ninth." She said the date softly, almost to herself. "March ninth," she repeated. "That was the day I was to see Andrew in Hawaii. Now, I'll see him in a coffin." She began to cry again. She glanced over at the vase still holding Andrew's flowers. They were dead, too, and she couldn't bring herself to throw them out.

Chapter Twenty-One

Nighttime Visitor

"They prevented me in the day of my calamity:
but the LORD was my stay."
Psalm 18:18

The Past

March 07- March 09, 1970

Carrie Emeline was at home in Franklin with her parents and her four siblings when the call came in from Pastor Palmer that Andrew's body had arrived exactly on schedule at the First Methodist Church of Franklin. Carrie Emeline, her parents, and siblings bundled up to walk the few blocks to the church.

"Are you sure you don't want me to drive you?" asked her father.

"I'm sure, Daddy. I need the exercise, and it's only three blocks. I want to feel the wind in my face."

Pastor Palmer and his wife Mary greeted the family in the foyer when they arrived, along with Captain Hensley. "You have our condolences,

Carrie Emeline," Pastor Palmer murmured, and Mary hugged her.

Carrie Emeline looked to the front of the church and saw the casket on a riser. She ran as fast as her bloated body would allow, down the aisle and looked in. "Oh, Andrew." She slumped over the glass top casket, crying uncontrollably.

Her parents and siblings stood back in the lobby, allowing her privacy, as she cried, they themselves crying, too.

Finally her mother walked forward and placed her arm around her daughter. "Carrie Emeline, please come and sit down. This is not good for you, or the baby."

Dazed, she obeyed her mother and allowed her to lead her to the front pew. The moment was surreal, and the family gathered around her with consoling words. They all heard the interruption at the same time. The sound began in the church foyer. They looked in the direction of the thump, thump, thump they heard coming down the aisle toward them. The noise was made from a cane used by a soldier in his Class A dress army uniform. Captain Hensley stepped forward.

"May I help you, sergeant?"

The soldier saluted his superior and Captain Hensley returned the salute. "Sir, my name is Sergeant Marcus Taylor. I was on the mission with Sergeant McConnaughey when he was killed. Our buddy, Specialist Four Gerald Staats, was killed the same day. I was shot in the arm and leg and returned to the States to recover. I've been granted leave to attend the funerals of both my army buddies."

He then turned to Carrie Emeline, and she stood. "Marcus," she said while wiping her eyes, "thank you for coming."

He hugged her. "I'm so sorry, Carrie Emeline. Andrew was a good man, and a far better man than I. Believe me, I wish it had been me instead of him."

They stood and held each other as the family watched. Marcus comforted Carrie Emeline with gentle pats on her back, while she cried on his shoulder.

Although he had metal pins in his left leg and left arm, Marcus was asked if he'd like to be a pall bearer. He immediately accepted. The other five men were Christopher, Lily's husband John Demeter, Ken, Chris, and close family friend Eugene Scott.

The visitation was held for four hours on the evening of Sunday, March eighth. At many times that evening, the church sanctuary was overflowing into the lobby, with the townspeople wanting to pay their respects. Carrie Emeline held up well, but the family was worried about their daughter's health, so close to the birth of the baby. It did give them some comfort that Dr. Beasley, their friend of many years, stayed the entire four hours. Dr. Beasley shared the family's concerns about Carrie Emeline and the baby.

The next morning was a cold, windy day. Promptly at eleven o'clock, the funeral began. There was not enough room in the church, so chairs were crowded into the foyer. Pastor Palmer preached the service, so that Carrie Emeline could have both her parents beside her. There was not a dry eye in the house when he finished. Free-standing divider screens were placed around the coffin, so the family would have privacy in the final goodbye.

When the mourners walked outside and down the church steps to the limousine, the wind whipped at them and the women and children struggled to stand. A light drizzle of rain began to fall, causing a quick drop in temperature. Umbrellas shot up. Mindless thoughts ran through Carrie Emeline's head. *"Blessed are the dead that the rain falls on."* She heard her mother quote the phrase many times, from F. Scott Fitzgerald's *The Great Gatsby*.

Ken, Carrie Emeline's twin, offered his arm to

her, and she gratefully accepted. The cars were lined up as far as the eye could see. She knew at that moment the pall bearers were loading Andrew's body into the hearse. When the family had settled in the limousine, the hearse pulled out from behind the church and their driver followed. The slow procession led them the short distance to Greenlawn Cemetery where the cars encircled the cemetery on all sides.

More random mind-numbing thoughts filled Carrie Emeline's head. *Andrew enjoyed running with me through the cemetery. He'll be near our deceased family members and friends, which I pointed out to him. Have you introduced him to them, Jesus? Has he reunited with his parents?*

Captain Hensley escorted the family to the tent. The wind whipped the top of the tent and the tent poles swayed. Captain Hensley was true to his word and had no intentions of leaving them yet. He promised to see them through the burial. The pallbearers carried Andrew's body to the stand. Carrie Emeline thought about the six-foot deep hole under the stand. *Andrew's not here, is he Jesus? He's with You.*

Pastor Palmer officiated over a short service, and the seven men in Class A dress uniform lined up several yards away from the tent.

At the first crack of the rifles, Carrie Emeline

flinched. She knew it was coming, but it still startled her. She heard the second order to fire. "Again!" *Crack!* "Again!" *Crack!*

Two uniformed officers began folding the American flag draped atop the casket. They handed it to Carrie Emeline. In a stupor, she watched the long, slow, final salute, demonstrating their deep respect. When the taps began, she cried uncontrollably. Ken helped her to her feet, and through blurred eyes she viewed the faces of family and friends, men and women alike, also crying. Knowing they felt her pain, she loved each and every one of them.

Following the funeral, Sergeant Marcus Taylor said goodbye and hugged her. He explained he was leaving to join the Staats family in Dayton, Ohio for the funeral of their other fallen comrade's visitation that evening, and his funeral in the morning. "I'm leaving the army when my tour of duty is complete in August. I promise to come and visit you in Louisville. We can discuss Andrew's time in Vietnam if you like."

"I would like that, Marcus, and thank you for being here."

"You're welcome," and he kissed her goodbye on the cheek.

Captain Hensley again expressed his sympathies and goodbyes, too. "Mrs.

McConnaughey, if you need me for anything, please don't hesitate to call me." He gently patted her hand.

"Thank you, Captain Hensley, for everything."

That night, Carrie Emeline slept in her old bedroom at her home on South College Street, and dreamed of Andrew. She awakened with tears streaming down her cheeks. She rolled over and checked the time on the clock. It was three o'clock, and way too early to get up and awaken her family. She turned on the bedside lamp, reached into the drawer of the night stand, and picked up all of Andrew's letters to her, that she had wrapped in a red ribbon. Sitting up, she propped pillows behind her.

Two hours later she had not reread even half of his loving letters. Closing her eyes, she laid her head against the pillows. She heard her name and opened her eyes. A bearded old man in farmer's overalls sat in the chair. "Who are you?"

"An old family friend."

"I'm dreaming."

"Maybe."

"Are you Lydia Grace's angel?"

"Yes, and yours, too."

"My husband's dead."

"Yes, he is."

"I'll never be happy again."

"Yes, you will Carrie Emeline."

"How?"

"You must remember to place your faith in the Lord Jesus, and not people or things."

"That's hard."

"I know, but you are going to be fine."

"How long will it take?"

"That's up to you, Carrie Emeline. In the meantime, you have a beautiful baby boy to raise up to know Him."

"A boy?"

"Yes."

She closed her eyes and pondered his words. When she reopened her eyes, he was gone as quickly as he came.

Chapter Twenty-Two

Andrew Michael McConnaughey

"I wait for the LORD, my soul doth wait, and in his word do I hope."
Psalm 130:5

The Past

Monday, March 13, 1970

Four days later, Carrie Emeline was asleep when her labor began. Jerilyn had given her a loud hand bell to ring if the labor started at night, or if Carrie Emeline needed her for anything.

The first pain was a quick jolt, and Carrie Emeline rose up in the bed. She glanced at the clock, and it was four in the morning. She lay back down, not wanting to disturb anyone's sleep. Surely she was in the early stages of labor. Her back began to ache, and she had stomach cramps. The next pain was thirty minutes later, and it forced her to sit up again.

Perched on the edge of the bed, her feet dangled over the side. *I must remain calm. This is all normal. Mom's always up by five thirty. I can wait longer. It may even be a false alarm. He's not due for another twelve days.* She began breathing deep and slow. The next pain was twenty-five minutes later and more intense. She rang the bell. Within a minute, footsteps ran down the hall. Carrie Emeline felt her breath coming harder and faster.

Jerilyn looked her daughter over from head to toe. "Tell me about the pains, honey."

After giving her mother a quick run-down, Jerilyn helped her off the bed to walk. Carrie Emeline knew she was shaking, but she couldn't help it.

"It's okay, honey, you've got a while to go. Let's go to the bathroom. I'm going to draw you a warm bath."

When the water was ready, Jerilyn helped her daughter into the tub. Carrie Emeline sank into the warm water and began to calm down — until another pain hit that lasted longer than the previous ones.

She stared wide eyed at her mother. "Should we call Dr. Beasley?"

Jerilyn patted her daughter's hand. "Not yet, honey. Try to relax. This can take a while. Take deep breaths."

At six o'clock Christopher gently knocked on the bathroom door. "Everything okay in there?"

"Everything's fine, dear. Carrie Emeline is in labor. She's still got a ways to go."

After twenty minutes the water was tepid, and Jerilyn helped Carrie Emeline from the tub. Three hours later the contractions were seven minutes apart and lasting about a minute each time. Jerilyn and Christopher were each walking her in the hallway when her water broke.

Jerilyn nodded to her husband. "It's time to get Dr. Beasley, Christopher."

Christopher and Dr. Beasley rushed back to the house, and Carrie Emeline was back in bed with old towels and old quilts underneath her. Time passed slowly for Carrie Emeline. Each pain was now knocking her out until the next pain. She had previously informed Dr. Beasley that she would be having her child with no medications. She read that medication for her also medicated the child. She had insisted she wasn't having her baby drugged, and no way was she changing her mind now, in spite of the pain.

She asked her father to stay, and he held her hand. With a death grip on her dad's hand, she screamed again. Jerilyn panted with her, and held pillows behind her daughter.

Carrie Emeline glanced at the clock. It was eleven o'clock. *Dear God, please make sure my baby is okay. I already love him. I can't lose him, too*. She looked down at her dad's hand and saw that it was bleeding. "Daddy, I'm so sorry."

He smiled at her, and with his other hand, he patted his daughter's hand. "It's okay, my sweet girl." He laughed. "Your mom did this several times to me, too."

"You can push now," Dr. Beasley said. Jerilyn helped her daughter, lifting the pillows behind her back.

Following several pushes, Carrie Emeline lost count, but she knew her child was born. "He's a boy, isn't he, Dr. Beasley?"

"You're right, Carrie Emeline. You have a little man."

She smiled and watched as Dr. Beasley rubbed her baby's back, and almost immediately he began to cry. Her mom wrapped her son in a towel, and Dr. Beasley then suctioned out the baby's nose and mouth. "He's got a good set of lungs," chuckled Dr. Beasley, "just like his mother when I delivered you." He placed the baby across Carrie Emeline's stomach, and Jerilyn tucked a quilt around him. Dr. Beasley and Jerilyn attended to Carrie Emeline.

Carrie Emeline rubbed her crying baby. "It's okay, baby. You'll be okay. Mama loves you. I'll take good care of you, I promise." She looked at her dad, and she saw him wipe a tear.

After about fifteen minutes, Dr. Beasley clamped and cut the cord. He then handed the baby to Jerilyn. She had previously prepared a bucket of hot water, now warm, and a stack of clean towels to wash Carrie Emeline, and a large roaster pan in which to bathe her newest grandchild. Jerilyn bathed the infant in the makeshift tub. She then dried and diapered the little boy, slipped a gown on the tiny body, and handed him to Dr. Beasley to check his heart and lungs. She removed the old towels and old quilts from the bed, washed Carrie Emeline, and changed her gown.

Ten minutes later, Dr. Beasley announced, "Everything seems in order, Carrie Emeline. Congratulations to you. Please bring your son to me in a couple of days, and I'll check him further."

Christopher rose too. "I'll walk you out, Dr. Beasley."

Jerilyn swaddled the baby in a small quilt and placed him beside Carrie Emeline. While he suckled, Jerilyn brushed her daughter's hair. "You look about as fresh as possible for a new mother." She smiled at Carrie Emeline and looked fondly on her newest grandson. "I'd better ask your father to come back in. He gets very nervous when babies are born."

As soon as Christopher entered, he kissed his daughter on the cheek, and then kissed the forehead of the swaddled baby, now sleeping, and lying next to his mother. "What's my grandson's name?"

"His name is Andrew Michael McConnaughey: for Andrew, of course, but I'll call him Drew."

"It's a fine name, Carrie Emeline. I know Andrew would be proud of his son. I love you, honey," he added as he stroked her cheek.

"I love you, too, Daddy."

"Always know that your mother and I are here for you. You will forever be able to count on us ... for anything and any time."

"I know, and I love and appreciate you both," she said, smiling at her father, and then she gently kissed her son's soft cheek.

Chapter Twenty-Three

A Revelation

*"How long wilt thou forget me, O LORD? for
ever? how long wilt thou hide thy face from me?
How long shall I take counsel in my soul, having
sorrow in my heart daily? how long shall mine
enemy be exalted over me?"*
Psalm 13: 1-2

The Present Day
Monday
December 02, 1974

Although Carrie Emeline said she wasn't ready to
talk, one hour later she called her mom and asked
her to return. Over four years had passed since
Andrew's death, and Carrie Emeline planned to
be open with her mom for the first time. Actually,
it felt good to be talking it out with her mom. She
had kept too many emotions bottled up inside her
for much too long. Carrie Emeline's tears
subsided, and her mother's presence calmed her.

"I never really grieved Andrew. The funeral,
then Drew's birth four days later, and then

Marcus coming into my life, teaching again, and then Angela's birth. All those events left me with no time to spend grieving Andrew. I thought that was probably a blessing in disguise, but it wasn't. One needs time to grieve a loved one. That's what I've been doing today. An anonymous person once wrote, 'Every day shared with the ones we love is a gift for which to be thankful.' Mom, I *am* thankful for the days I shared with Andrew, and all my family, and friends. Down deep, I know I've been blessed."

With a big sigh she hung her head and continued. "Marcus was not what he appeared to be. There is a great deal about the marriage I didn't tell you or Daddy, or my sisters and my brothers. Ken probably would have bodily hurt Marcus if he knew. I was ashamed to tell you, and I've been bitter."

Another huge sigh escaped from Carrie Emeline. "In the beginning, Marcus was loving and attentive, and I did learn to care about him and later love him. Then I discovered he harbored a controlling nature. He kept telling me what to do, as if I were a child. I thought it was cute at first, but as it progressed it wasn't cute anymore."

"What do you mean, controlling?"

"Oh, it started small. In the first week he changed my name to Carem. Shortly after, for instance, he would say, 'Let me fix your scarf. It's not tied properly.' Or, 'You really don't intend to wear that, do you?' And constant criticisms when I drove, as if I'd just received my driver's license. I'd suggest a place to eat dinner, and he might say, 'You really don't want to eat there, do you?' After a while, I was worried about having any sort of conversation with him. Sometimes I felt more like his little girl than his wife. But it was when we began to have aggressive arguments, and he became abusive physically, and with his language, that I was alarmed and sometimes scared. A dark side that I didn't anticipate appeared."

"He hurt you?"

"Yes, but initially it only happened when he was having a nightmare. Sometimes, when he had nightmares, he hit or kicked me in his sleep."

"Did Marcus drink excessively?"

"Yes, later on. He didn't when we first married, and when he did begin drinking, it was just one beer. Then it became nightly, with hard liquor, and in the past two years he didn't stop until he was falling down drunk. He was out drunk the night Angela was born. I couldn't get in touch with him. Mr. White, my neighbor, took me to the hospital. You and Daddy already know that Marcus didn't show up until Angela was ten hours old, *and* he was hung over."

She paused, wondering how much to tell. "This last summer he hurt Drew. Marcus was having a nightmare and hit me. Drew tried to get between us. Marcus slapped him and Drew hit the nightstand. A heavy metal lamp fell on his head. I called the police, and Marcus was arrested. I changed the locks and filed a protection order against him. I also filed for divorce. Many times I wished he'd never come around after he left the army ... except I wouldn't have Angela. Now, I'm having trouble forgiving Marcus."

"I want to help you, Carrie Emeline. Please tell me everything about Marcus from start to finish."

She rubbed her temples, sniffed, and her eyebrows knit together. When her chin quivered, she feared she would not be able to control herself. When she could finally speak, only "Okay, Mom," came out at first, and very soft. "Looking back, I think I was first attracted to Marcus when he came to Andrew's funeral, although only in friendship. I was just so happy to see one of Andrew's buddies ... someone I could talk to about Andrew. Really, it all began when he came to visit me back in August, 1970, after he was discharged from the army. He told me that Andrew, Jerry and he made a Christmas pact on Christmas day in 1969 while they were together in

Vietnam. If any of them were killed in battle, whoever survived would visit and help each other's family."

Another sigh escaped. "This will take a while, Mom."

Jerilyn smiled. "I have plenty of time for you, honey."

"Thank you, Mom. I know now that I need you and your advice. I should never have hidden this information from you two. I once told Andrew that you and Daddy were my rock. Here goes...."

Chapter Twenty-Four

Marcus Taylor

"Little children, let no man deceive you."
1 John 3:7

The Past

Friday Morning

August 07, 1970

Morning bath time was always pleasurable for Carrie Emeline and Drew. Drew could now sit up for a few seconds on his own, and Carrie Emeline propped plastic tub pillows around him so he could splash and play in the two inches of water. She squeaked his rubber ducky, and the laughter was beautiful music in Carrie Emeline's ears. His plump arms grabbed for the toy, he squealed with laughter, and then splashed the water.

The doorbell rang, interrupting their fun. Carrie Emeline grabbed the towel folded on the shelf, wrapped it around Drew, and hurried to the door. When she opened it, she smiled at the sight of Marcus, in civilian clothes.

"Marcus! It's good to see you. You promised

you'd come, and you were true to your word. Please come in."

"Hi, Carrie Emeline. It's good to see you, too." He kissed her on the cheek, and walked into her home.

"Please have a seat. I was bathing Drew, my son. Let me get him dressed, and I'll be right out. Make yourself at home."

She was back within ten minutes and found Marcus viewing the family pictures on the fireplace mantel, walls, end tables, and book shelves. Many of the pictures were of Andrew, and lots of baby pictures of Drew.

Except for the straight, collar-length black hair and dark brown eyes, Marcus brought visions of Andrew to her mind. Their tall, athletic builds were similar, and Marcus even dressed casually like Andrew in jeans, a button down shirt, and gym shoes. She couldn't help thinking of Andrew, with his army buddy now standing in her living room.

Marcus turned toward her and watched while she sat Drew down in the playpen, propping pillows around him. After winding the musical Noah's Ark mobile, Drew laughed at the animals as they revolved around in a circle.

"What's his name?" asked Marcus.

"Andrew Michael McConnaughey, but I call

him Drew."

"Good name. I'm sure Andrew would be pleased."

"Actually, Andrew and I chose his name when we were still in Germany. I shortened it to Drew. I couldn't bear to call him Andrew."

"I can understand that." A moment of silence passed while they watched the antics of Drew who was laughing and cooing while reaching toward the animals to try and grasp them with his chubby little hands.

"So, Marcus, since you're in civilian clothes, I assume you're either on leave or have left the army? At Andrew's funeral you did say you were not re-upping for another tour of duty."

"Yes, I've left the army. With the metal pins in my arm and leg, I'll probably never walk again without a slight limp, or have one hundred percent use of my arm. It was best that I didn't sign up again."

"Well, I definitely appreciate you coming to visit me. Would you like a cup of coffee, or some iced tea?"

"It's still early, so I'd love a cup of coffee."

"Please keep an eye on Drew, while I get the coffee."

"Certainly."

She was quickly on her feet and returned a

few minutes later from the kitchen with a tray holding a carafe of coffee, cream, sugar, and two mugs. She set the tray on the coffee table. Marcus settled beside her on the sofa.

She tucked her hair behind her ears and smiled at Marcus. "I must look a mess. Drew gets me wet when I bathe him, splashing in the tub, but we have so much fun. I think I have as much fun as he does."

"You look fine, Carrie Emeline. You're still the beautiful girl I met in Germany. How have you been?"

She blushed before she answered. "Well, I stay busy. Drew keeps me hopping, but he's a good baby. We take naps together, and I play classical music on the stereo while we nap."

"It sounds like you enjoy being a mom."

"I do. Outside of Andrew, Drew is the best thing that could happen to me. I thank God every day that if Andrew had to die, at least he left me with his child."

"I can see how happy Drew makes you. You're in a much better place than when I last saw you. I'm glad you have Drew." He cleared his throat before his next words. "I wanted to come see you, as I said I would. I want you to know that you meant the world to Andrew. I can't tell you how many times he thanked Jerry for suggesting he spend his leave at Christmas Hotel. He always said the best thing that ever happened to him was meeting you."

She knew her eyes teared, and she willed them not to spill over. She nodded. "Thank you, Marcus. I feel the same about Andrew."

He cleared his throat. "I also came here to tell you about the pact Andrew, Jerry, and I made together last Christmas."

"A pact?" she asked, and she knew she looked puzzled. "Andrew didn't tell me in his letters about a pact."

"I'd better start at the beginning. Bob Hope arrived in Vietnam to entertain the troops, and the three of us were fortunate enough to attend. We had a great time, and it took our mind off the war for one night. However, the next day we got serious again. The three of us made a pact. We all agreed that if any of us died over there, whoever survived would periodically check up on the other's family." He showed her the slip of paper in Andrew's handwriting with her address.

"Yesterday, I visited Jerry's family in Dayton. Well, at least his mother, Mrs. Staats. She's still grieving. Mrs. Staats said she still hadn't returned to work. Last night I drove down here from Dayton. I really didn't know if you'd be here in Louisville or in Franklin. I took a chance and stopped here first."

Carrie Emeline smiled and nodded to show she was paying attention. "Actually, Marcus, I did spend a month in Franklin after Andrew's death, before coming home. My mother was a big help for me with Drew. He was born four days after the funeral. Now that I'm home, I've even been thinking about teaching again for the next school season, beginning in September, after Labor Day. I've been in touch with my elementary school and they have a third grade class for me to teach, if I want it. I need to let them know in the next week. I just need to decide about daycare for Drew."

"Ahem." Marcus cleared his throat again. "I suppose now is the time to let you know that there was ... a ... there was more to the pact. Andrew asked me to more than check on you. Since I was your age, Andrew ... uh ... asked me to marry you and be a father to his child. That was his wish. He wanted to make certain ... that ... uh ... you and his child was well taken care of."

Silence. Completely stunned, all Carrie Emeline could do was stare at Marcus. Finally she said, "It's hard for me to grasp Andrew asking that of you or anyone, even though I know he cared a great deal about you. This is life-changing. Are you sure you understood what he meant?"

"I'm sure. Don't you believe me?" His expression appeared sad and puzzled at the same time, as if she had hurt him by not trusting him.

"I'm sorry, Marcus. I didn't mean for you to think I was accusing you of disingenuous behavior. But, Marcus, don't you want to marry someone you love?"

"Love is not necessary. Up until a hundred years ago, many marriages were arranged by the parents. Why not a marriage arranged by the first husband? We can always have a marriage in name only. A marriage of convenience, if you like. I'm willing, if you are. I'm not working at the present time, and until I find a job I can also be Drew's caregiver, so you can teach again. I'm a good cook, and I can take care of the house, too. In the army I was a mechanic, so I can keep our cars running. And who knows, but that love won't eventually follow?"

She sat back and blinked her eyes several time. "Whew. This is a bit overwhelming. I never dreamed Andrew would make a pact such as that."

"I wouldn't lie to you, Carrie Emeline." He grimaced as if he was offended by her suggestion.

"Oh, Marcus, I'm sorry. I didn't mean to hurt your feelings. I wouldn't intentionally do that. It's just that I've been taken by surprise. This is so unexpected."

"Do you want me to leave, Carrie Emeline?"

"Why, no, Marcus. In fact, you probably have nowhere to go until you find a job. Why don't you stay here, and we'll discuss this more? I have a spare bedroom. Let's try to get to know each other better. Obviously Andrew cared a great deal about you to even suggest this. Maybe I can learn to care that much about you, too."

Marcus smiled. "I'll get my pack from the car."

Chapter Twenty-Five

A Marriage of Convenience

"But the fruit of the Spirit is love, joy,
peace, longsuffering, gentleness,
goodness, faith, Meekness, temperance:
against such there is no law."
Galatians 5:22-23

The Past

August, 1970

Over the course of the next week, Carrie Emeline and Marcus spent almost all of their time with each other and with Drew. Carrie Emeline thought it might be an acceptable solution for Drew's care, and for being able to return to teaching. Marcus was correct about his knowledge of cooking. In fact, he now cooked all the meals. She informed the school she would take that class when school resumed the day after Labor Day.

Marcus stunned her one evening by whispering in her ear, "By the way, Carrie Emeline is certainly a mouth full. Andrew told me you were named after a girl born in the nineteenth century. I thought of a name that I've created out of your names. I want to call you Carem. It's the first syllable of your two names."

"Well ... I suppose ... it's okay. I've always been called Carrie Emeline. It's kind of the way of the South. Even my little sister is still called Lydia Grace." She was mostly surprised that he didn't first ask her permission.

"Well, I like Carem, so it's settled. It'll be my special name for you."

"Okay," she agreed, but reluctantly.

On Tuesday, August eighteenth, Marcus stated, "We need to get married, Carem. I'm afraid the neighbors are looking at you as if I'm ruining your reputation. Let's go get a marriage license and our blood tests today." He smiled and added, "And I promise to be a good father to Drew."

"Well, since you're going to live here and care for Drew, that's probably best. I'm sure you'll be a good father to Drew, but are you certain you want this ... arrangement ... between us? Also, let me again remind you that the marriage would be in name only." She knew she was still dragging her feet to go forward in this commitment. *Maybe I want Marcus to back out.*

"Yes, Carem. I understand what I'm entering.

I promised Andrew I would look after you and his child. I intend to keep my word."

Carrie Emeline smiled and tried to quell the uneasy feeling in the pit of her stomach. Andrew had wanted this, and she appreciated Marcus's commitment to his friend, and that he was willing to take on such a responsibility.

I shouldn't be afraid. This is like my mom, when my biological father was killed at Pearl Harbor, and she married Christopher. However, Mom fell in love with Christopher before the wedding. Maybe Andrew was my past and Marcus my future. I'll accept his proposal.

Three days later, after the blood tests came back, Marcus suggested going to a justice of the peace. "We should take care of this today, Carem. Today is Friday, and we shouldn't wait any longer. We may not be able to do this on Saturday."

She knew that the smile she displayed was false, and probably looked so to Marcus. She closed her eyes and envisioned Andrew. *I hope you really meant that Christmas pact. Oh, silly me. Marcus was his buddy.* She opened her eyes. "Okay, Marcus. We'll do it."

Two hours later, following the very impersonal ceremony, and no family member present except Drew, Carrie Emeline became

Mrs. Marcus Taylor.

Oh, Andrew, I hope you really meant for me to do this.

*****

She called her parents the next day and spoke to her dad. He peppered her with questions. "You married him? I don't understand. Isn't this rather sudden? How well do you know him?"

She explained the Christmas pact to them. She accepted the fact that those were Andrew's wishes, and it was an answer for her to return to teaching and have a caregiver for Drew.

"But it happened so quickly," said her father. "You really don't know him well."

"Andrew knew him well enough to call him one of his two best friends. Besides, I didn't know Andrew long before I married him. Also, what about you and Mom? How long was that? Sixteen days, I was told." *Oh my, I'm now being confrontational to my dad.*

Dad paused before responding to my rude questions. He was kind, though. *"Touché."* Another long pause. "Is he a Christian?"

Trying to soften her tone, she answered his questions. "That's not been discussed. If Andrew felt he's the man to raise Drew, then I'm okay with that. I do know Andrew spoke to both Marcus and Jerry about God. I can only hope he reached them before he and Jerry were killed."

"Did you pray about this ... this marriage of convenience?"

She inhaled and blew out her breath. This was not going very well, but she could hardly blame her dad. "No, but I'm okay with this arrangement, Daddy. Please don't worry."

"Do you love him?"

She sighed. "Daddy, up until a century ago most marriages were arranged, *and* still are in many cultures."

"Okay, Carrie Emeline. You're a grown woman, so I won't lecture you on what the Bible says about being unequally yoked."

"Thank you, Daddy. I appreciate that. Please don't worry. It's going to be okay."

"I really hope and pray it will be, Carrie Emeline."

Chapter Twenty-Six

Teaching Again

"He that hath no rule over his own spirit is like a city that is broken down, and without walls."
Proverbs 25:28

The Past

September, 1970

On the morning of September eighth, Carrie Emeline rose early to bathe Drew, get his breakfast, and then ready herself for the first day of school. First, she undressed Drew for his bath, and Marcus stepped into the bathroom.

"I'll do that, Carem. Drew's now my responsibility."

"Well, this is a special time for us."

"Well, it can *now* be my special time with Drew."

"Okay, I'll go to my bathroom to bathe and then get dressed. We can all eat breakfast together."

She had no sooner stripped off her clothes

when she heard the water draining out from the other tub.

After her bath, she dressed, and headed to the kitchen. Drew was in his high chair, with no snack on his tray. Carrie Emeline always gave him a cracker to chew on while he waited for his breakfast. She knew Marcus was aware of this.

"He didn't have enough time in the tub for his playtime."

"Were you timing me?"

"No, it's just that by the time he splashes and plays, and then I wash him. It takes a while. It's one of his favorite times of the day."

"I figured the point of a bath was to get clean. He's clean, Carem. Now it's time for breakfast."

Drew began to fidget in the highchair, and then he cried. Carrie Emeline handed him a cracker. "He likes a cracker while I prepare his cereal. That way he's occupied."

Marcus smiled at her. "You *do* spoil him, Carem. You really need to work on that."

Marcus set Drew's cereal bowl with the spoon on the tray of the highchair. "Let's see if he can figure out how to use the spoon."

Drew picked up the spoon, banged it on the tray, dropped it on the floor and laughed at the noise. Carrie Emeline laughed with Drew, got another spoon, and began to feed him.

"I guess your son wasn't able to figure it out yet."

"He's not even six months old, Marcus. You're going to need to feed him for now. Please make sure he has his vegetables and fruit for lunch. I've already made up his meals for the week. The vegetables and fruit are portioned in labeled freezer bags in the freezer. You'll just need to heat the bag in a pan of warm water."

"Why don't you just buy jars of baby food?"

"It's cheaper to cook the fruit and vegetables myself, *and* I know that it's just vegetables or fruit, with no added sugar or salt. I'll call at lunch time to make sure you two are okay."

He looked at her with half of his lip curling. "Do you really mean that you want to check up on me? Making sure I'm being a good dad, right?"

She bit her lip holding back the retort that nearly flew from her mouth. She smiled, hoping to disarm him. "No, of course not Marcus. I just want to make sure everything is going well with your first full day alone with Drew. Babies are not always easily cared for. They have their good days and bad days just like adults."

Before Carrie Emeline left for work, Marcus retied the scarf attached to her blouse. "There, Carem. Look in the mirror and you'll see it looks better."

Breathe. Stay calm. Maybe it's good that Marcus is taking control. I hope.

*****

After the first few days, it seemed that everything was going well. Carrie Emeline was enjoying teaching again, and it appeared that Marcus was doing his job as a devoted father *and* taking care of the house. Every evening when Carrie Emeline arrived home, Marcus was cooking dinner and Drew was playing in his playpen. Drew was a happy baby, so Carrie Emeline had no reason to feel he was being neglected. *Maybe this arrangement will work*, she thought, and she prayed.

Chapter Twenty-Seven

Changes

*"My beloved spake, and said unto me, Rise up,
my love, my fair one, and come away."*
Song of Solomon 2:10

The Past

October-December, 1970

Over the next few months, the days began to blend together. Oftentimes, Carrie Emeline arrived home from work and caught Marcus playing with Drew. Those were the times that melted her heart. She knew she was feeling closer to Marcus. They had settled into a routine like a family, in all ways but one. They were not living together as a man and wife. They were more like roommates, still maintaining separate bedrooms.

Carrie Emeline was not going home to family events. With Thanksgiving coming up, she was invited home, as usual, but chose to stay in Louisville with Marcus and Drew. She knew that her parents did not approve of her marriage of convenience, and she didn't want to stir up dissention with Marcus.

Carrie Emeline was the one who gave thanks at all meals and took Drew to church each Sunday. Drew loved Sunday school, and his teacher took turns holding her babies and read Bible stories to them. Carrie Emeline, Marcus, and Drew celebrated the feast of Thanksgiving alone. Marcus chose to go with them to church the Sunday before Thanksgiving, but later said it made him uncomfortable. That was the only Sunday he had attended church since their marriage. At times, Carrie Emeline tried to broach the subject of church and Jesus, but Marcus was not interested.

Some nights from her bedroom Carrie Emeline heard Marcus groan, cry out, sob, and sometimes scream in his sleep. Whenever she asked him about the disturbances the next morning, he'd just shrug it off and tell her not to worry.

Friday, December eighteenth was the last day of school for Carrie Emeline before Christmas break. When she arrived home, Marcus was finishing dinner, and Drew was in his playpen as usual. He had been sitting up for two months now and had just begun pulling himself up around furniture. As soon as he saw Carrie Emeline, he pulled himself up, bounced up and down, and began to laugh, while holding on to the side of the playpen.

"Ma Ma, Ma Ma, Ma Ma," he called over and over.

As Carrie Emeline picked him up, he wiggled in excitement, kicking his legs. "How's my little man?" Carrie Emeline hugged him to her and smelled his clean baby smells. *At least Marcus keeps him clean.*

Marcus peaked around the corner from the kitchen. "How was your last day of school for 1970?"

"Wonderful, but I'm ready for the break. We also need to get this house ready for Christmas. We really should get the tree after dinner. Drew is going to be so excited."

"Sounds good to me."

Marcus carried Drew when they walked through the evergreen tree lot to select their favorite tree — one that would also fit in the corner of their small living room. With the perfect tree chosen, the salesman tied it to the top of Marcus's 1967 Jeep Wagoneer.

Carrie Emeline placed a stack of Christmas record albums on the stereo. When Marcus brought up the Christmas decorations from the basement, trimming the tree commenced. Carrie Emeline had begun collecting ornaments since she left home for college ten years ago. Each year she added something unique and different. She also had the collection her mom gave her. For each of her children, her mom made an ornament every Christmas until they turned eighteen. Her mom was now carrying on the tradition with her grandchildren. She'd already called to say her first ornament for Drew was in the mail. For Drew's first Christmas, Carrie Emeline had his picture imprinted on an ornament and dated 1970. She planned on a distinctive ornament collection just for Drew for every Christmas until his eighteenth birthday, just like her mom did for her. She assumed he'd either go to college after high school graduation or enter the military like his two dads.

When the tree was complete with the ornaments and lights, Marcus plugged it in. Drew's eyes grew round with amazement, and his fat little cheeks broke into laughter. He clapped his hands and then pulled himself up in the playpen, holding onto the rail and bouncing. His baby laughter filled the room. Carrie Emeline smiled. *He looks so much like Andrew with his blond hair, twinkling blue eyes, and he's even developed that crooked grin. For the millionth time, thank you, God, for giving me Drew.*

*****

The next morning the three of them headed to the mall for gifts. It was exciting choosing gifts for Drew, and Marcus insisted on a train set. Carrie Emeline bought a baby walker so he could roll from room to room in safety.

Carrie Emeline pointed at the gifts in their cart. "You know we'll have to assemble some of these gifts together on Christmas Eve."

Marcus nodded. "I don't mind. It'll be fun."

On Christmas Eve they put Drew to bed at his normal bedtime of seven o'clock. Carrie Emeline loaded the stack of Christmas albums on the stereo: Christmas songs featuring Perry Como, Andy Williams, and Brenda Lee. Sitting on the floor together, she and Marcus first tackled the assembling of the baby walker. It wasn't too complicated. Carrie Emeline tied a big red bow around it and set it under the Christmas tree.

"How about some hot chocolate before we tackle the Flintstone car?" she suggested.

"Sounds great to me."

She returned with the chocolate, and they sat together on the floor and assembled the car. Carrie Emeline laughed. "I suppose we didn't need to buy the baby walker. This car will serve the same purpose, and Drew will probably prefer it."

"Well, the baby walker collapses, so we can

take it with us if we visit anyone."

Next they unloaded the train with all the village displays. Carrie Emeline shook her head and waved her hand over the parts. "Wow, there's a lot of pieces to this."

"I know, but I had a train with a village when I was a child. I think Drew is old enough to be fascinated with it. My parents always made sure the train was part of the decorations each year, and it circled the tree. They purchased it my first Christmas."

She looked at him and cocked her head. "You never speak of your family. Where did you grow up?"

"In the beautiful Northwest. I hail from the seaport town of Bellingham, Washington. My parents own an upscale restaurant on the bay."

"It sounds like a great place to grow up."

"It was. We snow skied in the winter, and in the summer we swam, water skied, and fished in the bay. It was one adventure after another."

"Do you have brothers and sisters?"

"I have three brothers and one sister. Sally was the last one born — and picked on unmercifully by her four older brothers, but babied by our parents. In spite of her big brothers, she turned out to be a great girl, and the only one still in school, actually college, and living at home. She's twenty-two."

"Don't you miss your family?"

"That's another story," and he clammed up.

While Marcus set up the train track, Carrie Emeline designed the village, placing the houses, businesses, a church, streetlights, trees, and the people in the little village scene. Lastly, she added the couples skating on the frozen pond. Her mind briefly flashed on Andrew, and she smiled. When everything was complete, they sat back and admired their work.

Carrie Emeline made more hot chocolate while Marcus built a fire in the fireplace and lit four candles on the mantel. Setting the mugs on the coffee table, she took a seat on the sofa with her legs curled under her, and Marcus sat beside her.

"It's beautiful," Carrie Emeline murmured softly.

They had turned out all the ceiling lights and lamps. The Christmas tree sparkled with twinkling lights. The tree, fireplace, and the candles were all that lit the room. The only sounds were the train moving on the track around the tree and the Christmas songs playing softly.

"This is nice, Marcus. I don't know how I would have gotten through this Christmas without your help. I want you to know that I appreciate all you have done for Drew and me."

"Carem, it's been my pleasure. Because of you, I have a home, and companionship." He stared into her eyes. "I care about you, Carem. I want a real relationship with you. I want to be a *complete* husband to you."

Carrie Emeline closed her eyes and a tear trailed down her cheek. Marcus took her mug and set it on the coffee table beside his. She opened her eyes, and with his thumb, Marcus wiped her tear away. She stared into his dark brown eyes, unable to speak.

She lowered her head and a curl fell onto her cheek. Marcus tucked it behind her ear and lightly stroked her cheek. "Carem, I don't expect any more from you than what you can offer. I want you to know that I've loved you since Germany. I loved watching your love for Andrew. I thought then that if I could experience a woman loving me half that much, I'd be a very lucky man." He cupped his hands around her cheeks and leaned in slowly.

She understood he was allowing her to say no. He kissed her, and she realized she was returning the kiss. Thoughts flew around in her confused head. *He cares. He's my husband. He wants to be Drew's father. I should be his wife.*

He stopped and again looked into her eyes.

He rose, blew out the candles and extinguished the fire in the fireplace. She watched the last ember die, and allowed him to take her hand and lead her into his bedroom.

Chapter Twenty-Eight

Bellingham, Washington

*"Hear my prayer, O LORD, give ear to my
supplications: in thy faithfulness answer me,
and in thy righteousness."*
Psalm 143:1

The Past

1971

Outside of Marcus's increasing night terrors, they settled into a pleasant family routine. One morning in early May, at the breakfast table, Carrie Emeline broached a subject that had been on her mind for a while. "Marcus, school's out for the summer on May twenty-eighth. How about vacationing a month in Bellingham, Washington? I'd love to meet your family. We don't have to stay with them. We could rent a cabin on the bay."

He stood and turned away from her. "I don't know, Carem. I haven't been back in a long time."

"Precisely. That's why we should go. They probably miss you."

He turned back to her. "I really doubt that.

I'm rather the black sheep of the family." He leaned with his back to the countertop, his arms and ankles crossed.

"What do you mean? You joined the army and served your country. You weren't drafted, and you didn't leave your country and move to Canada, like so many did. I can't imagine any parents that wouldn't be proud of their son."

"It's things I did before joining the army. I was the bad seed. My brothers and sister went to church with my parents, and all of them got what you call *saved* at an early age. When I received my driver's license I began running with the wrong crowd, and carousing on weekends. My mom would sit up those nights crying and waiting for me to come home. I saw how my lifestyle tormented her. I barely graduated high school, but all my brothers have graduated with honors. They all went to college and have wonderful jobs in Seattle. My sister Sally will probably join the family business and will someday own the restaurant. My dad told me I had to leave the house when I graduated. He couldn't bear watching his wife suffer any longer. I joined the army because I had no skills, except as an auto mechanic. I wanted to get away and see the world. It was the best thing for me."

"Did you go home on any of your leaves?"

"No."

"Did you want to?"

"Not particularly."

"Would you go home for me?"

He changed the subject, throwing the question back to her. "I don't see you beating a path back to *your* home, Carem. Are you ashamed of our marriage?"

By hanging her head, she knew she had answered him. When she looked up he was gone.

*****

Three weeks later on a Friday evening after putting Drew to bed, Carrie Emeline broached the subject again. They sat together on the sofa drinking Chamomile tea. "Marcus, you're wrong about my feelings toward you. I'm not ashamed of you. I'm ashamed of me. In the beginning, when our marriage was just for convenience, I'll admit I was scared to discuss it with my parents. However, I did tell my dad the next day. My father asked a lot of questions, but said he wouldn't lecture me about my decision. But look at us now. We've become a conventional family."

Marcus remained silent.

"Marcus, I'll make you a deal. If we can spend a month this summer at your home, we'll go to my home at Thanksgiving or Christmas. We don't have to stay in my family home. We can stay at

Christmas Hotel. What do you say?"

He smiled, but she heard the sigh. "If it means that much to you, Carem, the answer is yes. When do you want to leave for Bellingham?"

She set her tea cup back in the saucer and hugged him. "Oh, Marcus, thank you! This is going to be the best vacation ever!"

In the middle of the night, Carrie Emeline awakened when the bed shook. Marcus was shivering and then began yelling incoherently in his sleep. Switching on the end table lamp, she touched him and called to him gently, "Wake up, Marcus. You're having a nightmare."

He flipped over toward her, knocking her hand away. Pulling his clenched fist back, he was about to hit her when he awakened. Surprise and then horror reflected on his face. Carrie Emeline began to cry.

Wrapping her in his arms he cried, too and kissed her face. "Carem, I'm so sorry. I didn't mean to scare or hurt you. Please forgive me."

She wiped the tears from her face. "I know, Marcus. You need to get help. These nightmares can't continue. What was this one about?"

"I don't want to talk about it." He rolled over. In a few minutes, he was breathing softly. Carrie Emeline lay on her back and looked up at the ceiling. *Help us, Lord. Please help us. Please.*

*****

On the eleventh of June, Carrie Emeline, Marcus, and Drew flew to Seattle, rented a car, and drove an hour and a half along the scenic water route up to Bellingham. At fifteen months old, Drew knew many words. Every time he saw a boat, and they were numerous, he'd point and yell, "Boat, Mommy!"

Just South of Bellingham, Marcus turned onto Chuckanut Drive. "There's something beautiful I want to show you." He pulled off to the side of the road and lifted Drew from his car seat. "Bring the camera, Carem. You'll want pictures. From this vantage point, you can see the San Juan Islands, the Olympic Mountains, the hills and forests of the Chuckanut Mountains, and several bays along the edge of the Salish Sea." He pointed in the direction of all the places.

"Wow, Marcus, this *is* beautiful. We have to get pictures of you with Drew and me for our vacation scrapbook."

He chuckled. "We have a vacation *scrapbook*?"

"We will, if this trip is as memorable as I believe it will be."

Thirty minutes later they drove up to the rental office to pick up the keys to the three bedroom log cabin they were renting for the next four weeks. Although Marcus's parents invited them to stay at their home, Marcus made it clear he preferred to rent the cabin on the bay. There was also a boat included in the price of the cabin. It would be docked, gassed, and waiting for them.

Marcus stopped at the local market so they could pick up supplies. After unloading and unpacking, he phoned his parents. They had flown out at six o'clock EDT that morning, with one layover to change flights, and it was now one o'clock PDT. They had been traveling for ten hours. Although Drew was able to sleep on the plane, he was clearly ready for an afternoon nap. Carrie Emeline was unable to console him, and he whined and cried relentlessly, as they grocery shopped.

Marcus's parents were overjoyed to hear that their son and his family arrived safely, and of course his parents wanted to see them immediately. Carrie Emeline could only hear half of the phone conversation, but knew what was being discussed.

"We're going to lay the baby down for his afternoon nap. Yes, we can come for dinner tonight. Not the restaurant? You want us to come for dinner at home? Okay, we'll be there. Bye."

"So what time's dinner, Marcus?"

"Mom asked us to come at six o'clock."

Marcus was nervous, as he chewed his lower lip and wrung his hands together. After all, he'd not seen his parents since he was eighteen years old, and he was now twenty-nine. The only contacts were the letters that his mother and his sister Sally wrote to him. He said his father and brothers had not written at all. Marcus admitted he rarely wrote, and when he did it was only to update them on new addresses.

Carrie Emeline and Marcus showered and dressed for the evening, while Drew napped. When Drew finished his nap, Carrie Emeline bathed him and dressed him in a matching shorts and shirt outfit, along with summer sandals.

They left the cabin promptly at five-thirty and arrived at the family home shortly before six. Positioned at least fifty feet from the curb, the three-story Victorian home sat on two acres in the Bellingham historic district.

"Marcus, your home is lovely. Is this the home in which you grew up?"

"The one and only."

Carrie Emeline stepped out of the car and stood on the sidewalk in front of the home, while Marcus released Drew from his car seat. The little boy took Marcus's hand, and they joined Carrie Emeline as she took in the site. The house was a creamy yellow with white trim and moss green shutters. Ten steps led up to the wraparound porch which encompassed the home on three sides. Two long rectangular sidelight windows with beveled glass and an overhead transom framed the heavy brown wooden front door.

Directly above the front door, a walk-out balcony with another wrap-around porch adorned the second floor, with another smaller balcony leading out from the third floor. The historic home gave Carrie Emeline cause for homesickness for her home in Franklin. However, she also looked forward to meeting Marcus's parents.

They climbed the steps and Marcus rang the bell. The front porch held five white rockers on each side of the door, along with many hanging flower pots, and several flower pots along the railing around the wrap-around porch. Matching swings hung from the ceiling of each of the side porches.

A smiling tall and slender man and his petite wife, both in their late fifties, opened the door. His mother ran to Marcus and he bent down for her embrace. She began to cry. "I've missed you so much, son."

She released him, and his dad stepped forward and shook his son's hand. "Welcome home, son."

The older couple then turned toward Carrie Emeline and Drew who stepped up on either side of Marcus. Marcus placed his arm around Carrie Emeline and took Drew's hand with his other. "This is my wife Carrie Emeline, but I call her Carem, and her son Drew."

Carrie Emeline couldn't help but notice he introduced Drew as *her* son and not *their* son, but decided now was not the time to address the comment. Mrs. Taylor welcomed each of them with a hug and a smile, and Mr. Taylor shook both of their hands. Drew was agreeable with the handshake, which Carrie Emeline figured was probably his first greeting in that manner.

"Please come in and make yourselves at home," said his mother smiling warmly. "I was just finishing dinner preparations. Marcus, you can take Carem and Drew into the parlor."

His parents exited the huge foyer and headed to the back of the house. The foyer was as big as rooms in most homes, with beautiful wide plank oak floors. A winding staircase graced the foyer, along with an antique grandfather clock. The two-story ceiling was at least twenty feet high. Marcus led them into the parlor filled with Victorian furniture.

"Is it okay to sit on the furniture?" Carrie Emeline asked, feeling somewhat apprehensive.

Marcus smiled. "It's sturdier than it looks. Mom wanted the house decorated in its time period of the mid-nineteenth century. My parents bought the home shortly after they married, and Mom spent years in antique stores finding the appropriate pieces to fill their home."

Carrie Emeline jumped up from her seat on the English Victorian settee to rescue a glass vase from the end table before Drew could grab it. "No, Drew, mustn't touch," she scolded. Picking him up, she walked around the room viewing the family pictures that adorned the mantel, tables, and walls.

Marcus stood beside her. A picture of four little boys in a gilded frame held a prominent spot on the mantel. The oldest of the four boys possessed an impish grin. She pointed at the little boy. "You didn't say you were the oldest, but I suspect that's you."

"Guilty as charged. We were all typical boys, pulling pranks, getting into trouble with our parents, but I was the instigator." He laughed. "Here's an example. The neighbor boy, Ronnie, built a tree house. Unbeknownst to Ronnie, I talked my brothers into helping me remove the ladder and hiding it, *while* Ronnie was in the tree house. He was stranded from morning until dark, when his dad missed him and went looking for him. With no ladder, his dad had to call the fire department to get him down."

"That's terrible!" but she had to laugh, too. "Did you ever tell Ronnie?"

"Yes, about five years later when I returned the ladder to him. My father found it up in the carriage house loft. I had actually forgotten about it until my dad asked me what it was doing there. Needless to say, I got in trouble five years after the crime!"

They turned their heads at the sound of footsteps on the stairs. A tall, slender, and very pretty brunette young woman ran down the steps. Laughing, she flew into Marcus's waiting arms. "If it wasn't for the pictures we exchanged over the years, I'd never have known you, Marcus. I'm so glad you're home!"

"It's nice to see you, too, Sally. You're certainly not eleven years old anymore. Time doesn't stand still," he added, with a definite sadness in his voice, on which Carrie Emeline picked up.

He introduced Sally to Carrie Emeline and Drew. Sally hugged both of them. "Welcome to the family, Carem," and she then stooped down to address Drew, "Aren't you just the cutest little boy!" Drew giggled from the attention.

Mrs. Taylor appeared, and announced,

"Dinner is ready. You have just enough time to wash up. Marcus, please show them to the downstairs washroom."

When they entered the dining room, Mrs. Taylor removed her apron and said, "I hope you like smoked salmon, Carem. It's fresh, caught right here in the Bellingham Bay."

"It sounds wonderful, Mrs. Taylor. It will also be Drew's first experience eating salmon. It's not exactly fresh at home. However, one of the things Kentucky is known for is its beautiful lakes. If you visit us in Kentucky, you'll have fresh catfish."

"We'd like that, and I hope Drew enjoys the salmon."

Mr. Taylor took his seat at the head of the table, with his wife on his right and Sally on his left. Twenty leaf-scrolled backed chairs with thick padded seats surrounded the huge mahogany table. *Probably from the Regency period,* Carrie Emeline surmised. Carrie Emeline and Drew sat beside Sally, and Marcus beside his mother. Mrs. Taylor had provided a highchair for Drew in anticipation of the visit.

Carrie Emeline swept the room with her eyes. It was easily twenty-five feet in length and fifteen feet in width. The ceilings throughout the home were probably ten feet, normal height for the nineteenth century Victorian homes in America.

Seascape paintings graced the walls of the room, and an antique buffet required at least half the wall space on the shorter wall in the room and stood nearly eight feet tall on long fluted legs. Two floor-to-ceiling windows on each side of french doors looked out onto a courtyard with several huge potted plants and several wrought iron chairs and two matching tables.

She looked up at the overhead candle and crystal light in the center of the ceiling. "Oh my, there must be at least five hundred crystal prisms in the light."

She didn't realize she spoke aloud until she heard Sally chuckle. "There are exactly five hundred and ninety-nine crystal prisms. I know, because I've polished each one and many times." She then sheepishly looked over at her mom. "There were six-hundred at one time, but I broke one when I was sixteen. Mom didn't know that."

Her mom just shook her head, but she reached across the table and patted her daughter's hand. "That's okay, dear."

It was at that moment Carrie Emeline realized Marcus was raised by loving parents. *I wonder what happened to make Marcus so cynical.*

Mr. Taylor took his wife's and daughter's hands. "Let's all join hands and I'll ask the blessing." Marcus and Carrie Emeline did as requested and bowed their heads with the others. "Dear Heavenly Father, we are thankful for this day that our son Marcus has returned home to us. Only Thou knowest how much he's been missed by his family in the past eleven years. I pray for an abundance of love and devotion in his marriage with Carem, and I pray that Marcus will be a very good father to Drew. God, please shower blessings on their little family. We thank Thee for the food Thou hast provided this evening for our meal, and blessings on the hands that prepared the meal. In the name of Jesus Christ Thy Son we pray, amen."

The others followed with their amens.

Carrie Emeline found it touching that Mr. Taylor prayed so beautifully for his prodigal son and his son's new family. It was wonderful hearing a man pray the blessing again. She didn't realize until that moment how much it was missed. She had been used to her father's prayers, and then the short time with Andrew, his prayers. As far as she knew, Marcus never prayed. Her father had called them unequally yoked, and rightly so. *Dear Lord Jesus, I can only pray that You have a plan and that someday Marcus and I will be equally yoked.*

Following the lovely dinner, Sally volunteered to wash the dishes, while Mr. and Mrs. Taylor took them on a tour of the gardens, along with added information for Carrie Emeline's benefit. Mrs. Taylor pointed to a building on the property. "The carriage house is situated at the rear of the property, with Mr. Bradley our caretaker's full-size apartment above. Mr. Bradley takes care of our gardens, the maintenance on the house, the restaurant, and even the cars. He's worked for our family for the past twenty-five years. Within five years after moving to this historic property, we realized we needed full-time help, especially when the babies began arriving. Mr. Bradley lived in the apartment with his wife, but she passed away two years ago. Mrs. Bradley helped with the children as they grew up, and she also did the cooking and cleaning for us. Mr. Bradley wanted to stay on after the passing of his wife, for which we were quite pleased. He's become like family to us."

Mr. Bradley was tending one of the many flower beds when the family strolled into the yard. He was bent over, trimming a bush when he saw Marcus. With a huge grin on his face, he straightened, brushing the dirt off his hands onto his work pants. "Is that you, Marcus?"

"It is, Mr. Bradley."

The two men shook hands and then patted each other on the back. "It's so good to see you here again. Mrs. Bradley, God rest her soul, would have loved to see you, too. She thought the world of all you kids."

"I'm sorry about your wife, sir. You have my condolences." Marcus paused a moment and placed his arm around Carrie Emeline. "I'd like for you to meet my family, Mr. Bradley. This is my wife Carrie Emeline, but I call her Carem, and this little boy is Drew."

"Nice to meet you, ma'am," and he tipped his straw hat to her. Bending toward Drew, he shook the little boy's hand, causing Drew to laugh. "Hello, little shaver. When your dad was a young rascal, he liked to dig in the flower beds with me. Maybe you can visit with me for a few hours one day, and I can show you." Drew smiled big, showing off the twelve teeth he possessed. "How long will you and your family be staying?"

"A month," replied Marcus.

"Make sure you bring the little one around. He'd probably enjoy digging in the dirt."

"I'll do that, Mr. Bradley."

*****

Over the next four weeks, the little family visited Sally's college, Western Washington University in Bellingham, spent many days on the lake fishing or swimming, and hiking on the various trails at Whatcom Falls Park. Marcus purchased a carrier for Drew, so that he could enjoy the experience from Marcus's back, and not get tuckered out. A stroller wouldn't work on the trails, and Carrie Emeline and Marcus intended to take him with them everywhere they went. They spent nearly every afternoon boating in the bay or swimming around the dock at the cabin. So that Drew could safely play in the water with them, Marcus purchased water wings for him.

Every Friday night they were invited to the Taylor family home for dinner, except on their last Friday night in town. For the last night, Mrs. Taylor invited her other three sons up from Seattle along with their wives and children. They ate dinner at the Taylor family's restaurant, where they joined together six tables and positioned them so they overlooked the bay. Marcus greeted his three younger brothers: Nicholas, Timothy, and Noah, and met their wives and children for the first time. Mrs. Taylor had the waiters take pictures of the family gathering, totaling seventeen people.

Their father asked the blessing as the family all held hands around the table. "Dear Heavenly Father, I am humbled that my family could all be here together tonight." His voice grew hoarse and he paused to clear his throat. "It's a day Mrs. Taylor and I have dreamed of for many years. I'm thankful for the wives of my sons and all the beautiful grandchildren they've given us. Watch over them, Lord. Thou entrusted five children in our care as they grew to adulthood, and now they are returned to Thy care. I pray that each member of my family will know Jesus Christ as his or her Lord and Savior, and train their own children to know Thee as his or her Lord and Savior. I pray this in the name of Jesus Christ, amen."

The family echoed their amens.

The night before leaving Bellingham, Carrie Emeline and Marcus put Drew to bed and sat out on the back porch of the cabin, sipping lemonade. The moon was full and shone down on the shimmering water. They relaxed, listening to the crickets, tree frogs, and a hoot owl off in the distance, relishing in the companionship of each other's company. *The vacation has been perfect,* thought Carrie Emeline. *I don't think Marcus has had one nightmare since he's been here. This trip has been good for him.*

Marcus seemed to be in deep thought, too. Carrie Emeline took her husband's hand. "A penny for your thoughts."

After a moment he said, "I need to work, Carem. I've enjoyed taking care of you and Drew, but I need to be the man of the house as the provider, too. I know auto mechanics. I could probably work at any dealership in Louisville. I know there are decent paying jobs in that field. I might be able to work my way up into management, and maybe eventually own my own shop. What are your thoughts?"

"Marcus, I think that's a good plan. You'll be working at something in which you excel. I want that for you ... for us." She held his hand and they said no more, simply enjoying the peace and quiet of the summer evening on Bellingham Bay.

Chapter Twenty-Nine

Unequally Yoked

*"Be ye not unequally yoked together with
unbelievers: for what fellowship hath
righteousness with unrighteousness? and what
communion hath light with darkness?"*
2 Corinthians 6:14

The Past
Thanksgiving, 1971
In September 1971, Marcus obtained employment
at one of the major Louisville car dealerships as a
mechanic. Drew was placed in the care of a
retired couple who lived at the end of their block.
The couple was also the care-givers for two of
their own grandchildren, and Drew was given the
best of loving and quality care. Along with the
couple's grandchildren, Drew also called the
kindly couple Grandma and Grandpa White. It
was the ideal solution for Carrie Emeline and
Marcus, and they could each work without
worrying about Drew's well-being.

As promised, Carrie Emeline, Marcus, and Drew drove to Franklin for the Thanksgiving weekend. Thanksgiving fell on the twenty-fifth of November, so they would be off from the twenty-fourth and return to work and school on the twenty-ninth. They left Louisville on Wednesday morning and arrived at Christmas Hotel for their stay on the fourth floor.

Carrie Emeline's brother Ken and his wife Loretta had already claimed room #7, the family's private room. "Well, Marcus, what are your first thoughts of Christmas Hotel?" Carrie Emeline asked, as they stood on the curb in front of the building.

"Amazing. It's beautiful. It's old, but I can see it's so well maintained. The Italianate architecture is distinct in every way. Architects certainly added more detail back then to their work than they do now. It's too bad that in major cities many of these old buildings have or will be torn down. *Progress* they call it. I call it a real shame. Your Christmas Hotel is as spectacular as you led me to believe."

The Taylor family entered the building. Mom and Dad were sitting on their stools behind the desk, and Chris was filling out paperwork. Carrie Emeline set Drew down on his feet, and she held out her arms to her family, as they ran to her.

"Oh, Carrie Emeline, I'm so happy you came home," said her mom, blinking back the tears that threatened to spill over. She then looked up at Marcus. "Welcome to Christmas Hotel, Marcus," and Mom hugged him.

Her dad and brother hugged her, and then Dad held out his hand for Marcus to shake. "Welcome to Christmas Hotel, Marcus." Leaning down to Drew, he smiled. "I hardly know you, Drew. You're such a big boy." He reached to pick him up, but Drew shied back, hiding behind Carrie Emeline's legs. At nearly two years old, he was somewhat cautious around strangers, and Carrie Emeline had not been home since Drew was a month old.

At that moment, Carrie Emeline realized that she missed her family, and she was sorry Drew didn't know them. That was very wrong of her, in spite of what they felt about her marriage to Marcus. She saw the hurt expression on her dad's face.

She smiled and tried making light of it. "He'll warm up to you, Daddy. It won't take him long."

Her dad returned her smile with no comment.

Chris didn't attempt to pick up Drew, but offered to shake the child's hand. "I'm your Uncle Chris, and I'm happy to meet you, Drew."

Drew returned the handshake, smiling

timidly.

"Thanksgiving dinner will be at home tomorrow at noon," said her mom. "I hope you three will come earlier to spend some time with your brothers and sisters, and nieces and nephews, before we eat. Drew needs to meet his many cousins. It'll be a wonderful day for all of us."

"Certainly, Mom. We'll be there early. I'd like to help in any way with the dinner. I realize there will be a lot of us this year. I'm sure Drew will enjoy watching the traditional Macy's Thanksgiving Day Parade on the TV with his cousins, too."

Chris handed Carrie Emeline the key to their room, and she led the way for Marcus and Drew.

*****

The next morning, Carrie Emeline, Marcus, and Drew arrived at the Wright family home at eight-thirty. When they pulled up to Carrie Emeline's family home at 210 South College Street, Marcus whistled. "It's beautiful, Carrie Emeline. The balcony above the front door even reminds me of my family home, and I love the Italianate architecture. Although my family home is Victorian, I see our parents have similar tastes."

"I thought the same thing when I first saw your family home. You're going to meet a crowd of people. I hope it's not too intimidating."

"It didn't seem to bother you at my home meeting my parents, all my siblings, and their spouses and children. I'll be okay."

She kissed him. "Thanks, Marcus. I appreciate that."

Carrie Emeline rang the bell, no longer feeling comfortable just walking in. Lydia Grace opened the door. "Welcome home, Carrie Emeline. Since when do you ring the bell at home?" She smiled and the two sisters hugged.

"It's good to see you, too, Lydia Grace."

Lydia Grace turned to Marcus. "It's nice to see you again, Marcus, especially under much more pleasant circumstances than a funeral."

He nodded. "It's nice to see you again, too, Lydia Grace."

"This little guy must be Drew. I'm your Aunt Lydia Grace. It's nice to meet you," and she attempted to hug him. Drew again shied back, and he held onto Carrie Emeline's legs. "That's okay, Drew. I was frightened of strangers when I was little, too. I suppose you and I have that in common." That being said, Lydia Grace did coax a smile from Drew.

"Drew, your cousins are lined up in the living room watching the Macy's Thanksgiving Day Parade. Would you like to meet them?" Lydia

Grace pointed in the direction and he peered around his mother's legs.

Brian, his oldest cousin, stepped into the foyer. "Come on in, Drew, you can sit with me. I'm Brian."

Drew looked up to Carrie Emeline for approval, and she nodded to go on. Brian took Drew's hand and introduced him to his three sisters, Teresa, Mary Beth and Ellie. Ellie was the closest to Drew's age at three and a half years-old.

The morning went well, and Carrie Emeline breathed a sigh of relief. She hadn't realized how nervous she'd be with Marcus encountering her family, in spite of what he had professed. The men gathered in the living room and watched the parade. Carrie Emeline hugged her twin Ken and his wife Loretta, who now had a six-month-old baby girl named Jenna whom Carrie Emeline had not met. She then hugged her older sister Lily, and Lily's husband John. Marcus stood beside her and shook hands with all of them.

The women gathered in the kitchen. The pies were baked the night before, and the casseroles were being prepared while the turkey cooked. Christopher and Jerilyn had remodeled their kitchen seven years earlier, so they now had a double oven with plenty of space to cook the Thanksgiving feast.

The three Wright sisters and their sister-in-law Loretta set the large dining room table with the best china, crystal, and linens. The five older grandchildren would be seated at an extra table laden with the everyday dishes and glasses, but baby Jenna would sit in a high chair beside her mother Loretta.

The adults and children held hands while Christopher asked the blessing. After settling in their chairs, Jerilyn asked, "Lydia Grace, it's time we met that boyfriend of yours. When is that going to happen?"

Lydia Grace smiled at her mother and winked. "Maybe at Christmas, Mom. We'll see. He comes from a small family, and I don't want to scare him off. I've met his parents, and I know you would like them. Don't worry, Dad, they're all Christians, so you don't need to fret if we married."

Everyone at the table froze, and tried to avert their eyes from Carrie Emeline and Marcus. Carrie Emeline could see that Lydia Grace regretted her words as soon as she spoke them. Lydia Grace shot her that 'I'm sorry' look.

Marcus dropped his head and said nothing throughout the meal. When the meal was finished he put on his coat and left the house.

"Mom, please watch Drew while I go talk to

Marcus."

"I'm so sorry, Carrie Emeline," said Lydia Grace, with pain on her face. "I didn't mean to hurt you and Marcus."

Carrie Emeline patted her little sister's hand. "It's okay, Lydia Grace." She threw on her coat and hurried out the front door. She saw Marcus at the corner, and he was just turning onto West Cedar Street. She broke into a jog to catch up with him. "Marcus, wait," she yelled, but he kept walking and did not look back. When she caught up with him, she placed a hand lightly on his shoulder.

"Back off, Carem. I'm in no mood for talking." He threw her hand off, his lip curled, and his tone was so harsh that it alarmed her.

"Marcus, please. We need to talk."

"Go back to your precious *Christian* family, Carem. Remember, we're unequally yoked. Isn't that what your sister meant?"

"She's already apologized. It was just a slip of the tongue. She meant no harm."

"Meant no harm? Is that all it was to *you*?"

"Marcus, it's just that it was the way we were taught. It was as natural for her to say as breathing."

"I need to cool off. I'm going back to Christmas Hotel to pack. Say goodbye to your

family, or I'm leaving and driving home *now* —
and without you and Drew."

She stopped and watched him walk away.
Tears streamed down her cheeks. *Dear God, help
us. I'm so scared. I don't know what to do. The
most innocent occurrence will set him off.*

Chapter Thirty

Return of a Night Visitor

*"For he shall give his angels charge over
thee, to keep thee in all thy ways."*
Psalm 91: 11

The Past

January to August 1972

It was late on a cold January evening, the visit to
Christmas Hotel for Thanksgiving just a bad
memory. Drew was fast asleep when Carrie
Emeline joined Marcus on the sofa for a cup of
tea. Taking a deep breath, not knowing how he'd
take the news, she just blurted it out. "We're
going to have a baby, Marcus."

He set his tea cup down. "A baby, huh. Is that
what you want?"

She was puzzled. "I don't understand. I
thought you'd be thrilled."

"I thought you were on the pill. What
happened?"

"We talked about this, Marcus. At my last
check-up my doctor said that it wasn't wise,

because it could now be detrimental to my health to take the pill after age thirty, which is what I'll be in four months. I stopped the pill three months ago. You knew that."

"So, *voila*, you're pregnant. Just like that." He snapped his fingers for emphasis. "When's it due?"

"My due date is August seventh."

"You can always get rid of it. I'm sure we can find someone to do the deed."

"You can't be serious," she said in horror.

"I didn't think you would. Looks like I'll need to earn more money." He mocked and curled his upper lip. "With another kid to take care of, you won't be going back to teaching in September. You'll have it made if you have a baby every year! You'll just keep my nose to the grindstone!"

"Marcus, please. This is our baby we're talking about. And our baby is not an *it*."

"Oh, good grief, Carem. You are such a pro-lifer!"

"What's wrong with loving babies whether born or in the womb?"

He would not answer. He just scoffed and shook his head.

*****

The nightmares worsened, and Marcus quit coming home directly from work. "You've been drinking again, Marcus."

"So what?" he slurred.

"It's become a bad habit. Drew even said to me yesterday that Daddy smells funny."

"Tell the brat not to worry about it."

*****

"Marcus, wake up." She gently shook him. "You're having another nightmare."

Still sleeping, he raised his leg and kicked her so hard she fell from the bed. The nightmare continued. Carrie Emeline did not go back to bed, but sat curled up in a chair and watched Marcus as he tossed and turned, occasionally yelling out, but she couldn't make out his words. His body shook, and about thirty minutes later he finally relaxed.

She was still sitting in the chair when the alarm went off. With his eyes closed, Marcus eventually turned it off after three clumsy attempts. Then he saw Carrie Emeline in the chair. "What're you doing over there?"

"Marcus, we've got to talk."

"Oh, good grief, can't a man get some peace around here?"

"Your nightmares are getting worse, Marcus, not better. When are you going to talk to me about them, or at least speak to a professional?"

He sat up in bed, ran his fingers through his

hair, and stood. "Let it go, Carem." He walked into the bathroom. She heard the shower running and knew that the conversation was over — at least for him.

*****

In the evening of August sixth, Carrie Emeline was home alone with Drew when the contractions began. *It's six o'clock. He should have been home thirty minutes ago. He must be at the bar, again.*

She fed Drew and put him in bed at eight o'clock. At eleven o'clock Marcus still wasn't home, and the pains were now twelve minutes apart. She called Mr. and Mrs. White, who arrived within minutes. Mrs. White took one look at her and asked in obvious anger, "Where's Marcus?" Carrie Emeline knew the Whites were aware of his drinking.

"He hasn't come home, yet." Carrie Emeline saw the anger change to pity in her expression, and at that moment she hated Marcus.

"I'll stay with Drew, and Mr. White will drive you to the hospital."

It was now one o'clock in the morning and a doctor and nurse had just checked her again. She heard whispering in the background. "If she doesn't dilate, soon, we'll need to do a C section." They left the room.

Carrie Emeline closed her eyes, and when she reopened them she saw an old man wearing farmer's overalls sitting in a chair. "I've seen you before."

"Yes, you have."

"Am I dying?"

"No, you'll be just fine."

"Is my husband here?"

"No."

"Is the baby okay?"

"Yes, she's fine."

"She?"

"Yes. She's a beautiful little girl."

Carrie Emeline relaxed and drifted off for a minute, but the next pain jarred her awake. The doctor and nurse were back in the room, and the old man was gone.

"Mrs. Taylor, it's time to push."

After four tries, Carrie Emeline birthed her baby.

"You have a little girl, Mrs. Taylor," the doctor announced.

"I know," and she smiled.

The nurse leaned over her. "Just rest, dear, and we'll check and bathe your baby."

Carrie Emeline was given a quick glimpse of her daughter and then drifted off to sleep. She was more tired after delivering this baby than with Drew. *I guess I'm getting old.*

The sun peaked over the horizon at six o'clock, and she was in a room with one other mother. The other mother was nursing her baby and looked over at Carrie Emeline. "Oh, you're awake. It must have been a long night for you."

Carrie Emeline just nodded. She pressed her call button for the nurse. "I need to see my baby."

"Don't try to get up. Just stay there and I'll bring her to you."

Ten minutes later the nurse returned with her baby in a rolling, portable hospital crib. The nurse gently lifted the swaddled baby and handed her to Carrie Emeline. Opening the blanket, she had her first complete look of her daughter. She had straight black hair like Marcus. She checked her body, her fingers and toes, and then rewrapped the blanket. "You're perfect. Oh, my little angel," she cooed aloud. The morning had now dawned. "Angel — Angela, the morning dawn. Your name will be Angela Dawn. Angela Dawn," she repeated. "It fits, sweetheart."

She snuggled against her daughter, and kissed the top of Angela's downy head. Then she called her parents.

Chapter Thirty-One

Angela Dawn

"Wine is a mocker, strong drink is raging: and whosoever is deceived thereby is not wise."
Proverbs 20:1

The Past

August 07, 1972

Following his all-night drunken binge, Marcus arrived home and discovered his wife and Drew were not there. He went looking for Carrie Emeline at Mr. and Mrs. White's home. Crossing her arms, Mrs. White informed him his wife was at the hospital and had delivered *his* baby. She wasn't very pleasant conveying the information. It was a Saturday morning, and Marcus didn't have to work that day, so he didn't change his disheveled clothes. He finally arrived at the hospital when his daughter was ten hours old.

When Marcus walked into Carrie Emeline's room, he was greeted by her parents. *Oh good grief. I'm probably going to get a bad husband lecture. Wait until they find out I slept in the car last night.* He was aware that he smelled of alcohol, stale tobacco, and his clothes were rumpled.

Surprisingly, Carem appeared happy to see him. He glanced into the portable crib and saw the baby was asleep.

Carrie Emeline smiled. "We have a daughter, and I chose a name for her. I hope you will approve. How about Angela Dawn? She looks like a little angel, and she was born the moment the sun dawned. Do you like it, or do you want to think further about her name?"

Carem looked so happy that he decided not to dash her hopes, especially in front of her parents. "Angela Dawn is fine. I'm sorry I wasn't here for you, Carem. The guys and I got a little carried away last night."

Carrie Emeline changed the subject, but her parents glared at him. "Drew is staying with Mr. and Mrs. White until Angela and I are released to go home. My parents have offered for me ... and the children, of course to go home with them for a few weeks. That way you can work without worrying about the children and me at home."

"If that's what you want, Carem, then go with your parents. Keep in mind that I'm capable of taking care of all of you in the evening, and Mrs. White would help while I'm at work."

Christopher and Jerilyn had said nothing up to this point, but Christopher now spoke. "Carrie Emeline would receive excellent care along with the children at our home. Dr. Beasley's office is two blocks from our home in case of an emergency. Don't you think it would be better for your wife and children to stay temporarily with us?"

Marcus thought Christopher's tone was a bit curt, so he decided to disagree. "I think Carem and the children should be at home, but thank you for the offer," he answered in a stern tone.

Two days later, Marcus left work at noon to bring home his wife and baby from the hospital. Marcus was quiet during the drive. He had not brought Drew with him. Carrie Emeline asked, "Did Drew stay the last two days with Mr. and Mrs. White?"

"Yes. I thought it was better for him. He went to church with the Whites on Sunday, and of course I had to go to work this morning."

"I can't wait to see him and have him meet his little sister. He's going to be so surprised."

When Carrie Emeline and Angela were settled in, Marcus brought Drew home. Drew ran to Carrie Emeline and they hugged and kissed. Angela lay in the cradle beside Carrie Emeline's chair in the living room. It had been Drew's cradle as a baby, which her father and Chris built for him.

"Are you ready to meet your baby sister?"

A huge smile spread across his face. "Yes, Mommy."

"Well, have a seat on my lap, honey. Maybe Daddy can hand her to us." She looked at Marcus. He had not yet held his daughter.

"I'm not in to holding or picking up small babies. They squirm, cry, and make messes."

Carrie Emeline stared at him, hardly believing he could speak in such an uncaring manner. In a controlled voice she finally said, "This is not just *any* baby, Marcus. She's *your* daughter."

Marcus snarled, turned, and stomped out of the room and into their bedroom. Exasperated, Carrie Emeline nearly cried, but she knew she needed to be strong for her children. "Get down, Drew my sweet. Mommy will pick up Angela, and then you can get back on my lap and we'll both hold her."

With Drew comfortably settled back on her lap, she placed Angela in his arms. "Now hold her head like this, honey," and she showed Drew how to cradle his little sister's head. "Angela can't hold her head up on her own yet. She's going to need our help."

Drew did as he was instructed. Angela woke

up and made gurgling baby sounds to him, and he laughed. Then Angela began to cry, and Carrie Emeline realized she needed her diaper changed. Marcus entered the room.

"She needs her diaper changed, Marcus. Do you want to help like you did when Drew was in diapers?"

"No, I'm going out."

Carrie Emeline heard the tires squeal as he raced out of the driveway. Turning to Drew she smiled. *I must remain calm. I don't want to scare my children.* "Well, you and I can change her diaper, Drew. Come help Mommy," and Drew followed as Carrie Emeline carried Angela to the nursery.

Chapter Thirty-Two

Vacation Suggestion

"Destruction and misery are in their ways: And the way of peace have they not known: There is no fear of God before their eyes."
Romans 3: 16-18

The Past

1973

They did not visit Franklin, Kentucky at Thanksgiving or at Christmas. After the Christmas holidays, Carrie Emeline returned to school to finish out the year, with Mrs. White caring for Angela, along with Drew and her own two grandchildren.

"Are you certain that a five-month old baby will not be too much for you with Drew *and* your two grandchildren?"

"Not at all, dear. Drew is almost three, and he's such a good boy. One of my grandchildren is now in kindergarten in the morning, and the older is in first grade all day, so I won't even have them all at the same time. I'll be fine. Please don't worry about the children, Carrie Emeline. I love Drew and Angela just like my own grandchildren."

"Thank you, Mrs. White. You and Mr. White have certainly been a blessing to me."

The months passed quickly, and before Carrie Emeline realized, Friday, June first had arrived, and school was dismissed for the summer. Carrie Emeline had an idea that would hopefully help Marcus. She had finished cooking dinner for the family, and Marcus actually arrived home right after work that day.

Following dinner, and after the children were in bed, Carrie Emeline proposed the vacation subject. "Marcus, I can't tell you how much I enjoyed the month we spent at your family home in Washington. Your parents have written several times with an open invitation for us to come again. They would love to meet Angela. You have accrued three weeks of vacation days, so how about a visit in July?"

The silence was deafening. Carrie Emeline realized this subject wasn't going to please him. When he finally spoke, he was belligerent, condescending, and sarcastic. "If they've wanted to meet Angela, they've had ten months in which to do it. I say they're so busy with the grandchildren that *matter* to them, that they're just speaking empty words. If they want to meet her, they can come here."

"Marcus, they have their restaurant to operate. They can't just pick up and drive or fly more than halfway across the country. I don't work summers, and you have three weeks' vacation time. It makes more sense for us to travel to them."

"Let me be perfectly frank with you, Carem, and say this slowly so that you can understand simple words. I-have-no-desire-to-go-to-Washington-and-visit-with-my-parents."

A few expletives interlaced his sentence, and Carrie Emeline was horrified. Marcus was changing into a monster. This was the first time she heard the foul language. She was speechless, and an evil grin slowly spread on his face.

"There, I've said it, Carem. Do ... you ... understand?" His tone was cold, his eyes narrowed, and his lip curled.

"Yes, Marcus, I understand completely. You don't have to treat me like a child."

"Good. I'm going out." He was out the door before Carrie Emeline could utter another word.

She sat stunned for the next few minutes. The tears rolled down her cheeks. In the hallway she heard little feet, and then they stopped. She turned and saw Drew. "Mommy, why was Daddy being mean to you? You're crying."

Carrie Emeline was even more appalled to see that Drew had heard at least part of the conversation. "What did you hear, honey?"

He crawled upon her lap and wiped tears from her face. "I heard him say mean things. Is he mad at you?"

Carrie Emeline knew she needed to carefully select her own words. She didn't want to turn Drew against Marcus. "Honey, Daddy is just tired. I'm sure he didn't want to sound mean. Daddy will be okay and soon be back to himself. Please don't worry."

"I'm scared, Mommy. Last week when Angela cried, he called her my stupid sister. When I said she wasn't stupid, he called me a brat and told me to shut up."

"Don't worry, honey. Go back to bed. Mommy will take care of everything." She watched him walk back to his bedroom. *Dear Lord, what do I do? The stress is getting to me.*

*****

The next morning she told Marcus what Drew had told her. He hung his head. "I don't remember saying that, Carem. Maybe Drew imagined what he thought I said. He does have an imagination."

Carrie Emeline inhaled a deep breath and blew it out. "You've got to see someone for help, Marcus. We can't go on like this."

"I'll check with some of the guys and see where to go. I'll get help, Carem. I promise."

I don't believe him anymore.

Chapter Thirty-Three

Danger

*"Look not thou upon the wine when it is red,
when it giveth his colour in the cup, when it
moveth itself aright. At the last it biteth like a
serpent, and stingeth like an adder."*
Proverbs 23: 31-32

The Past

June 14 and 15, 1974

One year later, the situation was not getting any better. In fact, it was worsening. Marcus was now hanging out nightly at the Veterans of Foreign Wars Club — better known simply as the VFW. He rarely came home before two o'clock in the morning. On this particular night Carrie Emeline sat alone in the living room, praying.

Dear Heavenly Father, I don't know how much more I can take. One day blends into the next. Drew is afraid of Marcus, and frankly, so am I. Angela has even tried to protect her brother when Marcus has said unkind things to Drew. She tells her daddy not to say mean things to Drew. Maybe, subconsciously, Marcus resents Andrew's son. They're children, Lord. They shouldn't have to witness Marcus's bad behavior.

I don't think Marcus truly loves any of us. I don't think he loves himself. I've been as patient as I possibly can. I abhor divorce, but no one should have to live like this. Help us, Lord. I certainly can't handle Marcus on my own, and I've prayed for Your help so many times. I've stood by Marcus for nearly four years. I can't do it anymore. I need You, Lord. Do You hear my prayers? Please intervene. In Your Son Jesus's name, I pray, amen.

Tonight she'd confront him.

He stumbled in the door, saw her sitting in the semi-darkness and slurred, "What ya doin' sittin' in the dark?" and he hiccupped.

"I'm just thinking about us."

"Us, huh?" Hiccup.

"You drink too much, Marcus."

"Oh, really? Aren't you Miss high and mighty?"

"You've missed two weeks' work already this year from hangovers. You've been reprimanded twice. I fear they'll fire you."

"So, what you're really saying is that I'm worthless? I'm not bringin' in 'nough money?"

"You're a bad influence on the children."

"Those brats don't care."

"Please don't call our children brats. I don't ever want to hear those words from your mouth again. In fact, I think you should leave our home." She stood and crossed her arms.

He stumbled toward her and stopped toe-to-toe in front of her, trying to balance. He spat the words, mockingly, "You're that 'b' word that disgusts you." He slapped her, and she fell back in the chair.

Placing her hand on her face, she watched him stagger off to the bedroom. "Marcus, please. We have to talk."

"Shut up, Carem."

"Dear, Lord, he's evil!"

That night, Carrie Emeline slept in the twin bed in her daughter's room, alongside Angela's crib. She lay in the dark staring up at the ceiling. From the dim glow of Angela's nightlight, Carrie Emeline could just make out the Disney characters on the walls and the stars on the ceiling. She remembered years ago, when her sister Lydia Grace was eight years old, she once counted stars to fall asleep. *Maybe I'll count the stars on Angela's ceiling tonight.*

Angela's favorite Disney movie was "Snow White". "She has black hair like me, Mommy." Therefore the theme of this room was recently changed to "Snow White". Snow White and her friends the seven dwarfs were pictured on the walls and the sheets and the comforter in the crib and the twin bed sheets and comforter in which Carrie Emeline now lay. Matching curtains hung in the single window.

She had not slept in this bed since Angela was four months old. When Carrie Emeline and Angela arrived home from the hospital and Angela awakened in the night, with no help from Marcus, it had been easier to get up, change Angela's diaper, and put her back in bed with her and nurse her. Many people said not to nurse a baby in the bed, but Carrie Emeline knew she wouldn't fall back asleep. Back then, she spent the time praying while Angela nursed, and now she spent this night praying.

Angela was almost two, and Marcus still had not gotten help for his problems. As usual, he'd broken his promise. Carrie Emeline had been reading about Marcus's symptoms in the school library. She was nearly positive he had Post-Traumatic Stress Disorder, or PTSD. The articles she devoured all reported the same symptoms: night sweats, shivering, terrible nightmares, suicidal, controlling behavior of spouse and/or children, denial, and drug and/or alcohol addiction.

Marcus experienced nearly all of the symptoms. She had prayed for him a very long time. *Where are you, Lord? Why haven't you answered my prayers? Are you there? Do you hear me? Am I alone in this, Lord?*

The next morning, Carrie Emeline slipped out of the bed before the children awakened. When she entered the bedroom she and Marcus had shared, the alarm was blaring, but Marcus was oblivious to the noise, and he was snoring loudly. The air smelled foul from his sour breath. She had made up her mind, and she wanted him out of the house today. She turned the light on to the dimmest switch. Gently she shook Marcus on the shoulder, trying not to startle him. He awakened, wild-eyed and clearly panicked. He jerked her arm, throwing her onto the floor. Jumping on top of her, he began pounding her head on the floor, and choking her. His lip curled, and a dark and evil scowl appeared on his face.

Help me, Lord! "Marcus, wake up!" she cried out.

He pulled back his fist to hit her, when a body jumped between them. *Oh, God no, it's Drew!* Marcus tossed Drew aside like he was a limp dishrag. Drew's body hit the nightstand with such force it knocked the heavy metal lamp off onto his head. Blood spurted everywhere.

"Marcus, wake up!" She hit him square in the face with her fist.

Marcus froze, dazed. He looked down at Carrie Emeline who was coughing and bleeding on the floor below him, and turned toward the crumpled body of Drew lying against the wall. The next sound he heard was pitiful.

"Daddy?" said the soft voice. Angela stood in the doorway holding her doll tightly to her chest, tears streaming down her face.

Chapter Thirty-Four

Emergency

"God is our refuge and strength, a very present help in trouble."
Psalm 46:1

The Past
June 15, 1974

"Let me up, Marcus," Carrie Emeline demanded in a controlled and forceful voice. Marcus rolled off Carrie Emeline, and she crawled to her son. "Drew, baby. Drew, wake up." The blood was spattered on the wall, the floor, and underneath him. "Get a towel, Marcus," she commanded with as much authority as she could muster.

Marcus returned with the towel and she tied it around Drew's head, adding pressure. "Call an ambulance!" she yelled at Marcus. "*And* then call the Whites."

Marcus obeyed, and picked up the phone book in the night stand, found the emergency number in the front, dialed the phone, and then phoned the Whites. Within ten minutes the ambulance and the police were at the door. When Marcus let them in, Carrie Emeline sat in their living room in the rocking chair, holding her bleeding and unconscious son on her lap, ignoring the blood running from her own head wounds.

Angela stood beside the chair and kept asking, "What's wrong with Drew, Mommy? You're bleeding, Mommy." Carrie Emeline could see Angela was scared and placed one arm around her.

Mr. and Mrs. White hurried into the house seconds behind the police. The paramedic who drove the ambulance wrapped Drew in a blanket and another paramedic held the towel pressed to Drew's head. Carrie Emeline saw Mrs. White, and was relieved. "Mrs. White, please take Angela home with you. I've got to go to the hospital with Drew."

Turning to the police officers she said, "I need to file charges against my husband. He attacked my son and me."

Carrie Emeline climbed into the ambulance beside Drew and watched out the window as one of the officers handcuffed Marcus and led him to the police car. The other officer climbed into the ambulance and took down her account of the attack, as the ambulance sped away.

Carrie Emeline relayed to him an abbreviated

version of when the occurrences began, and up to the present day. While talking to the officer, Drew began to stir. The paramedic spoke softly. "I'm sure he's got a concussion, ma'am, but don't worry. The doctors will check him thoroughly."

"Thank you." While Carrie Emeline continued her report to the officer, the paramedic wrapped her head with gauze. The amount of blood she lost was minor compared to Drew.

When they arrived at the hospital, she and Drew were whisked away. She heard the officer's parting words to her. "When you are able, please come to the station and file a restraining order. You'll probably want to change the locks at your home, too."

"Thank you, officer, for everything."

Drew was quickly hooked up to numerous machines, with tubes covering his little body. The hospital had a neurologist on duty, and he immediately began barking out orders. Blood was ordered along with a series of x-rays. Watching the nurses shave and bandage Drew's head naturally alarmed Carrie Emeline. He looked so small and frail, and the tears ran down her face. She didn't leave his side, only moving whenever a nurse checked his vitals or changed his head bandages. Carrie Emeline was told she would need several stitches to her own head injuries, but she told the medical team to concentrate on Drew. Her own care must wait.

While they were giving Drew a unit of blood, Carrie Emeline held his hand and prayed aloud, not caring who heard. "Dear Heavenly Father," she stopped to catch her breath, "please don't take my son. I'm not ready to give him up. I know he's in Your hands. I understand that only You know how long any of us will live. I love him so much. Please, God, give me strength."

She held her breath when the heart monitor alarm pierced the stillness in the room. Nurses and doctors poured in, and one took her hand, leading her out of the room. Watching the heart monitor through the window into his room, she saw the flat line. One doctor performed CPR, but when the paddles touched her son's chest, Carrie Emeline screamed, and then she fainted.

When she awakened, a nurse held her hand. "He's alive, Mrs. Taylor. We got to him in time. Our cardiologist just checked him and doesn't believe Drew's heart is damaged, but he has ordered a chest x-ray as a precaution. His little body has just been traumatized. His blood pressure simply dropped too low, and then his heart stopped. Drew is resting easy. Now we need to see to your own head."

She refused to leave Drew, so a nurse tended

to her care in Drew's room. The nurse partially shaved the back of her head, and at the moment she was receiving the necessary stitches, Dr. Peters, the neurologist arrived to speak to her.

"As you know, your son's been through an ordeal, Mrs. Taylor. Not only did he lose blood when he was attacked, but he watched his mother being attacked. That is enough trauma for one little boy. I want to keep him under observation. I don't know how long he'll need to stay, but I assume that your husband is out of the home?"

"Yes, doctor. I understand he's in the county jail. I've filed assault charges, and I'll be obtaining a restraining order. When I return home, I'll have the locks changed."

"As you are aware, Drew has suffered a concussion. A concussion is a type of traumatic brain injury that can alter the usual and normal functioning of the brain. Drew's concussion was caused by the heavy metal lamp you described that fell on his head. His concussion can trigger headaches, dizziness and neck pain. Concussions are considered mild brain injuries, and often result in short-term impairment such as memory loss and disorientation, along with potential for more serious complications."

Carrie Emeline stared at the doctor, not saying anything but imagining the worst.

"When your son is released, I need you to closely monitor Drew for a few days to look for any warning signs such as an inability to recognize people, or one pupil becoming larger than the other. That might indicate the injury is more serious than we currently believe. Having a concussion increases the risk greatly of having a repeat injury. I know how this happened, Mrs. Taylor. I wish only the best for you and your family. Good day, Mrs. Taylor."

"Thank you, Dr. Peters."

When the doctor had gone, Carrie Emeline called Mr. and Mrs. White to give them an update. Mr. White brought her a change of clothes. When she entered the restroom to wash and change, she saw the bruises on her face, throat, and arm, and felt the back of her shaved head and the stitches. *God help me, but I hate him for what he's done to us!*

Three days later, Drew was released. Mr. White picked up Carrie Emeline and Drew and drove them home. Mr. White then took Drew to his home to join Angela, and Carrie Emeline drove to the police station where she filed the restraining order against Marcus. He was in a cell, but she was not ready to visit him, if ever. She had begged him for over three years to get help, but he always refused. She now had to protect her children and herself. She could only pray for Marcus. He was in God's hands.

The locksmith arrived later that day.

Chapter Thirty-Five

Divorce

*"But they that wait upon the LORD shall renew
their strength; they shall mount up with wings
as eagles; they shall run, and not be weary; and
they shall walk, and not faint."*
Isaiah 40:31

The Present Day
December 02, 1974

Carrie Emeline watched her mother's face express
the pain which she herself felt. "Carrie Emeline, I
can't believe it. This is awful. I can't imagine how
a father can do this to his wife and children."

It had taken Carrie Emeline over five months
to share the horrendous story with her mother,
and in one day it had all poured out. "I'm not
sticking up for him, but I think he may be sick,
Mom. I've been reading a great deal about Post-
Traumatic Stress Disorder. It's known as PTSD.
I'm not condoning what Marcus did, because he's
had many chances over the years to seek help.
He'll lie to me and promise he's going to get help,

and then he doesn't."

Her mother gripped her hand tightly.

Carrie Emeline sighed and continued. "Mom, I've dropped the abuse charges, but I'm having a real problem forgiving Marcus. My heart says he's sick, but he hurt our children and me. He could have killed any of us. All because he refused help. There were moments when I have actually hated him.

"The first year with Marcus, I did learn to love him, but I knew even then that something was wrong. Before we married, and he was staying in the guest room, I often heard him cry out in his sleep. I knew he was having nightmares. At that time, they were not nearly as frequent as in these past couple of years.

"I pray for Marcus and our family constantly, but I have children to protect. I filed for a divorce in late August." She rose and walked to the desk. In one of the drawers she pulled out papers and sat down by her mother.

"Here are the papers. They arrived on November first. I have yet to sign them," and she hung her head. When she looked back up, she was crying. "Oh, Mom, I feel like such a failure. This is not what I wanted. I really hoped to have a good marriage with Marcus. No, I didn't fall head over heels in love with him as I did with Andrew, but it was a *healing* love.

"There was companionship. We had a wonderful time together on the vacation in Bellingham visiting his parents. He didn't even have the nightmares while we were there. I think he was at peace that he was finally home."

"Can you pinpoint when the nightmares worsened? Was it when he started the heavy drinking?"

Deeply exhaling again, Carrie Emeline pursed her lips and nodded her head. "Yes. It happened when I told him we were having a baby, and he hinted for me to get an abortion. Maybe he was overwhelmed with married life. Drew *and* a baby meant just one more problem to Marcus. All I know is that he needs help, and it's up to him to ask. He has to choose the path he wants to walk. All I can do is to continue praying for him."

"Have you seen Marcus since you filed the restraining order?"

"No. I'm not even certain he still has his job. Early in August I received a call from his boss that he had not shown up at work. He asked me to get a message to Marcus. I couldn't lie. I told him I hadn't seen Marcus since June."

"Well, honey, if his boss called you in early August, Marcus had probably been going to work, at least at that point."

"That's true. I have since heard from Marcus. He wrote me a letter." She rose again and retrieved a single tablet size sheet of paper from the desk. "Here's what he wrote."

August 18, 1974
Dear Carem,

I'm sorry, and I deeply regret what has happened. I hope you and the children are okay, especially Drew. I can't believe I hurt you and Drew like that. I know Angela saw it, too. I love and miss all of you. I realize I've wronged my family.

I know there's a restraining order against me, so I won't attempt to see you or the children. I hope someday you and the children can forgive me, but I'll understand if you can't. I can't forgive myself for what I did.

If you need to get in touch with me, my address is:
2210 Bank Street Apt 3D
Louisville, Kentucky
40212

Sincerely,
Marcus

"It was because of this letter that I had an address to file and deliver the divorce papers. Otherwise, I would have had to take a chance that he was still at the dealership, and serve the papers on him at work. I didn't want to do that."

"Do you have the proof he received the papers?"

"Yes, he signed for them from the delivery service. I haven't heard back from my lawyer that they've been signed, but again, I haven't signed mine either."

"Do you intend to sign them?"

"I don't know, Mom. I'm terribly confused. Divorce is such a dreadful word. I've always loathed divorce, thinking couples don't try hard enough. Now I think differently. I've been praying about it, but I've not received an answer."

"Honey, when I pray about something and I have no answer, I usually just wait. Eventually an answer will come. Be patient, Carrie Emeline. Wait on the Lord."

"Thanks, Mom. I love you."

"I love you, too, honey. Please come home with me. I've enjoyed looking after the children for the past few days, but they need their mother. You need your children, and your father and I want to take care of you. Are you ready?"

She nodded. "Yes, I'm ready, Mom."

Chapter Thirty-Six

The Unsigned Papers

*"The LORD executeth righteousness and
judgment for all that are oppressed."*
Psalm 103:6

The Past

Friday morning
November 01, 1974

Marcus checked his watch. "Who could possibly be at the door at eight o'clock in the morning?" he mumbled aloud.

"Are you Marcus Quinton Taylor?"

"Yes," he answered warily.

"Would you please sign for the receipt of these papers?"

"What are they?"

"Don't kill the messenger. They're from the office of these attorneys." The delivery driver pointed to the four names on the outside of the envelope: Lockwood, Jones, Smith, and Mann.

Marcus signed and accepted the papers. He slowly closed the door. He knew what was in the envelope. He sat down at the small table in the room he rented on the attic floor of an old house in the downtown business district. He took a sip of coffee, delaying the inevitable.

Four and a half months ago, his life took a drastic turn for the worse. *I nearly killed my wife and Andrew's son. Andrew; one of the best men I ever met. I may as well have spit on his grave. He loved me like a brother. I've put his wife, his son, and now my own daughter through my hell. Yes, my own personal hell. They don't deserve this.*

Another brisk knock on the door. He slowly opened it. It was his landlady. "Mr. Taylor, if you don't pay your rent today you're going to be out on the street. I won't have you paying two weeks late again. I can rent this beautiful room to *anyone.*" Her puffy face was stern, she pursed her lips, her eyes narrowed, and her hands rested on her ample hips. He knew that look from a woman.

Her last name was Hogg. A nasty remark formed, but he bit his tongue. He needed this room. "I get paid today, Mrs. Hogg. I'll have the rent by five o'clock."

"See that you do, Mr. Taylor. Good day." She turned and marched heavily down the steps.

Good day, yeah, right. It was a good day until these papers and you showed up.

Marcus paid his rent that night, and wound up at the VFW afterwards. He only had a couple of drinks there, and left without speaking to anyone. He unlocked the front door of his temporary home and climbed the four flights to the attic room. The house had probably once been beautiful, but now it was just a run-down place where mostly divorced men rented rooms. He had the choice of living in a nicer room on the second floor, but it was also $40 more every month. Each of the four floors had one bathroom to be shared by the four or five rooms on each floor. That was one advantage to the attic floor: there were only three rooms here on the top floor, and currently the other two rooms were vacant, but already let and about to be occupied.

His room was furnished with a bed, lamp, night stand, dresser, and a small table with two chairs. He purchased a mini refrigerator, hot plate, coffee pot, and a clock radio. He kept his coffee, cream, sugar, and bread all in the refrigerator, along with a package of bologna. The house had mice that he heard sometimes at night. If he turned on the bedside lamp after dark, the roaches fled to their hiding places. Although Mrs. Hogg sprayed monthly, and set out mouse traps, the vermin never completely went away.

He brewed his coffee in the morning, went to

work, and at night he brought home a fifth of cheap bourbon, stored it in the refrigerator, and drank until he passed out. Every weekday he repeated the routine. On weekends he hung out at the VFW in the evenings, and slept all day.

Tonight was different. He still had not opened the envelope. It lay on the table where he left it that morning before work. He poured a glass of bourbon, switched on the radio, and sat at the table. The envelope now beckoned him. He finally picked it up, holding it for a moment. Then he tore it open. It contained a three-page document full of legal jargon which could only be completely deciphered by another attorney. However, he understood the gist of it. Carem wanted a divorce, and he couldn't blame her. He was now thankful he had written to her and given her his address. He would not have wanted the papers served at his employment.

He took a hefty swig of the bourbon and sat back in the chair, closing his eyes and rocking on the back two legs. He caught the end of Barbra Streisand singing "The Way We Were."

"Memories may be beautiful, and yet what's too painful to remember, we simply choose to forget. So it's the laughter we remember whenever we remember the way we were."

Marcus recalled the laughter and the peaceful evenings with Carem on the lake in Bellingham, Washington. He smiled. *That's what I'll choose to remember tonight.*

Chapter Thirty-Seven

The Awakening

"Be not forgetful to entertain strangers: for thereby some have entertained angels unawares."
Hebrews 13:2

The Past
Sunday morning
November 03, 1974

Marcus forgot to turn off the alarm, let alone change the clock radio from radio to alarm. It was seven o'clock and the booming voice of a preacher filled his head the first thing that morning. He could have turned him off, but he lay there and listened.

"With God, you can put away the old man and become a new man! Let God renew your mind and your spirit. Let God speak to your heart. God is righteous and holy."

While the choir sang "Standing on the Promises," Marcus listened to the words of the old hymn by Russell K. Carter, and remembered his home church in Bellingham, Washington.

*Standing on the promises of Christ my
King,*
Through eternal ages let His praises ring,
Glory in the highest, I will shout and sing,
Standing on the promises of God.

Standing on the promises that cannot fail,
*When the howling storms of doubt and
fear assail,*
By the living Word of God I shall prevail,
Standing on the promises of God.

Standing on the promises I cannot fall,
List'ning every moment to the Spirit's call,
Resting in my Savior as my all in all,
Standing on the promises of God.

*Is there hope for me? Does God help deceitful
men? I deceived Carem. She believed my awful
lie to her because Andrew and I were friends. I
knew Andrew was Carem's one true love. If she
ever had any love for me, I killed it. I wish I had
the power to change things.*

He had a crazy thought — at least it seemed
crazy to him. Not too far from him was a church
he passed on the way to work. It was actually in

walking distance. *I'm going to church today.*

When he arrived at Shawnee Baptist Church on the corner of 38th Street and Market Street in downtown Louisville, the adult Sunday school class was just ending. He sat on a pew in the rear. As the worship service congregation filed in, the preacher greeted them, and then he sought out Marcus on the back pew and shook his hand. "Hi, I'm Pastor Lonnie Mattingly. Welcome to Shawnee Baptist Church."

"Thank you, Pastor Mattingly."

Marcus sat back and watched the people enter and receive each other, and found it uplifting when they welcomed him, too. He realized they were genuine in their happiness to see him and meet him. Again, he thought about his home church in Bellingham. *They were good people, too. My father was a deacon in his church. Where did I go wrong? What was my problem, Lord? I suppose I can speak to You, since I'm in Your house.*

Following several more hymns, Pastor Mattingly addressed the congregation. "Please stand for the reading of God's word, and turn to Matthew chapter sixteen, verses twenty-five to twenty-six."

Thankfully, there were Bibles in the slots beside the hymnals, since Marcus owned no

Bible. He turned to the passage as Pastor Mattingly read in a booming voice: "'For whosoever will save his life shall lose it: and whosoever will lose his life for my sake shall find it. For what is a man profited, if he shall gain the whole world, and lose his own soul? or what shall a man give in exchange for his soul?'"

Marcus heard none of the sermon. He was thinking about his life. *I was fortunate in having two of the best parents ever, and the best siblings. I realize I had a wonderful life growing up, but I was told I had a rebellious spirit. That's probably true. I know I always wanted to do everything my way, including setting my own boundaries. My parents' rules and teachings meant nothing to me. It wasn't until I entered the army that I realized I had to conform. Actually, it wasn't so bad. Until Vietnam.* He shook his head. *Lord, I didn't come here to think about Vietnam. How have I profited? Well, I married Andrew's wife under false pretences. Then I fell in love.* At that he returned the Bible to the slot, rose, and bolted from the church.

He wandered the streets, not wanting to head back to his lonely sleeping room. Standing on a street corner, he watched people walk in and out of the local tavern. Drawing a deep breath, he sauntered through the door and sat down on one of the bar stools. Smoke filled the room, even though two overworked fans rotated overhead. The barmaid was fortyish with graying hair pulled into a stringy ponytail. "What can I gettcha, honey?" Her voice was deep and strained, and she coughed or cleared her throat after every couple of words. Too many years spent smoking, he guessed. She looked tired and too thin.

"I'll have a double shot of bourbon, straight up." He laid a ten dollar bill on the bar.

She poured the alcohol into a small glass and set it in front of him. Picking up the bill, she walked to the cash register, rang up two dollars, and returned eight dollars change.

"Hey, Gert," someone at the end of the bar yelled, "bring me another. And bring one for my buddy Ralph here, too."

"Hold your horses, Al. I'll be right there." She winked at Marcus, "If ya need anything else, honey, just yell."

Obviously, this was the local watering hole, and everyone knew each other. A couple more guys walked through the door and Al called out to them. "Hey, Pete and Jim, come on down here. How ya guys been?" He slapped them both on the back.

Is this what you want? Marcus heard the question in his head. It must be the alcohol, he thought.

Don't you want to get your wife back? Don't you miss Drew and Angela? It was nice having family care about you, wasn't it?

"Stop it!" he yelled and covered his ears. Conversation in the bar halted. The men and Gert turned to stare at him. He realized he had spoken aloud. Picking up his change, he left a dollar on the bar, and made a fast exit.

Just wonderful. Now I'm hearing voices. He walked across the street to a park and sat on an empty bench. A flock of ducks and Canadian Geese swam on a pond in front of him. Some of the birds toddled around the pond, and one of the ducks waddled up to him. "I don't have anything, buddy. Sorry."

An old man walked by and turned toward Marcus. "Yes, you do." He reached into a covered container hanging on a pole, grasped a handful of grain, and then closed the container and handed some to Marcus. "The park's maintenance department supplies the grain, so we can feed them. I like to come here and watch the birds. It gives me time to think. Mind if I sit down, young fella?"

Marcus moved over and the old man sat. He wore farmer's overalls, suspenders, a plaid shirt, a long gray beard, and a large floppy hat. He chuckled every now and then as the birds drew closer, waiting for him to throw more grain. Marcus threw some out, too. The old man leaned back. "Pleasant autumn day isn't it, young man?"

Marcus checked the surroundings. He hadn't even noticed the weather. The park was full of old trees; mostly oak, elm, ash, walnut, and maple. The leaves of varied colors of red, gold, brown, and yellow nestled in piles on the ground and many still clung to the tree branches. A gust of wind tossed some of the leaves into a swirl along the path in front of the pond. The sun shined overhead, and the temperature was probably close to sixty.

"Yes, it's a pleasant day," Marcus answered the old man.

"You come here often, son?"

The old man was certainly friendly, and Marcus wasn't sure he wanted to get into a conversation with a stranger. *Oh, what the heck. What else do I have to do?* "No, actually this is my first time in this park. I didn't even know it existed before today."

"I like to come here, and sometimes over to the Ohio River. Anywhere there's water. I just enjoy the ducks and geese. It's a great place to relax and to think." He turned back to Marcus. "What brings you to the park, son?"

"Actually, I had nothing else to do." He threw out more grain.

"A nice young man like you must have some family and friends."

Marcus looked down and mumbled, "I had a wife and two children."

"I'm sorry, son. Did they die?" the old man asked gently.

"No, but they're dead to me. I ran them off. They're gone for good."

"If they're still living, and you want them back, nothing is impossible with God."

"I don't think God wants to bother with me. I haven't exactly been the best of his creation," Marcus scoffed.

"None of us are perfect. 'For all have sinned, and come short of the glory of God.' We are born imperfect little beings. Do you know about Jesus Christ, son?"

Marcus sighed and thought before answering. "I grew up in church. My parents and siblings are Christians. My wife is a Christian." He scoffed again. "I'm the lost cause."

"You're not a lost cause. God will meet you where you are, when you're ready. Are you ready, son?"

Marcus stared at the old man, and then he rose, and threw the remaining grain on the ground. The ducks and geese swarmed the granules. "It was nice talking to you." Marcus walked away.

Chapter Thirty-Eight

Behold Your New Life

*"And he shewed me a pure river of water of life,
clear as crystal, proceeding out of the throne of
God and of the Lamb."*
Revelation 22:1

The Past

Sunday Morning
November 10, 1974

On Saturday evening, before going to bed, Marcus did it again. He forgot to turn off the alarm and change the clock radio from radio to alarm. It was seven o'clock and the booming voice of the preacher again filled his head. "For all have sinned, and come short of the glory of God."

"Wow, that's what the old farmer quoted to me last Sunday. I wonder if he was really a farmer. It's certainly a coincidence ... or is it? Now I'm talking to myself again."

After dressing, he checked his image in the bathroom mirror. Frown lines had formed around his mouth, and there were more lines in his forehead than he remembered. He brushed his teeth, combed his hair, and he headed out to the local bakery. They would have donuts and coffee, and he knew where he was heading afterwards.

Twenty minutes later, he sat on a bench outside the Shawnee Baptist Church. He deliberately timed it so the congregation would be settled in the pews. Listening to the choir sing "The Old Rugged Cross," caused him reflection. *I feel close to home here. This church reminds me of my family church.*

Why don't you go in?

"Huh?" he said aloud, and looked around. *I'm hearing voices again.*

Why don't you go in? Are you afraid?

"I'm not afraid of anything. Who *are* you?" he asked in a stern voice.

I'm your conscience. I'm always here. It's just been a long time since you've heard me.

I'm not dressed for church. I don't think they'll appreciate a guy in jeans and a sweatshirt.

I think you'd be surprised.

He finished his coffee and donut. Throwing the paper in a trash receptacle, he climbed the steps to the church.

Marcus took a seat in the back, while the music director led the congregation in a hymn. The man beside him smiled, and handed Marcus his hymnal and pointed to the verse they were singing. The man then turned to the woman beside him and shared her hymnal. Two little girls stood beside the woman.

Nice family, thought Marcus. He sang the last stanza and the chorus of "Shall We Gather at the River" along with the congregation.

> *Soon we'll reach the shining river,*
> *Soon our pilgrimage will cease;*
> *Soon our happy hearts will quiver*
> *With the melody of peace.*
>
> *Yes, we'll gather at the river,*
> *The beautiful, the beautiful river;*
> *Gather with the saints at the river*
> *That flows by the throne of God.*

"Please be seated," said Pastor Mattingly. "Shall we gather at the river of life? Heaven. A beautiful place. Is Heaven where you're headed? Do you want to dwell eternally with the Lord Jesus? Do you want to live where there are no more lies, no deceit, and no dishonesty? Do you want all your tears wiped away?"

At that, Marcus shed quiet tears. *Help me Lord Jesus. Please.*

I'm here.

Are you the voice in my head again?

I'm the Lord Jesus Whom you called upon.

I've done evil. I'm paying for it with terrible nightmares.

It's time to lay your burden down.

I've lost my wife and kids.

Maybe not.

I've hurt them. They'll never forgive me.

Do you believe in Me?

Yes, Lord Jesus, I believe in You.

Do You want to be made whole?

Yes, Lord.

Do you want the salvation only I can offer?

Yes, Lord. Please forgive me and save me.

You are forgiven, my son. Behold your new life.

Marcus wept. *The old man said that You'd meet me where I am, and when I'm ready. Thank you, Lord, Jesus.*

Chapter Thirty-Nine

Pastor Mattingly

"They prevented me in the day of my calamity: but the LORD was my stay. He brought me forth also into a large place; he delivered me, because he delighted in me."
Psalm 18: 18-19

The Past

Monday, Evening
November 11, 1974

After work the next day, Marcus headed straight to the church. There was a side door and a sign on the side of the building that read church office. The door was unlocked. Marcus stood in the doorway and was greeted by a woman at a desk off from the entryway. "Please come in. I'm Nancy Mattingly."

"My name is Marcus Taylor. It's nice to meet you, Mrs. Mattingly."

"I don't believe I've seen you before. Are you here to see my husband?"

"Yes, please, if Pastor Mattingly is available. I

wouldn't want to interrupt."

"Oh, you wouldn't be interrupting. My husband is always available for anyone wishing to speak to him. Please follow me. He's in his office."

Marcus followed her down the short hallway. Opening a door, she said, "You have a guest. This is Mr. Marcus Taylor."

Pastor Mattingly rose behind his desk. "Please come in, Mr. Taylor." They shook hands. "Please have a seat." Pastor Mattingly pointed to the chair across from his desk.

In the doorway, Mrs. Mattingly asked her husband, "Would you like me to bring water, tea, or coffee?"

"I'll have coffee, dear. What would you like, Mr. Taylor?

"Coffee would be just fine."

Within a few minutes she was back with a tray holding a carafe of hot coffee, two mugs, cream and sugar, and two spoons. "I'll just leave you two men at your business." She discreetly exited the office.

"I've seen you at the church the past two Sundays, Mr. Taylor. How may I help you?"

Marcus smiled. "I see you know when a new sheep has joined the flock."

"I try to know each and every person who enters my doors. You've been leaving before I can talk to you."

"Let's suffice it to say that the Lord gave you sermons for me. As my father would say, 'He knows who will come through the doors and what they need.'" Marcus expelled a huge sigh. "I need someone to talk to, and I felt led to come here today."

"You can tell me anything, Mr. Taylor. Please take your time."

"I got saved in your church yesterday, Pastor Mattingly."

A huge smile broke out on the pastor's face. "Marvelous! Tell me what happened."

Marcus relayed both visits to the church and the mysterious encounter with the old man. "Do you think he was an angel?"

Pastor Mattingly smiled. "The Bible speaks of entertaining angels in Hebrews 13:2. 'Be not forgetful to entertain strangers: for thereby some have entertained angels unawares.' It's certainly possible, Mr. Taylor."

Marcus spent the next hour telling Pastor Mattingly about some events in his life. However, it was now nearly six-thirty and Marcus realized that the pastor probably had supper waiting. "I don't want to take up any more of your time, Pastor Mattingly. It's late, and I know it's probably past your suppertime."

"Mr. Taylor, why don't you join us for supper? My wife makes a wonderful pot roast; unless you have somewhere else to go."

Marcus thought about going back to the sleeping room with only a radio for companionship. "I'd relish having supper with you and your wife. Evenings are rather lonely for me."

An hour later, Marcus produced a huge satisfied smile. "Thank you, Mrs. Mattingly. Your husband was correct; you do make a marvelous pot roast."

"Thank you, Mr. Taylor," she beamed from the compliment, and flashed her husband a loving smile.

Following dinner, Pastor Mattingly asked Marcus, "Would you like to join me in my study for further conversation?"

"Yes, sir, I'd appreciate that."

"Mr. Taylor and I will be in the study, dear."

His wife smiled and nodded knowingly. "I'll be in shortly with the coffee."

Marcus began telling Pastor Mattingly his life story, and they talked until eleven o'clock. Marcus looked at his watch. "Oh my, I apologize. I had no idea the time. Please forgive me!"

"No need, Marcus."

Several hours earlier Marcus had asked the

pastor to drop the "Mr. Taylor" and call him Marcus. In return, Pastor Mattingly said Marcus could address him as just Pastor. Pastor turned around and viewed his bookshelf. "Do you have a Bible, Marcus?"

"No, sir, I don't."

"I'll give you one of mine. It has notes I made in the margins. I hope you find the notes helpful."

"Thank you, I'm sure I will."

"Also, why don't you stop by each night after work, and we can talk. Except on Wednesday, when we have prayer and Bible study. It begins at six o'clock. I hope you'll join the congregation. It will be helpful for a new convert."

"Thank you, and I'll do that. I'll see you tomorrow evening."

Chapter Forty

Harrison Chapman

"Thy testimonies also are my delight and my counsellors."
Psalm 119: 24

The Past
Monday
November 18, 1974

Marcus met with Pastor Mattingly every evening after work, and attended Bible study on Wednesday evening, and worship service on Sunday morning. On Saturday he worked with the pastor and other men in the church, doing janitorial work. Pastor had explained that each Saturday the men gathered, cleaned floors and bathrooms, while the women dusted every wooden area of the church. In the summer, the men also mowed the church lot and weeded the flower beds.

It was now a week later, and Marcus felt transformed. The nightly sessions with Pastor Mattingly had renewed his spirit. However, he still had nightmares some evenings; usually after a loud noise, such as a car backfiring. The nightmares were always the same. Andrew and Jerry had been his best buddies, and he'd watched both of them die within minutes apart. Many nights he re-lived that fateful day in battle. It was something he could never discuss with Carem. After all, Andrew was her beloved husband.

Tonight he would not be meeting with Pastor Mattingly. A meeting had been arranged with a counselor, who was a church member. This counselor was a former Korean and Vietnam War veteran, and he specialized in counseling veterans of foreign wars who had Post-Traumatic Stress Disorder. The counselor agreed for Marcus to come to his home for an hour Monday and Tuesday evening after work. Marcus still planned on attending Bible study at the church Wednesday evening.

He checked the address on the sheet of paper. Yes, he was at the correct address, which was only three blocks from the church. He walked up to the door and rang the bell.

A distinguished gentleman in his late forties or early fifties opened the door. He had short hair graying at the temples, and was dressed in a business suit.

"You must be Marcus Taylor."

"I am, sir."

"As you are aware from our pastor, my name is Harrison Chapman. Please call me Harry."

"Please call me Marcus." The two men shook hands.

*****

On Monday and Tuesday, the two men spent each night holed up in Harry's home office. By late Tuesday evening, Marcus's brain was spent. His mind hurt from reliving all the battles.

"I've always been in control, at least before Vietnam. The war was a situation I couldn't control. The day my two best friends died, I watched helplessly. I ran to Andrew, and then a moment later I ran to Jerry. I couldn't save them. I applied pressure on their wounds. I watched the light fade from their eyes. Then I, too, was wounded in my arm and leg." Marcus tried not to cry, but he couldn't help himself.

"It's not your fault, son. You did the best you could do. War is tough. War can bring any man to his knees."

Marcus withdrew his handkerchief from his pocket and wiped his eyes. "Speaking of bringing men to their knees, Andrew talked to us about Jesus Christ. I wanted nothing to do with Jesus. Sometimes Andrew was relentless, and I told him to back off. He was my best friend. What was wrong with me?"

"You weren't ready."

"When I came home, the nightmares began. I kept having flashbacks of that day in particular. I was surrounded by people who didn't have a clue about war. If you haven't been there, you can't possibly imagine what it's like. I grew more and more depressed. In Vietnam, I was always on my guard. However, Christmas Eve, 1969 was wonderful. We were fortunate to attend the Bob Hope Christmas show in Vietnam. Connie Stevens traveled with him as his special guest, and the show was an amazing respite from the war. The next day, which was Christmas Day, Andrew, Jerry and I made a pact. We were in total compliance. If any of us didn't make it back, whoever remained would visit the family of the one ... or two that died. We all agreed and shook on it. I never dreamed that I would be the one remaining. Andrew was the Christian with a wonderful wife and a baby on the way. God wouldn't let him die. But he did die. I don't know if Jerry got saved. He was so young, just twenty that Christmas." Marcus stopped and looked at Harry. "I'm sorry. It's hard."

"I understand, Marcus" responded Harry. "I'm here to listen and try to help. I'm here for you. Please continue."

"In 1970, March, I was still in the Army, and I was granted permission to attend Andrew's funeral, and Jerry's the following day. I knew Andrew's baby was due soon. In August, after leaving the army, I visited Andrew's widow. I told her about the pact. I took it a step further and I lied to her by telling her that Andrew wanted me to marry her and raise his child if he didn't make it back. As I said, when I came home all the nightmares and everything else began. Initially, I couldn't work for all the flashbacks. Before visiting Andrew's widow, I attempted a job in a machine shop. Every time I heard a noise, I had a panic attack. That's when I devised the plan to coerce Andrew's wife to marry me.

"I used her for a meal ticket, but then I fell in love with her. However, the nightmares worsened. I didn't drink alcohol in the beginning, but I did later. I just wanted to sleep through the night without a nightmare. I know now that all I was doing was self-medicating." He stopped again. "I'm a Christian now, Harry. When I awaken from a nightmare, Pastor Mattingly told me to say 'Devil be gone!' I must admit, it helps. Pastor calls it the 'power of prayer.'"

"Well, I agree with Pastor Mattingly. There are medications on the market, but I like to lean on prayer first. Also, talking about it helps, especially discussions with other veterans. I hold a veterans' group therapy meeting every Thursday evening at six o'clock here at my home. I'd like you to come. You'll meet foreign war veterans from World War One, World War Two, Korea, and Vietnam. You'll find that many of these men waited years before seeking help. They thought they were being brave by ignoring it, but later found they were brave for facing up to it. Post-Traumatic Stress Disorder is nothing to be ashamed of, Marcus. PTSD has been around since war began. Whether you want to call it shellshock, battle fatigue or PTSD, it must be faced and dealt with. Will you come to the meeting this Thursday?"

"I'll be there."

"You're going to recognize many of these men from church. They were graduates of Pastor Mattingly's counseling before coming to me. I have a feeling you'll find them to be just what you need."

Chapter Forty-One

Veteran Therapy

"Where no counsel is, the people fall: but in the multitude of counsellors there is safety."
Proverbs 11: 14

The Past

Thursday
November 21, 1974

The men gathered in a large room in the basement of Harry's home. Harry's wife served the refreshments, welcomed the men, and then excused herself. Marcus counted twenty-one veterans.

All the chairs had been placed in a circle. Harry stood and greeted the group. "You may notice that we have someone new here tonight. Marcus, would you like to stand and tell us anything about yourself?"

Marcus stood. "My name is Marcus Quinton Taylor, and I was honorably discharged from the United States Army in 1970. I fought in the Vietnam War, and I was wounded."

Harry addressed him. "Marcus, all these men fought in foreign war battles. You're not going to feel alone here. No matter which war, they would all say that war is hell. There's nothing romantic about it, as some movies or books like to portray war. These are brave men, and many suffered in silence for years before finally seeking help. When someone new arrives, these men like to share their experiences. It helps them, and it helps the new attendee. Emmett, as the oldest member of the group, would you like to share first?"

Emmett stood, using a cane.

Harry put up his hand. "You don't have to stand, Emmett."

"I know, but I want to," the elderly man replied in a quivering voice. "It's important for the youngsters to know who came before them, and I want them to hear me loud and clear.

"My name is Emmett Howard Coleman, and I began my service on the eighth of June, 1917, as a private in the American Expeditionary Forces — or AEF — of the first division of the United States Army. I had just turned nineteen. All I knew about war was that my dad died on the first of July, 1898 in the Battle of San Juan Hill during the Spanish-American War, along with two uncles. I never knew my dad. I was born two weeks before he died. I knew nothing about the reality of war. There was no family member or friend to discuss war. War appeared exciting to a young nineteen-year-old. I thought I was going on an adventure.

"We sailed from Hoboken, New Jersey on the fourteenth of June, 1917. One of the first things General Pershing asked of us was to parade through the streets of Paris on the fourth of July, 1917 to the grave of Gilbert du Montier, the Marquis de Lafayette. Colonel Charles Stanton gave a speech and you may be familiar with his famous final words in the speech, 'Lafayette, we are here!'

"The first division was an untrained group of men. General Pershing worked hard to turn us into fighting men, so we could give aid to the British and French, and fight the Germans. Our mission was to assume the allied line from Saint Mihiel to Belfort. Our first mission was deemed successful, which brought encouragement to the first division.

"However, it was the Meuse-Argonne battle that ended the war and was the bloodiest battle of the war. It lasted forty-five days from the twenty-sixth of September until Armistice. I watched four of my buddies die beside me." He had to stop. His eyes teared, he slowly shook his head, and his voice became hoarse. "Excuse me. I can still see them die." He coughed to clear his throat. "They were ages nineteen to twenty-one. I always wondered how I survived. We were in the same trench.

"I spent years fighting what was known as shellshock following what we dubbed the Great War. When I returned home, I resumed my relationship with my high school sweetheart. I was twenty-three and Lillian was twenty-one when we married. I was assigned to Fort Knox, Kentucky to finish my stint with the army. I even considered becoming a lifer. However, the nightmares and alcohol were ruining my marriage. Lillian left me several times, before she finally called it quits after eleven years. She took our two boys and moved home with her parents. Both of those boys grew up and fought in World War Two. Neither of them made it home. I blamed myself for a long time. I never raised the boys, so I couldn't tell them about the horrors of war. They may have romanticized war as adventure as I once had. All their mother told me in her final letter was that John and Matthew were gung-ho to go fight the Germans. Just like I was.

"It wasn't until I got saved and later joined Shawnee Baptist Church in 1951, that my outlook on life changed. Jesus got hold of me, and He never let go. In 1953 I joined a counseling group with Spanish-American War, other World War One, World War Two, and Korean War vets over at Fort Knox. The nightmares finally stopped, although I can still recall images of battles; as I did tonight. I do my best to help other vets when I can. Another plus to my story was when I met Rebecca at Shawnee Baptist Church in 1954. I was fifty-six and she was forty-two. Although, she was a Korean War widow with two boys and a girl under the age of eight, she was willing to bless me with a boy and a girl. I've been privileged to have raised these five fine children with Rebecca. I thank Jesus Christ for my life, my redemption, and the deliverance from the nightmares. I thank Jesus Christ for my new life.

"I'm now seventy-six, and in spite of the cane my health is fairly good. It's just the arthritis in my right knee. You see, I was shot in the knee in that last battle. The wound played havoc with the knee, but I'm alive in Jesus Christ." He held up his cane and looked up. "Thank you, Jesus, for saving me."

As he took a seat, a rousing applause broke out from the other men, and they thanked him for his service.

Marcus heard four more stories: two from World War Two vets and two from Korean War vets. They also spoke of nightmares, night sweats, alcohol and/or drug abuse, attempted suicide, and family violence. They all had many of those symptoms in common. They all, also, were saved by the grace of Jesus Christ.

After two hours, the group broke up for the evening. "Who would like to give the closing prayer," asked Harry.

"I would," said one of the World War Two vets. "Dear Heavenly Father, we thank You that You are here for us each and every day. We thank You for the redemption of our sins through Your Son Jesus Christ. We thank You for the blessing of Harry, allowing us to use his home for our weekly meetings. It's comforting for all of us to get together and share the comradery of other war buddies. It doesn't matter from which war we hail, we have Jesus Christ in common, and it's Jesus for whom we live. Thank You for having Marcus join our group. I hope this group is as beneficial to him as it's been for the rest of us. In the name of Your Son Jesus Christ we pray ... amen."

The others added their amens.

Harry stood and addressed the men. "Before we leave, I have an announcement. Next Thursday is Thanksgiving, and the ladies of Shawnee Baptist Church are cooking a dinner for any of us that would like to attend. It will be held in the church's basement at five o'clock. You can bring a guest or come alone. Everyone is welcome. Please let my wife know at church next Wednesday evening how many will be in your party, so the ladies can prepare enough food for everyone. I hope to see you there. Until we meet again, God bless you all and have a good evening!"

Chapter Forty-Two

Thanksgiving Day

*"The righteous cry, and the LORD heareth,
and delivereth them out of all their
troubles. The LORD is nigh unto them that
are of a broken heart; and saveth such as
be of a contrite spirit."*
Psalm 34: 17-18

The Past

November 28, 1974

Marcus wasn't the only man without a wife at the Thanksgiving feast. He sat with two other Vietnam War vets, Mike and Bob.

"Are you married, Marcus?" asked Bob.

"Yes, I am ... at least for now," he added.

"I'm divorced," said Bob. "I'd be happy to share, if you'd like to hear my story?"

"Yes, I would," answered Marcus.

"Here's the brief synopsis. Deborah and I were high school sweethearts, and we married immediately following graduation. Deborah was the best wife a man could have, and I know she loved me, and I loved her. I was stationed at Fort Knox when my time was up in Vietnam, and she and I acquired a small apartment on the base. Before Vietnam, I had never been a drinking man, or violent in any way, but that's what I became when I arrived home. I wasn't the same man, and I refused help. Deborah couldn't handle the change in me, and this new behavior didn't sit well with her. After a year, she filed for divorce and returned to our home town — Birmingham, Alabama.

"After Deborah left, I nearly re-upped for Vietnam, but my army doctor noted in his report about my PTSD, and my refusal to get help. The army asked me to resign my service, but in exchange they offered an honorable discharge. Even the army no longer wanted me." He shook his head.

"I continued drinking, and my behavior became more violent. I lost two jobs. That was when Mike here stepped in." Bob smiled, and slapped Mike on the back. "Mike was an army buddy from Fort Knox. He knew exactly what to do. Mike encouraged me to get help, as he'd done. He brought me to Harry's meetings. I finally realized that I wasn't alone. However, these men had something I didn't, and that was Jesus Christ. I have all these men to thank for leading me to the Lord. I now attend Shawnee Baptist Church with them. I'd hoped I might even get Deborah back. I contacted her, but she'd remarried. She'd moved on, and I knew that's what I needed to do, too."

"Here's *my* brief story," said Mike. "I was going through PTSD when I left Vietnam. I did everything that Bob described, except I wasn't married. The army told me to get help or get out. I chose the help. I wanted to be a lifer, but I *didn't* want another tour in Vietnam.

"At first I met with a doctor on base at Fort Knox. He recommended the therapy group situation with Harry. These men led me to the Lord, too, and I joined Shawnee Baptist Church. I feel like a new man; and by the way, I'm seeing Jackie Thompson, a Christian girl from the church." He grinned. "I'm going to ask her to marry me."

Bob looked thrilled. "That's great news! I've seen you two together, and Jackie's a wonderful lady. I wish you both all the best." He turned to Marcus. "Would you like to share your story, Marcus? Mike and I are good listeners."

Marcus saw the genuine concern in their eyes, and he definitely needed some buddies. He hadn't allowed himself to get close to any men since Andrew and Jerry. It was time. "At the moment,

I'm still married. My wife has served divorce papers on me, but I haven't signed them. The papers arrived on the first of the month, and apparently she's not signed her copies either."

He inhaled deeply and let his breath slowly escape. "My wife was married to one of my best friends. His name was Andrew, and we were stationed in Germany together. That's when I first met her. She was over for a visit. She's beautiful inside and out, and she loved Andrew. I wasn't jealous of Andrew, but I might have been a bit envious. However, I knew she was married to a wonderful Christian man.

"Andrew and I were reassigned to Vietnam, along with another buddy, Jerry." He stopped to catch his breath and his eyes teared. His voice was hoarse when he spoke again. "Like what happened to Emmett in World War One, during a battle I watched them both die beside me, just minutes apart. That was nearly five years ago, but yet sometimes it was like yesterday."

Bob nodded consolingly "I understand, Marcus."

Mike added, "As Christians, war is as close to Hell as *we'll* ever see, thank God."

Marcus cleared his throat and continued. Explaining their Christmas pact, he then added, "We all exchanged addresses of those family members. The day they died, I was shot in my arm and leg. After the doctors patched me up, I asked for leave to attend the funerals of Andrew and Jerry. My request was granted. They'd planned to send me back to the states, anyway. When I saw Andrew's wife, Carrie Emeline, I was saddened for her. She was understandably in pain, and I really wished it had been me that died. Andrew was a much better man than I.

He stopped to clear his throat and wipe his eyes. "In August 1970, I was honorably discharged. This is where it gets rough, and I'm now ashamed of myself. I remembered Carrie Emeline's beauty, and I hatched a plan. Let me back up some. When she was in Germany, she and Andrew conceived a child. That child, a boy, was born a few days after Andrew's funeral. Five months later I showed up on Carrie Emeline's doorstep with every intention of persuading her to marry me." Marcus saw the surprised look in their eyes. "I told her about the pact, but I carried it a step further."

After explaining the falsehood, he stopped again, and ran his fingers through his hair. "I'm not proud of what I did, but if she believed me, I had a place to live. I had no job, so I thought she could be my meal ticket if I played my cards right. I was a snake, and she invited me into her home.

Then I fell in love with her, and it was too late to tell her the truth.

"However, the nightmares grew worse and I became violent, like most people with PTSD. I hurt Carem. That's what I call her. I was physically and emotionally abusive. The last straw for Carem was the morning I hit Andrew's son, Drew and beat her, too. I had awakened from a nightmare when I began the assault. I am not making excuses, I should have gotten help and Carem begged me to do so. I sent the boy to the hospital. I nearly killed the child. Carem kicked me out. I did call the hospital anonymously to check on Drew, and thankfully, he lived. Carem filed assault and battery charges, and placed a restraining order on me. She later dropped the charges, and I was released from jail. However, she didn't rescind the restraining order.

"I don't blame Carem for her decisions. She needed to protect the children. You see, we have a daughter, too. My daughter Angela saw me hurt her mother and her brother that morning. She's only two, and hopefully she forgets. Drew is almost five. He'll probably never forget, and I know Carem won't forget. I'd do anything to get them back."

"Carem might not forget, but she may forgive you," said Mike. "You said that Andrew was a

Christian, but what about Carem?"

"She's a Christian." He hung his head. "She shouldn't have married me. The Bible talks about being unequally yoked. When we first married, we called our union a marriage of convenience. Carem hardly spoke with her parents about the marriage. I think she was afraid of the disapproval from them in marrying a man she barely knew. I met her parents, and they're good Christian people. They would never have shown condemnation toward her. They accepted me as Carem's husband." Marcus finished his testimonial. Tears pricked his eyes.

"Let's pray," suggested Mike.

The three men bowed their heads, and Mike led the prayer. "Dear Heavenly Father, You know Marcus's heart which is now heavy with guilt and grief. He realizes that deceiving his wife was wrong. We thank You for the salvation Marcus has experienced — in fact, the salvation all three of us have experienced through Your Son Jesus Christ. We know You have forgiven all of us. We pray Carem and Drew can find it in their hearts to forgive Marcus, and that he will soon see them and his daughter again. We also thank You for the group and our wonderful church we all attend. Both the group and our church have helped all of us through the PTSD that we share. God bless

Marcus, Bob, and me as we move forward in our new lives. In the name of Your Son Jesus Christ we pray ... amen."

Marcus and Bob echoed their amens.

"Go forward with God, Marcus, and know that you and your family will continue to be in our prayers," said Mike, and Bob nodded in agreement.

Chapter Forty-Three

Decisions

"Trust in the LORD with all thine heart; and lean not unto thine own understanding. In all thy ways acknowledge him, and he shall direct thy paths."
Proverbs 3: 5-6

The Present Day

December 01 and 02, 1974

Three days after Thanksgiving and sharing his situation with his two friends, Marcus was dressed and in his hallway where he encountered Mrs. Hogg, his landlady. She had the ever-present scowl on her face. "You haven't paid me for December, Mr. Taylor."

"It's Sunday. Can't you at least wait until tomorrow?"

"If you were worried about paying rent on Sunday, you should have paid yesterday." She crossed her arms and tapped her foot, clearly annoyed. She grudgingly acquiesced. "Okay, I'll let it go ... again. *But* I want the rent money before you go off to work in the morning. As I previously told you, I can rent this lovely room to anyone."

"I'm sure you can," he responded with sarcasm. Immediately he was sorry for his poor attitude. *That was the old Marcus.* "I'm sorry, Mrs. Hogg. I'll have the rent money in the morning."

Following church, Marcus walked to the park. Dipping his hand in the seed box he took a seat on the bench and waited for the ducks and geese to come to him. It didn't take long before they waddled along the path toward him. Absent mindedly, he threw the grain. He actually hoped the old man might come. He bowed his head.

Dear Heavenly Father, I have now had the divorce papers for a month. I don't want to sign them, Lord. I love my wife and my children. Is there any hope for reconciliation? Or at least her forgiveness? I think Carem did love me at one time. I pray, Lord, that You will help us overcome the many obstacles we face. Please, show me the way.

He sat with his head bowed, trying to collect his thoughts as he continued to pray. *I can't go to Carem. There's that restraining order. I don't want to call her. I need to see her in person, but how is that possible? I don't want to go to jail for violating the order.* He paused, realizing the answer. *I've got it! Why didn't I think of this before? Probably because I didn't have You to lead me before, Lord. I need to talk to her father. Thank You, Jesus! Amen.*

On the corner, Marcus stopped at a phone booth. Pulling three dimes from his pocket, he placed the three calls to Harry, Mike, and Bob. He told them his decision and asked for each man to pray for him, and to pray that if Carem would not reconcile, at least for them to remain friends for the sake of the children, and rescind the restraining order. Whatever is in the Lord's will, Marcus said he would accept the outcome.

Next, he returned to his sleeping room and packed a suitcase of clothes, his shaving kit, and made himself a lunch for now, and one for the next day. He didn't want to take the time to stop at a restaurant on the drive down to Franklin. He was going to be ready to leave first thing in the morning, after paying his landlady, and after stopping by work.

He prayed his boss would understand that this leave of absence was very important, as he would be off for the entire week. The remainder of the day he spent in prayer and reading the Bible Pastor Mattingly had given him.

*****

The next morning after paying Mrs. Hogg, Marcus stopped by his work to explain why he needed a leave of absence. His boss understood the situation and was fine with Marcus's need of the leave from work. Marcus was on the road to Franklin by nine o'clock. The heavy morning traffic on I-65 slowed him down. What was normally a two hour drive would undoubtedly cost him an extra half hour on the interstate. *I need to be patient, Lord. I'm just so excited to get this behind me. Actually, I'm excited at the prospect of possibly seeing Carem.*

When he arrived at the Elizabethtown exit, where they normally ate on the drive to Franklin, he pulled the sandwich from his lunch box. Munching on the sandwich, he continued his journey, and his thoughts rested on his family. He pictured Carem with Drew and Angela. Carem was such a good mother. She was so patient and loving toward the children. She rarely scolded them. She had a way of shifting Drew's temper tantrums into laughter. When Angela's two-year-old bad baby-behavior grew defiant, Carem could maneuver the situation into a fun playtime. He wished he'd been more patient with the children. He tended to yell and admonish. Of course, that made the situation worse.

He had noticed in the past couple of years

how Carem made sure he was never alone with the children. He knew that she had quit trusting him with them; and rightfully so. His drinking had turned him into a tyrant. He certainly didn't set a good example. Andrew would have been such a good father. He'd already been a great husband to Carem.

I've let Andrew down. I was so wrong for what I did, Lord. I should have gotten help much sooner. Please help me rectify our lives. Please give me wisdom, and help my faith stay steady. Please help Carem and the children to trust me again. Please help them to forgive me. I know I don't deserve a second chance, but forgiveness would be sufficient for me, Lord Jesus.

He pulled his 1967 Jeep Wagoneer into a parking spot on the East Cedar Street side of Christmas Hotel. After removing his suitcase, he walked up to the front door. Opening the heavy door, he saw that Mr. Mullins was on duty behind the desk.

"Hello, Mr. Taylor," greeted Mr. Mullins. "Are you here to see Mrs. Taylor?"

"Mrs. Taylor is here?" asked Marcus, clearly puzzled. He expected her to be at their home in Louisville with the children.

"Yes, she's staying in the family's room number seven. Would you like me to call her?"

"Ah ... no. Are the children with her?"

"I believe they have been staying at the family home, sir."

Marcus was now really puzzled. *Carem left the children, and she's here at Christmas Hotel. That's not like her.*

"Will you be joining Mrs. Taylor, sir?"

Unmistakably, the news of the separation was not general knowledge. "No, Mr. Mullins. Do you have a room that I can have on one of the upper floors?"

Mr. Mullins was now the one to appear bewildered, but he was very professional and he quickly recovered. "Yes, I have a room on the fourth floor, sir. Room number forty-seven is available. Please just sign in here, and I'll carry your suitcase."

"That's okay. I'll take the elevator, and I'll carry my suitcase. Please don't tell Mrs. Taylor or the family I'm here. I'll just surprise them."

"As you wish, sir." Mr. Mullins handed him the key, and Marcus hurried to the elevator. If Carem saw him here, in breach of the restraining order, he knew he'd be in serious trouble.

Chapter Forty-Four

Comfort

"Blessed be God, even the Father of our Lord Jesus Christ, the Father of mercies, and the God of all comfort; Who comforteth us in all our tribulation, that we may be able to comfort them which are in any trouble, by the comfort wherewith we ourselves are comforted of God."
2 Corinthians 1:3-4

The Present Day
December 02, 1974

Carrie Emeline and Jerilyn walked down the Christmas Hotel staircase and approached the front desk. Jerilyn smiled at their assistant manager. He'd been with them many years, and was a faithful, loyal, and dependable man whom she and Christopher also considered a dear friend. "Good evening, Mr. Mullins. My daughter and I are headed home. If you need Christopher or me, you can reach us there. We'll be having dinner at home with Carrie Emeline and our two grandchildren tonight."

"Have a good evening to you and your family, ma'am."

"You, too, Mr. Mullins."

As soon as Carrie Emeline walked in the front door of the family home, both children attacked her. "Mommy, Mommy," they both yelled in excitement. "I missed you, Mommy," said Drew jumping up and down, and Angela echoed his sentiments.

Carrie Emeline knelt down to their level and hugged both children. "I'm sorry I stayed away from you two for so long. I promise you it won't happen again. I'm better, thanks to Grandma." She looked over their heads and smiled at her Mom.

"Your mommy just needed some much needed rest," explained Jerilyn. "However, I could use some help with dinner. Who wants to help?"

"I do," they both chorused.

"Well, let's head to the kitchen and find something to prepare. Any suggestions?"

Drew yelled out displaying huge and rounded eyes. "Hot dogs and ice cream!"

Angela clapped her hands. "Pizza, Grandma!"

Jerilyn chuckled. "We'll see," and the children bounced behind her to the kitchen.

*****

Marcus paced in his room at Christmas Hotel. He was anxious and scared, because the old desire to drink returned. He remembered Pastor Mattingly's words, 'Devil be gone!' That's what Marcus yelled, and immediately a peace came over him. Opening his suitcase, he pulled out his Bible. Taking a seat in the chair in front of the window, he switched on the light and flipped to the back of the book to the Bible Concordance where he looked up passages for comfort. Turning to Second Corinthians, he read the first chapter, noting every place that spoke of comfort. He wasn't looking for comfort just for himself, but for his wife and children, too.

So Carem is here at Christmas Hotel, and separated from the children because of me. She has to be in agony. She would never leave her children for any other reason. With a broken voice, he began to pray aloud.

"Dear Heavenly Father, please be with my wife and our children. Please offer comfort for Carem. She has been through a great deal of sadness in her life. We don't know why Andrew had to die. He was a good man, and I was not. However, for some reason Andrew loved me. Did his prayers bring me to this moment in life? I know You don't make mistakes.

"I've hurt my wife, when I should have just

offered her comfort. Please watch over Carem and Drew and Angela. Please comfort them tonight and for all their days. In the name of Jesus Christ I pray ... amen."

Chapter Forty-Five

The Medicine of Laughter

"A merry heart doeth good like a medicine: but a broken spirit drieth the bones."
Proverbs 17: 22

Tuesday
December 03, 1974
The children were still asleep when Carrie Emeline awakened early to meet her parents downstairs. They were having their morning coffee and devotions on the sofa in the living room — something they'd done daily through all of Carrie Emeline's memories. They hadn't heard her come down the stairs, and she stood a moment to watch them. Her parents possessed a loving marriage straight from their shared love of God: a thirty-three year marriage of patience, passion, hard work. Two heartbeats working together to make one. A true marriage of 'until death we do part.' *They are the true meaning of the word marriage. It's the kind of marriage I*

always wanted. I had it briefly with Andrew. I hoped when we vacationed in Bellingham that I might have such a relationship with Marcus. I suppose it was not to be.

Her parents were holding hands and praying; calling the names of their five children, the spouses of their children, and their grandchildren, and praying individually for each of them. When they called out her name, they joined her name in prayer with Marcus.

Christopher continued, "And, Heavenly Father, lead Carrie Emeline and Marcus in whatever is Thy will, and *not* their wills. Please give them Thy divine wisdom. Have them consider the consequences of their decisions in the lives of Drew and Angela. We pray that Marcus will come to know Thee as his Heavenly Father."

There was much more to their prayer, but Carrie Emeline's thoughts were drawn to what her parents prayed for her and Marcus. *Thy will be done, Lord. Yes, that's what I pray, and I, too, pray for wisdom, and that Marcus will come to know You, Lord Jesus. Can it be, Lord? Will Marcus experience Your amazing grace? I pray that he can. I pray that his living nightmare will end. I would like our children to know a Christian father.*

When her parents finished their prayers, she walked into the room. Her father stood, smiled, and kissed her cheek. "Good morning, Carrie Emeline. Please join us for coffee and devotions."

She accepted the steaming hot mug of coffee her mother offered, and settled in the chair across from them, tucking her legs up under her. "Before we begin devotions, I need to say something."

Her mother set her mug down and turned to her daughter. "Go ahead, honey."

Carrie Emeline nodded. "I'm not ready to return to Louisville. Currently, I'd like to stay here with you. I don't want to be alone. I realize I need my parents during this time of indecision. Drew and Angela need the stability of being here with you two."

"Of course, dear. You're always welcome. This is your home."

"You can stay, as long as you need," added her father. "We love you, Carrie Emeline, and we pray for your future."

"I know you do, Daddy, and I appreciate you both so much. I thank God that I was blessed with you two for parents, and as the grandparents of my children. I'm going to dress the children, and when we finish breakfast I plan to enroll Drew in kindergarten here in Franklin. I don't want him to miss another day. He's enjoyed school in

Louisville, and he's done so well. Although he's a little younger than the others in his class, he's managed to keep up. I suppose having a teacher for his mother hasn't hurt, of course," At that, both she and her parents laughed.

"It feels good to laugh. I haven't done much of that lately. The Bible says 'A merry heart doeth good like a medicine: but a broken spirit drieth the bones.' That's been me. I've forgotten the merry heart, and I've let a broken spirit dry deeply into my bones. I haven't chosen the healthy path, and that needs to stop now. I must get my life back on track for the sake of myself *and* my children."

"Carrie Emeline, whatever you decide, your mother and I will stand beside you. Let's pray."

Immediately following breakfast, Carrie Emeline drove Drew to the Franklin Elementary School. Following enrollment, Principal Barnard escorted them to the kindergarten class of Mrs. Susan Best. Mrs. Best met them in the hall.

"I have a new student for you, Mrs. Best." Principal Barnard placed an arm on Drew's shoulder. "This is Andrew McConnaughey, but everyone calls him Drew."

"Drew, I'm very pleased to meet you." Mrs. Best's radiant smile was infectious. Carrie Emeline guessed she was probably in her early forties, and Drew smiled and took to her immediately. She then addressed Carrie Emeline. "I'll take good care of your son, Mrs. McConnaughey. You don't need to worry."

"Thank you, Mrs. Best. However, I'm Mrs. Taylor now. Mr. McConnaughey was killed in Vietnam."

Carrie Emeline saw the pain that flashed across Mrs. Best's face. "So was my husband, Mrs. Taylor. Drew and I will get along fine." She spoke in a soft tone of voice as she took Drew's hand and walked him into the classroom. Carrie Emeline watched through the window of the closed door as Mrs. Best introduced Drew to the class, and then seated him at the small desk closest to her desk.

Outside the classroom, Principal Barnard turned to her. "When you were enrolling Drew, I overheard you say that you'd been a third grade teacher in Louisville. Would you consider taking a third grade class here? I currently have one of my teachers out on pregnancy leave, so my only other third grade teacher is now teaching thirty-six students. I desperately need another teacher. If you're interested, do you have time to discuss the position with me?"

Carrie Emeline arrived back home at ten o'clock that morning. After explaining the job offer to her parents, her father had several questions. "If you take this position, your mother and I have no problem watching Angela, and then Drew, too, after his half-day at kindergarten. But what will you do about your home in Louisville, and your teaching position there?"

"I'm not going to do anything about the house until the divorce with Marcus is finalized. I'll call the school though, and take leave from my position for now. I did notify my school yesterday to let them know that I wouldn't be in this week. The school also knows Drew is with me, so he won't be counted truant. I'm certain Mr. and Mrs. White will watch the house for me until I make my decision of whether to sell the property or not."

Her mother scrutinized Carrie Emeline's face. "It sounds as though you're taking the position here."

"That's what I'd like to do, Mom. I told Principal Barnard I need to discuss the care of my children with the two of you. I also informed him I may only be able to teach until Christmas vacation. He was fine with that. Presently, I believe it's a good decision for me. I love teaching, and teaching will help relieve me of my constant thoughts of Marcus, not to mention relieving another third grade teacher of handling thirty-six students. I can only imagine how difficult this has been for her."

"When will you begin?" asked her father.

"Tomorrow morning. I can take Drew to his class, and I'll bring him home on my lunch break. That way we can all have lunch together, and then I'll return for the afternoon."

Her mom patted her hand. "Don't worry about the children. I, too, think this is a good decision for you."

"Oh, thank you both so much for your help. You have no idea how much I appreciate your support."

Her dad placed his arms around her. "We told you, we'd always be here for you. We love you and the children very much."

"Thank you, Daddy. I love you both, too."

Chapter Forty-Six

Confessions

"But if we walk in the light, as he is in the light, we have fellowship one with another, and the blood of Jesus Christ his Son cleanseth us from all sin."
1 John 1:7

Thursday
December 05, 1974
Marcus had mostly stayed in his room since his arrival at Christmas Hotel; not venturing out on the streets of Franklin often. Mr. Mullins informed him of the shifts that Chris and Carem's father, Mr. Wright, worked. He avoided going into the lobby at those times. If Chris or Mr. Wright had seen his name on the register, they had not confronted him.

He knew that most mornings Chris was on duty before his classes at Western Kentucky University in Bowling Green, Kentucky for three hours, and again after classes for four hours. Mr. Mullins worked some days, but mostly the third shift. Mr. Hanover was now in the rotation, as Mr. Wright no longer worked six days a week. He normally worked three or four shifts a week, and Mrs. Wright usually joined him.

Today at noon was to be Mr. Hanover's shift, but when Marcus stepped off the elevator in the lobby, he found himself staring into the face of Carem's father, Christopher Wright. He wasn't sure he was ready for this conversation, but now he had no choice. After all, it was why he came to Franklin.

Marcus stepped up to the lobby desk, and shook his father-in law's hand. "Marcus." Mr. Wright's face displayed no hostility, "I'm surprised to see you. I didn't notice your name on the register."

"I arrived on Monday, sir."

"Carrie Emeline didn't mention you were coming to Christmas Hotel."

"She doesn't know I'm here. I didn't know Carrie Emeline and the children were in Franklin, until Mr. Mullins told me when I checked in. I asked him not to say anything regarding my arrival. I actually came to see you, sir. Is there a time that we can talk in private?"

"Well, there's no time like the present, and we certainly have much to discuss. Mr. Hanover is in the office. I'll ask him to watch the front desk.

Have you had lunch, Marcus?"

"No, sir."

Christopher grabbed the key to room #7, ordered the lunch special for the both of them to be delivered to the room, and he led Marcus up the staircase.

Marcus had never been in this special room. He had only heard about it. Christopher unlocked the door, and they entered the darkened room. Christopher pulled a box of matches from the nightstand drawer, and lit the kerosene lamp. Marcus surveyed the room by the yellow light and was relieved to notice Christopher's smile.

A sheer curtain surrounded a high four-poster oak bed. The marble topped oak dresser held an attached matching oak-framed mirror. On a silver tray, a mother of pearl hairbrush, comb, and hand mirror rested on the ladies vanity. Heavy deep green velvet drapes pooled on the floor from four floor-to-ceiling windows. Christopher began the explanation of the room, as he had probably done many times over the years. "The room looks as it did the day Christmas Hotel opened in 1850. It's the only room of the sixty here in the hotel that has never been updated. Captain and Mrs. Bazell, the second owners of Christmas Hotel, purchased this hotel back in 1883 from the original owners, Mr. and Mrs. Thomas Hoy.

Captain and Mrs. Bazell's twenty-year-old daughter, Carrie Emeline Bazell, lived in this room until she died a few months after arriving with her parents."

"Carrie Emeline?"

"Yes. Your wife was named for their daughter."

Marcus was puzzled. "But ... she died before you or Mrs. Wright were born."

"Yes, she did. However, my wife felt a connection to her, as if she was a sister from another century, because of a diary the first Carrie Emeline wrote and my wife found. That's another story. Mrs. Wright and I also received Christmas Hotel as a wedding gift from the Bazells several months before they passed away. We're the third owners. There's a much longer and more involved story, but I suspect you didn't drive here from Louisville to discuss the history of Christmas Hotel. Please have a seat in front of the windows."

Christopher opened the drapes and lit the other kerosene lamp on the table between the two brocade chairs in front of the windows, the yellow flame adding to the old-fashioned atmosphere. A knock at the door signified their lunch had arrived. Christopher asked the waiter to set the food on the table in front of the window. He thanked and tipped the waiter, and the young man closed the door behind him.

Christopher and Marcus made small talk until they finished the soup and sandwiches. "Okay, Marcus, I'm ready to listen."

"I'm not sure where to begin, sir. All I know is that I felt compelled to drive here and speak to you."

"Let's begin with calling me Christopher instead of sir."

"Okay, Christopher, I can do that."

It was a long story, but Marcus wanted Christopher to know everything, including his thoughts and emotions. He began with his friendship with Andrew and Jerry, and the meeting of Carrie Emeline in Germany.

"I want you to know that I felt no lust for your daughter when Andrew introduced us in Germany, but I admired her devotion to Andrew. Andrew was my friend, a good man, and quite deserving of a wonderful wife like your daughter. I wasn't jealous of Andrew, but I envied their relationship. Their two hearts melded beautifully into one heart. It was wonderful to watch them together."

Marcus explained the Christmas pact on Christmas Day in 1969. "Andrew and Jerry were extremely close to their families, and when they exchanged the names and addresses, I saw the tears in their eyes. I knew they didn't want to die, but if they did, they wanted to ensure that their families received the needed closure. In my case, I was the proverbial black sheep of my family. Growing up, I was nothing but trouble for my parents. However, in the event of my death, I did desire to have my family visited by someone I knew and loved. I did love Andrew and Jerry. They were good buddies to me. I wanted my family to know I thought of them ... at least in the end.

"That wasn't meant to be. The two who should *not* have died ... did. Andrew was forever talking to Jerry and me about the Lord Jesus and His gift of salvation. Although I grew up in church, I didn't want to hear about Jesus and His death on the cross. I now wish I'd listened, and I sincerely hope that Jerry did. Jerry was so young, at just twenty.

"As you know, I was wounded that day, but the worst part was watching them die. I never hurt so badly for my two buddies, and I screamed at God. *'No, please take me instead!'* It was at that moment, when I lost focus on the battle, I was wounded." Pausing, he rubbed his forehead, blinked back tears, and hung his head, giving Christopher time to respond.

"First of all, Marcus, we don't know how long any of us will live. Only God knows that. You were saved from that horrible death for a reason. It was not your time."

"I know that now, but in the moment I didn't. At Andrew's funeral, and later Jerry's, I saw how many lives they each had touched. I was stunned at how many people turned out at the visitations and the funerals for both of them. I wondered if anyone outside of my parents and siblings would attend my funeral — if it had been me that died." He stared into Christopher's eyes. "Do you want to hear more? It's going to get harder for you."

Christopher returned the gaze and nodded. "Go ahead, Marcus. I want to hear it all."

"In August of 1970 I was discharged from the army, but honorably. I didn't want to go home to Bellingham, Washington. I attempted two jobs that didn't work out. That's when I remembered your daughter, the promise to visit her, and of course how beautiful she was. I devised a plan; a devious plan.

"When she welcomed me into her home that day, it was only because I was Andrew's friend. Possibly, for her, with me being in her home brought back some good memories of Andrew. I like to think so now. When I explained the Christmas pact, I took it a step further." Marcus watched Christopher's face when he retold the untruth. He saw the eye twitch, the brow pucker, and the teeth clinch, but the rest of Christopher's face remained stoic.

"So you lied to my daughter, Marcus. Andrew didn't give you permission to cajole his wife into marriage and raise his son?" Christopher's demeanor remained controlled, but his hands quickly balled into fists; however, just as rapidly, they relaxed. Marcus knew Christopher's words were spoken in righteous anger. After all, this was a beloved daughter. He knew Christopher had willingly become the father of Carem and her twin Ken after the death of their biological father at Pearl Harbor. Christopher had raised the twins as his own, with honesty and love. *Do I really expect this loving father to accept my admission of guilt with open arms?*

Marcus looked Christopher in the eye, and it was one of the hardest things he'd ever done. He had to admit his blatant lie to his wife's father. "No, he didn't."

"So let me get this straight, Marcus. You used the death of a Christian man, who was your army buddy, your friend, to deceive his wife?"

Marcus hung his head. "I did, sir. I make no excuses for the deception." He raised his head, and knew his eyes were tearing. In a hoarse voice he added, "What I did was wrong, and I confess that sin to you, as I've confessed my many great sins to Jesus Christ."

Marcus watched as Christopher scrutinized his face. *Please help show Christopher that I'm sincere, Jesus.*

Christopher's face relaxed. "I'm not your judge, Marcus. I believe you are being truthful. Do you love my daughter?"

"Yes, I love her with all my heart. I've wronged her and the children. I only hope that she will forgive me ... and Drew will forgive me, also. Has she discussed with you our four years together?"

"Not directly. She has told Jerilyn, who told me. Carrie Emeline arrived for Thanksgiving, but left our home and stayed in this very room until Monday. She's now at our home with the children. Her mother has told me Carrie Emeline's side of the story. I'd like to hear your side, Marcus." Christopher checked his watch. "It's now five thirty and my family expects me home for dinner. If you like, we can meet here tomorrow at noon and talk some more."

"I'd like that, Christopher."

"Do you want me to let Carrie Emeline know you're here at Christmas Hotel?"

"Not yet, please. I want to spend some time

with you first, and in prayer."

"I'm pleased to hear that, Marcus. If you'd like to use the chapel, it's always available. Just a heads up, though. Chris is off duty at six o'clock today, so wait until after he's gone before you go down. Mr. Hanover is on duty until midnight."

"Thank you, Christopher."

"I'll see you tomorrow, Marcus."

Chapter Forty-Seven

Questions and Answers

*"And ye have forgotten the exhortation which
speaketh unto you as unto children, My son,
despise not thou the chastening of the Lord, nor
faint when thou art rebuked of him: For whom
the Lord loveth he chasteneth, and scourgeth
every son whom he receiveth."*
Hebrews 12: 5-6

Friday
December 06, 1974
Christopher and Marcus met in room #7 the next
day, and Christopher provided another delicious
Christmas Hotel dining room lunch for them.
Christopher arrived armed with plenty of
questions.

"I don't want you to think I'm interrogating
you, Marcus, but I just want to understand your
side. My first question is: when and why did you
decide that you thought the marriage of
convenience should end, *and* you decided the two
of you should have a real marriage in every sense

of the word?"

Marcus took a deep breath and slowly released it. "That's a good question. I told you that I met your daughter in Germany, when Andrew introduced her. She was so beautiful and genuinely kind. Although her eyes were only for Andrew, she was polite with me. I really believe that was the groundwork of my love for her, but I didn't know it at the time. It was during the 1970 Christmas season following our marriage that I knew for certain the marriage of convenience was over ... at least for me. I was completely in love with my wonderful wife. At the time, I was the house husband and the caregiver for Drew, while she pursued her passion as a teacher. She was patient, loving and kind ... and did I say beautiful?" He received a warm smile from Christopher.

"It was the night that we put Drew's Christmas gifts together, and later drank hot chocolate in front of the fireplace. That night our marriage was consummated. However, because of me, we were happy for only short periods of time." Marcus stopped a moment and ran his fingers through his hair. "I have Post-Traumatic-Stress-Disorder ... or PTSD. Are you familiar with that affliction?"

"Yes, I am, Marcus."

"Carem, that's what I call her, had known about my nightmares ever since the first night that I had arrived in her home. She told me that she would sometimes hear me in her guest room crying out in my sleep, and tossing and turning in the bed. The PTSD didn't improve after I moved into her bedroom, in fact it gradually worsened."

"When were you diagnosed with PTSD?"

"I initially sought help from a pastor at a church near my sleeping room after Carem and I split up this past summer. He provided me with the name of a counselor of war veterans, who specialized in PTSD. I've since joined a weekly group in Louisville. There are veterans from four wars in the group."

"Did you resent Drew, because he's Andrew's son and not your son?"

"That's a tough question. At first, I was just a caregiver; nothing more. As the days went by, I began to enjoy Drew's company and have fun with him. He was a really good baby. He laughed a lot, rarely crying. He was happy, but I think that's because Carem is such a good mother. There is a strong bond between the two of them. I suppose I *could* have been jealous of that bond, because he was Andrew's son, but I wasn't. I loved Andrew, too, and I understood the bond."

"Are you now a Christian, Marcus?"

"Yes, I am. I was saved in that little church, Shawnee Baptist Church. However, I sincerely believe God has been planting seeds in my life for a long time. He's brought people in my life to help me ... I just didn't want to listen. I went to church when I was a boy at home in Bellingham, Washington, and my whole family is Christian. I entered the army, met Andrew, and he desperately attempted to lead me to the Lord. I've been married to Carem four years. She tried to get me in church to hear the Word. I refused.

"It took a horrible event — the morning I nearly killed Drew and hurt Carem, for the Lord to begin getting through to me in my hard head. I went to jail, I moved into a sleeping room, and I continued to drink. On two Sundays, I *accidentally*...." He chuckled. "Accidentally, yeah right. I left the radio on to awaken me, instead of switching it to the buzzer sound. Each of those times, the radio minister awakened me preaching in a booming voice. I was curious, and I listened. I sought a neighborhood church, and I found Shawnee Baptist Church. I entered on two different Sundays. On the second Sunday I asked the Lord into my heart."

Marcus dropped his head and wiped a tear. "I don't know if Carem or my children will ever forgive me, but I know Jesus has forgiven me when He came into my heart that Sunday. The Lord Jesus had to chasten and scourge me to bring me to my knees. Believe me, it's been worth it. I know now it was done out of His love for me. I just pray Carem and my children will forgive me. I hope they'll want to meet the new Marcus and Daddy."

"Let's pray for the Lord's will, Marcus."

The two men bowed their heads.

Chapter Forty-Eight

Mt. Vernon Missionary Baptist

"If any of you lack wisdom, let him ask of God, that giveth to all men liberally, and upbraideth not; and it shall be given him."
James 1:5

Sunday
December 08, 1974
Marcus awakened in his room at Christmas Hotel and opened the drapes. A bright and sunny morning met his eyes. Christopher had told him the family would not be having breakfast at Christmas Hotel today, so he decided to dress and head downstairs to breakfast.

By the time he arrived, the dining room was nearly full to capacity. The host found him a small table behind the kitchen door. "I recommend an omelet, today, sir," the waiter suggested. "The chefs make them on weekends. Here's the list, but you may request it any way you wish."

After checking the menu, Marcus chose a ham and cheese omelet filled with tomatoes, spinach, and mushrooms. The waiter brought coffee and orange juice, and Marcus sat back and watched the people around him.

Laughing, happy families filled the room in their Sunday best dresses and suits. Beside his table sat a family of four. The little boy looked to be about Drew's age, and the little girl, Angela's age. The mother was helping the little girl cut her sausage and eggs, and then added jelly on her toast. The father casually draped one arm around his son, and took a sip of his coffee. They were engaged in conversation between bites.

Another family's breakfast had just arrived and the family held hands while the father asked the blessing. *Carem always wanted me to ask the blessing. It just seemed hypocritical to me, Lord, because I wasn't a Christian. Carem tried so hard to get me to church. God bless her. She's such a caring wife. I love her so much.*

After finishing breakfast, Marcus walked to his Jeep Wagoneer parked down by the railroad tracks behind Christmas Hotel. He had taken the chance that Carem wouldn't see it back there. Although Christopher had invited him to church when he last met with him, Marcus was not ready to face Carem and the children. There was also the matter of the restraining order.

He didn't really know where he was going, but

aimlessly drove down a winding country road. He passed many cars of people who waved at him, and he waved back. *Friendly people.* He found a Christian radio station that played old-time hymns; hymns from his youth. Farms, barns, fences, and cows dotted the landscape. He came upon a small white church with cars parked all around it. He pulled off the road into the churchyard. "Mt. Vernon Missionary Baptist Church," he read aloud from the sign. It felt right when he turned off the motor and entered the church.

He took a seat on the back pew. The congregation sang a rousing hymn: "When the Roll is Called up Yonder."

It was a different sort of church to the ones he was used to. The people were robustly clapping, shouting, and praising the Lord throughout the service. When they heard the preacher say something in which there was an agreement, someone would heartily shout 'Amen, brother!', or 'Preach it!'

The message was on the Scripture James chapter one, verse five: seeking wisdom from the Lord by asking in prayer. Marcus thought about that.

I've never sought You, Lord, in prayer until I was saved. Lord, I've not called on You for help in my life until recently, but I'm calling on You now. I'm humbling myself, asking for Your divine wisdom. I don't know how to talk to Carem and my children. I beseech You to make a path for me. If she doesn't forgive me, I'll understand. I'll move on with my life wherever You lead me, Lord. However, if Carem forgives me and wants me to remain her husband, with Your help, Lord, I'll do my best to become a godly husband and father. Lead me with Your wisdom, Lord. I pray this in the name of Your Son Jesus Christ, amen.

The service ended with an old invitational hymn, "Just as I Am."

He listened to the words.

"Just as I am, without one plea,
but that Thy blood was shed for me,
and that thou bidst me come to Thee,
O Lamb of God, I come, I come.

"Just as I am, and waiting not
to rid my soul of one dark blot,
to Thee whose blood can cleanse each spot,
O Lamb of God, I come, I come."

I humbly come to You, Lord God. Thank You, Lord, for my salvation and for leading me to this little church. I feel Your comfort and Your peace. I pray that I'll meet with my little family soon. I thank You for the counseling from Your servant, Christopher. You have given him much wisdom and patience. I know You led me to seek him out. Thank You, Lord.

Chapter Forty-Nine

Counseling with Christopher

"Peace I leave with you, my peace I give unto you: not as the world giveth, give I unto you. Let not your heart be troubled, neither let it be afraid."
John 14:27

Friday
December 13, 1974
Marcus spent the morning in his room at Christmas Hotel. All week he listened to preachers and hymns on the radio, and reading the Bible Pastor Mattingly had given him. He appreciated the notes in the margin, as it provided him a better glimpse into some Scriptures. In the afternoons he took drives into the country and enjoyed the serenity. Originating from a seaside town, country life was a novelty to him.

The knock on his door surprised him, but he was pleased when he opened the door and saw Christopher. "Christopher, please come in."

"I'm not interrupting, am I?"

"No, not at all." He turned down the Christian music on the radio. "Have a seat, Christopher."

"I've been expecting you to contact me, Marcus. Please be assured, I haven't told Carrie Emeline you're here. However, I have told Jerilyn. We don't keep secrets."

"I don't mind that Jerilyn knows. I *am* curious as to what she thought when you told her."

"She only wants what's best for our daughter ... *and* for you, Marcus. I don't want to push, but when are you planning to speak to Carrie Emeline?"

He told Christopher about the church in the country. "I've spent the week in prayer, asking for godly wisdom. Whatever happens, I'm at peace."

"Well, here's my advice. Sometimes you just need to listen to your heart. You speak of the peace the Lord has given you. He says in the book of John chapter fourteen and verse twenty-seven: 'Peace I leave with you, My peace I give unto you: not as the world giveth, give I unto you. Let not your heart be troubled, neither let it be afraid.' Marcus, He's given you the peace, so now listen to the rest of the verse. You're using a troubled heart to prevent you from seeing Carrie Emeline. Let God pave the way for you, through prayer. I promise you, you've been on her mind. Although she's teaching school here at the Franklin Elementary during the day, you're not far from her thoughts in the evening. Just for your information, the divorce papers remain unsigned by her. Carrie Emeline has been troubled, too. She takes nothing lightly."

"I haven't signed my copy either. Where do you suggest I meet with her?"

"Right here at Christmas Hotel, in room number seven. Let Jerilyn and me talk to her when she gets home from school. If she's in agreement, I'll call you and I'll have us all meet."

"I like that plan, Christopher. Would you and Jerilyn stay with us for a while?"

"I think that can be arranged, son. Remember, Christmas Hotel is known as the place where miracles occur. Be at peace."

*****

"You've been meeting with Marcus, Daddy? I can't *believe* you've kept this from me!" Carrie Emeline was understandably hurt, but Christopher continued. Jerilyn had already taken the children upstairs before Carrie Emeline arrived home, so that father and daughter could talk in private.

"Honey, Marcus came to me for counseling. I assure you, he didn't even know you were in Franklin when he first arrived. He thought you'd returned to Louisville after Thanksgiving."

"How long has he been here?"

"Since December second."

"He's been here *eleven days*?"

"Yes, but I didn't see him until eight days ago, and it was by accident. He had trouble getting up the nerve to speak with me."

"*And* rightly so, Daddy!"

"Honey, you're judging. I really think you should hear him out."

"Daddy, you know what he did to the children … and to me. How can you be so forgiving?"

He stared into his daughter's eyes with a father's love. "The same way the Lord Jesus did for all of us."

Thirty minutes later, Drew and Angela were left in Chris's care at home, while Christopher, Jerilyn, Carrie Emeline, and Marcus met in room #7 at Christmas Hotel.

Carrie Emeline's first glance at Marcus was surreal. She wasn't certain what to expect. Her Mom sat on the bed, Daddy at the desk, which left the two brocade chairs in front of the window for her and Marcus. She was much closer to Marcus than she wanted. She reluctantly sat.

"It's good to see you, Carem."

She said nothing in return. Just nodded her

head.

"Ahem." Her father cleared his throat to get their attention. "Jerilyn and I are going to stay as long as you two like, but at some point you two will need to talk alone." He checked his watch and said, "It's now four o'clock. Who would like to speak first?"

Carrie Emeline lowered her head.

Marcus looked over at Carrie Emeline, and she looked in the opposite direction. "I will. Carem, I know you don't trust me, and that's understandable. I want you to know that I'm sorry for how I've wronged you and our children. God has forgiven me, and I hope you will, too. When I came home from Vietnam, I was troubled. When I look back on the things I did, I'm ashamed. The pact Andrew, Jerry and I made really happened, except for the latter part. I need to come clean with you."

As he confessed his transgressions, wild thoughts scrambled her brain. She finally turned toward him and interrogated him in an angry voice, "How could you lie about your best friend? You said you loved and cared about Andrew ... and me. Was it *all* a lie? How can I possibly believe anything you have *ever* said to me?"

Marcus rubbed his hands on his legs. "Because I never intended to hurt you, Carem."

"Never intended to hurt me? You've got to be kidding me. You set out to deceive me, and I fell for it, hook, line, and sinker. What a fool I am, to believe such deception!"

"Carem, I was wrong, but loving you is the truth. I do love you and our children, and I'm sorry I was unable to show it better."

"Show it *better*? That's a weak excuse, Marcus. So you know, I've read up on PTSD, so if you're now going to throw that into the mix of this conversation, I don't want to hear it. That was probably all a hoax, too." Tears pricked her eyes, causing her more anger, and this time at herself. *I'm not going to cry. God, I don't want to cry. Please help me.*

Marcus stared at her, and his voice was gentle. He tried to take her hand, but she slapped his hand away. "Believe what you want, Carem, but I do love you. I'm sorry for everything. Please don't shut me out. I got saved last month."

She returned his stare. *Is he telling the truth now, Lord? Can I believe this man?* "Marcus, I hope this is true for your sake. Salvation is nothing to lie about."

"It's true, Carem. Please hear what's happened to me since we separated."

"I feel as though I'm listening to a snake charmer, but go ahead," she said grudgingly.

Her father stood, walked to her mother and took her hand. "Carrie Emeline, I'm going to interrupt. Your mother and I are leaving you two, and we'll wait downstairs. You need to hear Marcus out, and Marcus, you need to let Carrie Emeline vent her anger and disbelief. She has every right. Carrie Emeline, you aren't the judge of Marcus, so please give him a chance to explain. That's all the advice I'm going to give you two, so please work out something, if not for yourselves, at least for the sake of your children."

Carrie Emeline nodded. "All right, Daddy. I feel like I've been properly chastised, but okay, I'll listen. You're right. For the sake of our children, we should come to terms with this situation."

Three hours later, Carrie Emeline's emotions were all over the place. Her heart wanted to believe Marcus, but her head said to pray about the right decision for this life-altering matter. After all, she was not the only one involved; she had children to consider.

"Let's go to dinner, Carem. I'm sure your parents would like to go home, too. I'm worn out. Can we call a truce for now?"

"Truce? Yes okay … for now. My mind is frazzled thinking about everything you've told me. Look, the dining room will soon close for dinner. I don't want to take you home to the children yet. Do you want to eat here at Christmas Hotel? The staff will still have some leftovers we can eat. Most of the diners will have left, too, so we'll have privacy. "

"The Christmas Hotel dining room is fine. I understand why you don't want me to see the children. After all, there's still that restraining order."

"I'll consider having it cancelled on Monday, Marcus. Let's see what happens."

In the lobby her parents still waited. Carrie Emeline kissed them both. "Thank you, but it's okay. You two can go home. We aren't going to kill each other."

Over dinner, they initially chatted with only polite conversation. Neither one wanted a heated argument in front of the staff.

"Your father told me you were teaching at the Franklin Elementary School. How's that working out?"

"It's wonderful. I have seventeen amazing little third graders, and three of them have parents whom I attended school with here in Franklin." With a chuckle she added, "It rather makes me feel a little long in the tooth."

"I'm happy for you. You're doing what you were gifted by God to do."

"Yes, I am." She cocked her head and studied his face. "You know, you even talk the godly Christian talk. Only a Christian would speak of being gifted by God for something. You really do appear to have made that one hundred and eighty degree turn since I last saw you." *However, appearances can be deceiving. I'll wait and see if he walks the walk.*

"I didn't do it on my own, and I still slip now and then." He chuckled, and then he told her about Mrs. Hogg, his landlady at the boarding house, and his ever-ending attitude toward her. "I do my best to stifle my mouth in her presence."

She laughed for the first time since their conversation began. "I might even slip now and then if she was *my* landlady."

They finished their dinner and walked into the lobby. Mr. Hanover was on duty.

Carrie Emeline approached the desk with Marcus close behind. "Hello, Mr. Hanover, it's nice to see you this evening." "It's nice to see you, too, Carrie Emeline ... and you, too Mr. Taylor."

Marcus nodded and smiled. "Thank you, Mr. Hanover. Have a good evening, sir." Turning to Carrie Emeline, he asked, "May I walk you home?"

"Why yes ... thank you."

"Let me go upstairs and fetch our coats."

The conversation on the walk home was civil. She pointed out some of the extra-special decorations in the store windows, and a few of the businesses on the square that had changed hands since he was last in Franklin.

At her door, with his hands in his pockets, he felt unsure of how to end the evening. "I appreciate you hearing me out, Carem."

"You're welcome, Marcus."

"By the way, when is your last day at school before Christmas vacation?"

"On December twentieth; one week from today."

He worked up the nerve to ask his next question. When he did, he rushed the words. "May I see you over the weekend, and maybe a night or two after work next week?"

She blushed and cautiously asked, "Are ... you asking me for a date, Marcus?"

He cleared his throat. "Uh ... well ... I guess I am. I want a new beginning with you. Is that possible? At least try to be friends ... for the sake of our children, of course."

She thought so long about how to appropriately answer his question that he looked down and shuffled his feet. "It's okay, Carem. I knew when I met with you that it was probably over between us."

With that she said, "Hi, my name is Carrie Emeline," and she offered her hand.

He smiled and took her cue, "Hi, Carrie Emeline, my name is Marcus. It's a pleasure to meet you," and they shook hands on her doorstep.

Chapter Fifty

Advice from a Wise Mother

"And Jesus said unto him, No man, having put his hand to the plough, and looking back, is fit for the kingdom of God."
Luke 9:62

Friday Evening
December 13, 1974

Jerilyn knocked on Carrie Emeline's bedroom door. "Come in." Carrie Emeline, now in her nightgown and robe, sat at her vanity table and brushed her hair. Her mother walked over, took the brush, and began brushing her daughter's hair.

"I always loved doing this for all my girls. Sometimes I miss the fact that my five children are grown. Even Chris, my baby, is nineteen. Where did the time go?"

"I suppose I'll say that about Drew and Angela someday. By the way, did you have any trouble putting them to bed?"

"Not at all. Drew requested *Where the Red*

Fern Grows and Angela requested *Charlotte's Web*. I told them they had to pick one tonight and one tomorrow. Drew was so mature, you'd be proud of him. He said, 'I'll be the gentleman and let Angela go first.'"

"Aw, Mom, that makes me cry. He's such a good big brother. That also causes me to miss Ken. After all, he's two minutes older than I am!" They both laughed. "You're right, Mom. They are growing up too fast and too soon."

"You know, dear, Marcus is probably saying the same thing. I realize that not getting help sooner for his PTSD was a poor choice on his part, but he's getting help now. Have you made a decision in letting him see the children?"

"What Marcus and I have decided on for the moment is baby steps for us, and prayer. We hashed out a lot tonight, but there's a great many issues to sort through. I don't want the children involved yet. I don't want to get their hopes up that their Daddy and I might get back together. At least Angela's hopes. I'm not sure about Drew. He may be afraid of Marcus. I need to have a discussion with Drew."

"You haven't talked to Drew about that morning?"

"I've tried several times. He just doesn't want to talk with me. He'll clam up as soon as I say anything."

"Maybe a counselor would help. Your father is a good counselor. It's also possible he misses Marcus, and he's afraid you don't. We won't know until he talks to someone. What about you, honey? Do you still love Marcus?"

"Oh, Mom ... yes ... no ... maybe. I just don't know. Daddy's right about one thing. I have wrongly been Marcus's judge and executioner for too long. However, I really should have left Marcus years ago. If I had, all that happened may never have escalated as it did. I was embarrassed about our private life. I didn't want anyone to know. I also considered divorce as being a failure. I was too proud to let anyone know I needed help."

She sighed. "Oh, Mom, I'm glad Daddy made me listen to Marcus today. I didn't know how much Marcus had changed since that terrible morning. I can see now he's a different man. He really *is* a Christian. He's trying so hard to do the right thing. I know I can't forget what he did, but can I truly forgive him? Can I trust him enough to let him back in our lives? I don't necessarily mean to live together again, but for visitations with the children."

"That's something you'll need to pray about, honey."

"Also, the much delayed grieving process I just went through for Andrew took a toll on me. I think I've always felt that Marcus should measure up to Andrew. I was so wrong. One man can't possibly be the same as another. How did you cope when my biological father died? You never really had time to grieve him before marrying Daddy. Did you feel like you were pitting the two men against each other?"

"Whew, that's a lot to answer. First of all, because Kenneth was in the war, I was always prepared for an injury or death, just like down deep you probably were with Andrew. It's hard to admit feelings like that."

Carrie Emeline nodded her head.

"Kenneth was my first love, and it was always expected, at least from our high school friends, we would marry. However, my parents didn't approve."

"I didn't know this tidbit of information, Mom. Why?" she asked, puzzled.

"Kenneth wasn't a Christian when we married, Carrie Emeline. My two marriages were somewhat a blended reverse of your two marriages. You married a Christian man first, and then an unsaved man second. Kenneth wasn't saved when we married, although he was saved before he died. *I*, on the other hand, was in a backslidden condition when we married. You know the rest of the story, about finding Carrie Emeline Bazell's diary, and her story that led me back to the Lord.

"I never compared Christopher with Kenneth. Everything happened so fast. I did grieve Kenneth, but Mrs. Bazell helped me through the process. Jesus said, literally, that once one puts his hand to the plow, don't look back. If you think about that, and picture the plows of Bible days, if you're plowing a row and look back, your rows will be crooked. I thought of it as not thinking too much about the past, because the past is behind us and can't be changed. But we *can* look forward and choose the right path for our future. We can make our paths straight to Him, the One who holds our hand.

"I believe that's what Marcus is accomplishing now. He told your father that even if you didn't forgive him, he would stay the course, whatever the Lord has for his future. He's not going to deviate. He just doesn't know that path yet, but he's praying about it. I suggest you do the same, honey."

"Thanks, Mom. I love you and Daddy so much."

Jerilyn returned the brush to Carrie Emeline and kissed her. "Your father and I are praying for you, for Marcus, and for the children. Through prayer, I know you and Marcus will make the right decision."

"Will you pray for us right now, Mom?"

"It would be my pleasure." Jerilyn took her daughter's hand and they bowed their heads. "Dear Heavenly Father, Carrie Emeline needs Your help to make the life-changing decision that's best for her and her children. Please help her decide if Marcus should return to her life and her children's and in what capacity. Help her know if they are to remain married or just be friends. Help her know in her heart if Marcus has told her the whole truth and if he's truly sincere and penitent. Lord, please help Carrie Emeline have peace in this great decision. Let her know Your will. In the name of Jesus Your Son we pray ... amen." Carrie Emeline softly added her amen.

"Thank you, Mom," she whispered, wiping her tears.

Jerilyn kissed her cheek. "You're very welcome, honey. God bless you and your little family."

Chapter Fifty-One

Visiting Angels Revealed

*"Let not the waterflood overflow me,
neither let the deep swallow me up, and
let not the pit shut her mouth upon me."*
Psalm 69:15

Saturday
December 14, 1974
Marcus awakened early, showered and dressed. After grabbing his Bible, he descended the staircase to have breakfast in the dining room. Chris was the manager on duty at the front desk, so Marcus stopped to talk. Whatever it was that Chris had been told about the situation, he didn't let it show.

"Hi, Marcus, I heard you were here! I hadn't checked the roster, and you've now been here for twelve days. I guess I'd better brush-up on my management skills!"

Marcus smiled and shook Chris's offered hand. "You're going to make a wonderful manager, Chris. I asked Mr. Mullins and Mr.

Hanover to keep it quiet that I was here, until I was ready to speak with your father."

"Well, they did their job by taking care of the guest's wishes. Are you heading to breakfast?"

"I thought I would, and then I plan to spend some time in the chapel — unless it's in use this morning for an event."

"No, it's available. No weddings scheduled today. Please feel free to take as much time as you like."

"Thanks, Chris."

Following breakfast, Marcus entered the chapel. After taking a seat on the front pew, he turned around to make sure he was alone, so he could pray out loud. He bowed his head in prayer. "Dear Heavenly Father. I came to Christmas Hotel to seek out my father-in-law for counseling. I thank You that I've received his acceptance. I thank You for the time I've spent with Carem. I pray she will forgive me. I pray my children will forgive me. I want their acceptance ... I crave their acceptance. I pray for Your direction for the remainder of my life. Where do You want me, Lord? Please let me know for certain. I want to do Your will. In the name of Your Son Jesus I pray. Amen."

He lifted his head and opened his Bible to the Book of Psalms and silently read chapter 69.

Without checking again that he was alone, he continued to pray out loud in a way that he had never thought possible. "Wow, Lord, this whole chapter could have been written for me, although I realize it's about King David. I was sinking in the mire, but You pulled me out. You always knew my foolishness; my sins were never hidden from You. I have been sinful, and an alien to my mother's children. I was the song of the drunkards. You redeemed my soul. David praised Your name in song and thanksgiving, and so do I."

"Is this seat taken?"

He looked up, surprised, realizing his unorthodox prayer had probably been overheard. Then he saw who it was, and smiled, "It's reserved for you, Carem. How long have you been here?"

"I arrived shortly after you, but I didn't want to interrupt your prayer, and then your reading. What book are you reading?"

"The Book of Psalms, chapter sixty-nine. It could have been written for me." He explained his thoughts as he read to her.

"So you feel that you're no longer stuck in the mire?" she asked softly.

"No, I'm not stuck anymore. The Lord picked me up and placed me on solid ground." His eyes teared, he tried to blink them back, and he swallowed before speaking. In a hoarse voice he said, "Carem, I'm so sorry for all I've done to you and our children. I'm so sorry I hurt you." Tears spilled down his cheeks.

She took his Bible and set it on the pew. Wrapping her arms around him, she held him as she did her children. They sat for a few minutes in silence.

Together, they walked out of the chapel. He returned his Bible to his room, grabbed his coat, and met her on the park bench across the street in the square.

Carrie Emeline fidgeted with her hands before she spoke. "I've a story to tell you, and it's hard to believe, but it's true. I've been visited on three occasions by an angel." She blurted it out quickly, watching his face for his reaction.

"Really? I do believe you, but you go first, and then I'll tell you why."

"The last time I saw him was on December second and he was sitting right here on this bench, feeding pigeons and doves. I knew he looked familiar, but at first I couldn't place him. Later, I remembered that he visited me the night I learned Andrew had died. That was the first visit, and he comforted me. I asked him if he was Lydia Grace's angel, and he said 'yes, and mine, too.' If you remember, I told you the story of Lydia Grace at age eight, and about her angel and her dog."

"Yes, I remember."

"The second time was in the hospital when I was in labor with Angela. It was a difficult labor compared to my labor with Drew."

He shook his head. "I'm sorry I wasn't there for you, Carem."

"It's okay; you are now." She smiled. "I remember asking the angel if I was dying and if the baby was okay. He said I was fine, and that my little girl was fine, too. That's why I wanted to call her Angela for the angel, and Dawn because she was born at dawn."

"You chose the perfect name for her. She *is* our little angel. If I did anything right in my life, it was producing Angela with you."

"We did do that right, didn't we?" She looked down as he took her hand, and she did not withdraw. "How was he dressed, Carem?"

"He always wore farmer's overalls, a heavy plaid shirt and a floppy hat."

"And a long gray beard?"

She nodded.

"I met him, too, Carem. This is unbelievable! We must have been visited by the same angel! Unbeknownst to us, God has been watching over our family from the beginning."

Her eyes widened in awe. "Wow! This is truly amazing! Tell me your experience."

He explained the meeting in the park in Louisville. "He must like feeding birds," and they both laughed. "He was dressed like you said. I think he wanted to lead me to Jesus right then and there, but I walked away. I wasn't ready."

"You know, Marcus, the Bible speaks of angels always around us. I feel so blessed."

"I do, too, Carem." They were quiet for a moment. He shifted on the bench and stared directly into her eyes, and said, "I have a question for you. I never asked you if I could call you Carem. I just told you. I've come to realize how wrong I was when I tried to control you in so many varied situations. So now I'll ask you. Do you mind being called Carem?"

This time she smiled a broad smile and laughed. "That's the sweetest thing you've asked me in a very long time. I'll admit I was a bit perturbed when you first informed me of the name you'd created for me. However, now that I'm used to you calling me Carem, I rather like it. But I don't anticipate my family calling me anything but Carrie Emeline. Carem will be your special name for me, and *your* family can continue to call me Carem."

"Thank you, Carem. I also realize that I have had a controlling nature toward you and probably others, too. I really regret that. I suppose I thought that I had to try to hold you close; not ever lose you, but I now know that I was pushing you away. I'm sorry."

She didn't respond at first. Finally, she cocked her head and looked at him. "Do you ever play, Marcus?"

"Pardon me?"

"I've never known you to play, such as to skateboard, snow or water ski, go ice or roller skating. I know we once swam and fished up at the lake in Bellingham, and did some hiking. That's the closest, and only time I've ever seen you play."

"Did you and Andrew play?"

"Yes, we spent time ice skating, building igloos, building snowmen ... and *this*." She jumped up, grabbed a handful of snow and threw it at him. Laughing, she yelled over her shoulder, "Tag, you're it," and she ran down the sidewalk with Marcus chasing after her.

Chapter Fifty-Two

Letter of Hope

*"Peace I leave with you, my peace I give unto
you: not as the world giveth, give I unto you. Let
not your heart be troubled, neither let it be
afraid."*
John 14:27

Thursday
December 19, 1974
Marcus opened the door to the knock. "Hi, Chris.
Good morning."

"Good morning, Marcus, I have a letter for
you. It must be from your parents' home. It's
postmarked Bellingham, Washington."

"Thanks, Chris." After closing the door,
Marcus took a seat in front of the window. *That
was a quick response. I only mailed their letter
last week.*

December 15, 1974
Dear Marcus,

It was so good to hear from you, son. Your father and I had no idea about the difficulties you've been through, concerning your health issues since leaving Vietnam. Of course we never dreamed what was going on in your marriage, either. You and Carem seemed so happy when you vacationed here. So now we're just grateful that you received the salvation of Jesus Christ, and we pray that Carem and the children can find it in their hearts to forgive you.

I want to let you know that if you decide you want to return home, the three bedroom cabin you and Carem rented during your vacation three years ago is now for sale. If you two reconcile, you might want to move back here and purchase it.

When Carem's family visits, they could always stay in our home. We certainly have plenty of room, with only Sally living here with us now. Also, your dad and I are considering retirement in the next couple of years. Perhaps you would consider taking over the family business. You worked in the restaurant during your teen years, so you'd just need to learn the management end of it. We always thought Sally would want to manage the restaurant, but it appears that she may have something else in mind for her future. It's just a thought. We wanted to make you aware, before we considered selling the restaurant.

We want to see Drew, and of course we have only met Angela in pictures. That's one of the drawbacks in owning a restaurant; it's difficult to take vacations. Please stay in touch. Dad and Sally send their love.
All my love,
Mom

He folded the letter and returned it to the envelope. *Go back home? Hmmm. That's something I hadn't considered. Manage the restaurant? Own the cabin? Carem, Drew, and I had such a good time on that vacation. It was the one time I was free from nightmares — until after I got saved. I wonder if Carem would move so far from her parents, and she just began the new job teaching here in Franklin.* He bowed his head in prayer.

The phone interrupted his prayer. "Hello?"

"Hi Marcus, it's Carem. Daddy's been talking to Drew, and Daddy wants you to come to the house. Are you busy right now?"

"Not at all. I'll be right there."

Five minutes later, Carrie Emeline opened the door for him and she stepped outside to speak with Marcus privately. "Daddy and Drew are in the living room talking, and Mom's upstairs with Angela. Drew said he wanted to see you. You need to take it slow and easy. I honestly don't know what to expect. I just know Daddy's been counseling him."

He nodded. "Okay. I'm ready. I'll be careful."

When they walked in, Drew stood with his back to the door and was facing Christopher on the sofa. Christopher took his grandson's hand. "Turn around, Drew."

Drew spun around, released his grandfather's hand, and faced his father. His lip began to tremble, his eyes widened, and then he began to cry. "Daddy!" Carrie Emeline stood back, waiting to see how this reunion would play out.

Marcus ran to Drew and knelt in front of him. Drew tentatively wrapped his arms around Marcus, and Marcus wrapped his arms around his son, pulling him close. Wrapped in each other's arms, they cried. Carrie Emeline and

Christopher watched the touching scene, tears on both of their faces.

"I missed you, Daddy. I'm sorry I was bad and you left home. I didn't mean to be bad. Please forgive me."

Marcus released Drew and held him at arm's length, staring at him. Tears streamed down Marcus's face, and he sniffed, "No, my son, *you* weren't bad. You did nothing wrong. Daddy was sick. I had to go away from home to get well."

"That's what Grandpa said. I thought I caused you to leave. Mommy and Angela have been sad, too."

Carrie Emeline grabbed tissues from her purse, wiped her own eyes, and handed tissues to her dad, Drew, and Marcus.

"I'm much better, Drew. I love you, son, and I've missed you so very much ... and Mommy and Angela, too. I am so sorry you thought you were to blame."

"I love you, too, Daddy. Please don't go away again." He looked up at his dad with pleading eyes.

Marcus looked up at Carrie Emeline, and she knelt beside them and hugged Drew.

"Daddy's not going anywhere, Drew," and she kissed Drew and then kissed Marcus. "Daddy's home now. He'll be here with us. He's not going back to Christmas Hotel either."

The peace and assurance of God filled her heart. She knew she'd made the right decision. Her mom was right.

Chapter Fifty-Three

Healing Decisions

"The heart of her husband doth safely trust in her, so that he shall have no need of spoil. She will do him good and not evil all the days of her life."
Proverbs 31: 11, 12

Friday
December 20, 1974
Lydia Grace arrived home early that morning, in time for breakfast with the family. Christopher asked Marcus if he'd like to ask the blessing. "Yes, I would, Christopher." Carrie Emeline smiled at him, and she felt her eyes begin tearing.

Marcus took her hand and Drew's, and Carrie Emeline took Angela's hand, and everyone bowed their heads. "Dear Heavenly Father, I thank You that my family is complete this morning and joined with Christopher, Jerilyn, and Lydia Grace. I've so much to be thankful for, but let me begin with forgiveness. I love my wife and children, and I'm so thankful that You brought us back together. I promise I will spend the rest of my life making sure they know how much they are loved and appreciated."

He squeezed Carrie Emeline's hand, and she returned the gesture. "I thank you for Christopher and Jerilyn; the best parents-in-law a man could have, and I look forward to getting to know Lydia Grace, Lily, Chris, and Ken this Christmas season. God bless this family, Lord, and in the name of Your Son Jesus we pray. Amen."

Everyone echoed their amens.

Carrie Emeline added silently, *Thank you, Lord Jesus. I've heard my husband pray, and ever so beautifully. I've waited a long time.*

Following breakfast, Carrie Emeline and Marcus strolled hand-in-hand around the square. Marcus pointed to an empty bench. "Let's have a seat on that bench." He pulled the letter from his mother out of his pocket and read it to her.

When he finished, he held her hand. "I'd like us to have a fresh start, Carem. Moving to Bellingham, Washington could be that fresh start. We were happy that month we vacationed there, and I'd like to take over the management of the restaurant. I'm sure you could find a teaching position, unless you'd like us to have more children and teach them yourself. I certainly don't want to rush you or overwhelm you. We've just reconciled. What are your thoughts?"

At first she said nothing. She knew that returning to Louisville was not an option. She would remember only the bad situations in her marriage to Marcus, and that wouldn't be good for their new start. However, she'd been offered a teaching position in Franklin, and she'd be close to her family. But how would that benefit Marcus? The time spent in Bellingham was wonderful for the both of them and Drew. It was a chance to start over and get to know Marcus's family. The thought of living in Bellingham filled her with great peace, and she knew God had directed her choice.

Still holding hands, she turned toward Marcus so she could look directly into his eyes. Using her other hand, she cupped his cheek. "I agree, Marcus. We can't go back to live in the house in Louisville. I thought Franklin might be an option, but in our case I think Bellingham is the best move for us. We were happy on that vacation, and you were at peace. I want that peace for the four of us, and for any more children God blesses us. If we can't break away from the restaurant for a vacation, I'm sure my family would love to visit us in the summer on Bellingham Bay. Who knows, maybe Sally won't leave, and you two can jointly manage the restaurant. That way, we could come home to Christmas Hotel for visits. I'll go wherever you go, Marcus. I love you."

"I love you, too. You own my heart, Carem," and he kissed her.

That evening, Carrie Emeline and Marcus met her parents and Lydia Grace in the living room. They announced their decision to sell the house in Louisville and move to Bellingham.

Christopher spoke first. "Of course we'll miss you living so far away, but I believe you've made a wise decision. A fresh start is the best for you two and your children."

Jerilyn hugged her daughter. "I agree with your father, Carrie Emeline. The memories in that house are too sad to return back there. You two need not look back, but forward. I left my family to marry Christopher, although it was only three hundred miles away and not twenty-five hundred!" She smiled at Carrie Emeline. "Hand to the plow, honey."

Carrie Emeline hugged her mother. "Thanks, Mom."

Christopher picked up Jerilyn's hand and kissed it. "Love is the key. This is what love means to Jerilyn and me. Love is real, it's unique for everyone, and it has the power to change our world if we let it." He looked at his wife and smiled. "Love is growing old, hand in hand, wrinkle after wrinkle. It's letting love win, always, no matter what."

He turned back to Carrie Emeline and Marcus. "Don't go to bed angry with each other, even if you have to stay up all night. Reconcile any differences daily. Don't raise your voices at each other.

"Tell each other 'I love you.' Don't just assume the other person knows it. Touch each other, hold hands, hug, and snuggle in front of the fireplace with a cup of hot chocolate on a cold winter evening. You may have a few of those in Washington," and they all laughed. "Be each other's best friend, and don't let anything or anyone come between you. Make certain God is at the center of your life together, and if you put God first in your lives, everything will fall into place. Raise your children to know the Lord."

Carrie Emeline wiped her eyes with the back of her hand. "Thank you, Daddy. You and Mom have set a great example for all your children." She looked over at Lydia Grace, who nodded her head in the affirmative. "By the way, Daddy, Marcus and I want to remarry, with you officiating in the chapel at Christmas Hotel. As you know, we were married by a justice of the peace. This time we want to do it right."

"I'd be happy to remarry you two. When are you planning to have the wedding?"

"Right away. The whole family will be here for Christmas Eve and Christmas. I checked with Chris, and he said the chapel was available on December twenty-third. If we can get Lily and her family, and Ken and his family together on the twenty-third, would that be okay with you?"

"Well, that's a Monday, so everyone should be able to attend."

"Do you want to invite anyone other than our family?" her mom asked.

"I'd love to invite Marcus's family, but I'm afraid the notice is too short."

"We can call them and tell them," suggested Marcus.

"Outside of our families, I really don't want to invite any others. I want this wedding small and intimate."

Her mom nodded. "I understand completely. When your father and I married in the Christmas Hotel chapel, we didn't have a lot of guests, either, just friends and family."

"May I wear your blue dress you made for your wedding with Daddy?"

Jerilyn smiled at her daughter. "Of course, dear. I knew some day that dress would be worn again."

Carrie Emeline wiped a tear and nodded. "So Monday, December twenty-third it is." Then she laughed. "I wonder how many people have actually married on a Monday."

Marcus hugged her to his side. "It doesn't matter, Carem. It will be our unique and special day."

Christopher took Carrie Emeline's hand, "Let's all pray," and they held hands and bowed their heads.

Chapter Fifty-Four

New Beginnings

*"Therefore shall a man leave his father
and his mother, and shall cleave unto his
wife: and they shall be one flesh."*
Genesis 2:24

Monday
December 23, 1974
Marcus's parents arrived the morning of the wedding. They flew into Nashville, and Chris picked them up at the airport.

They entered the lobby of Christmas Hotel with the same look of awe on their faces, as had numerous guests before them. Christopher and Jerilyn greeted them.

"Our daughter Sally was emphatic when she stated we *had* to be here, so she's taking care of the restaurant," said Mrs. Taylor.

"She also said we deserved a vacation at Christmas Hotel," added Mr. Taylor.

Jerilyn hugged them. "We're certainly pleased

you could be here. Christopher and I have reserved room number eight for your stay, which is right beside our family's permanently reserved room; the room in which Carrie Emeline will dress for the wedding."

"What time is the wedding?" asked Mrs. Taylor.

Jerilyn answered with, "Carrie Emeline told everyone five o'clock, so her twin brother Ken and his wife Loretta could drive in from Lexington. Our oldest daughter Lily and her husband John and their four children are staying at our home a couple of blocks away. After the wedding we can all have dinner in the dining room. It's only eleven. You two have time to rest, so you can be refreshed for the wedding."

"Thank you, Jerilyn," said Mrs. Taylor.

*****

At four o'clock that afternoon, the women gathered in room #7. Lily added the finishing touches on Carrie Emeline's hair, and Jerilyn zipped Carrie Emeline into her own pale blue wedding dress trimmed with delicate white lace on the sleeves and at the throat.

Lily ran her finger under her eye to catch a tear. "Carrie Emeline, you look so much like mother in that dress on her wedding day thirty-three years ago."

Carrie Emeline saw the look of confusion on her mother-in-law's face. "Mother Taylor, Lily was at the wedding, because Mom isn't her biological mother. Lily's mom died giving birth to her. I might also add that Christopher isn't the biological father to Ken and me. Our father, Kenneth Seifert died at the bombing on Pearl Harbor. However, the five of us children couldn't be any closer than if we'd all been born to the same parents. I'm sure Drew and Angela will feel the same way about each other years from now, too."

Lily hugged Carrie Emeline. "I couldn't have said it better, sis."

Carrie Emeline surveyed herself in the mirror. "I guess I'm ready. My dress covers the old, borrowed and blue, and my pearl earrings that Marcus bought me from Mallory Jewelers, covers the new."

Lily approached her with a blue garter. "You know I had to buy you a blue garter. After all, it's becoming my contribution to our family wedding tradition. A second something new and blue for you."

Carrie Emeline laughed and hugged her older sister. "Thank you, Lily. Yes, a blue garter must be your wedding tradition. Thank you."

Lydia Grace checked her watch. "I've got to

go. It's time for me to begin playing the organ."

A knock sounded at the door. Jerilyn opened it to greet Christopher, who announced, "Okay, places, everyone. I'm ready to walk my daughter down the aisle, give her away, and officiate the ceremony." He closed the door behind the women. "Are you ready, Carrie Emeline?"

She smiled at him. "I'm ready, Daddy. It's not the same as with Andrew, but I know it's right."

"Your mother and I have said that about our first spouses, too. I loved my first wife Ellie, and Jerilyn loved her first husband Kenneth. It's not guaranteed who we'll grow old with, but as long we love, that's what's important. Remember the words I spoke last Friday. Love is real, it's unique for everyone, and it has the power to change our world if we let it. Remember, love is growing old, hand-in-hand, wrinkle after wrinkle."

"Thanks, Daddy. I'll remember." She took a deep breath. "I'm ready now."

Lydia Grace played the wedding march on the chapel organ, and the family stood for Carrie Emeline. Marcus smiled at his bride, as he waited for her at the altar. Christopher gave his daughter's hand to Marcus and took his place at the podium.

Christopher began the ceremony. "Dearly

beloved, we are gathered together here in the presence of God — and in the face of these witnesses — to join together this man and this woman in holy matrimony, which is commended to be honorable among all men; and therefore is not by any to be entered into unadvisedly or lightly but reverently, discreetly, advisedly and solemnly. Into this holy state of matrimony, Marcus and Carrie Emeline now come to be joined.

"Through marriage, Marcus and Carrie Emeline make a commitment together to face their disappointments, embrace their dreams, realize their hopes, and accept each other's failures.

"Do you, Marcus Quinton Taylor, take Carrie Emeline Taylor to be your lawfully wedded wife? Will you live together after God's ordinance, in the holy estate of matrimony? Will you love her, comfort her, honor and keep her, in sickness and in health, for richer, for poorer, for better, for worse, in sadness and in joy, to cherish and continually bestow upon her your heart's deepest devotion, forsaking all others, keeping yourself only unto her as long as you both shall live?"

Marcus answered, "I will."

"You may place the ring on Carrie Emeline's finger." Christopher paused until Marcus had gently slipped the ring onto Carrie Emeline's finger.

"Do you, Carrie Emeline Taylor, take Marcus Quinton Taylor to be your husband — to live together after God's ordinance — in the holy estate of matrimony? Will you love him, comfort him, honor and keep him, in sickness and in health, for richer, for poorer, for better, for worse, in sadness and in joy, to cherish and continually bestow upon him your heart's deepest devotion, forsaking all others, keeping yourself only unto him as long as you both shall live?"

Carrie Emeline answered, "I will."

"You may place the ring on Marcus's finger."

Christopher resumed. "In the presence of God and these witnesses, I now pronounce you husband and wife. Marcus, you may now kiss your bride."

Marcus bent and kissed Carrie Emeline's lips. "I love you, Carem," he whispered.

"I love you too, Marcus."

The congregation applauded. Jerilyn had been holding Angela on her lap and Drew sat beside her, but now she released them to rush to their parents. Marcus bent and picked up Drew, and Carrie Emeline picked up Angela. The four of them walked out of the chapel as a family.

Epilogue

By the end of the year, Carrie Emeline and Marcus finish packing up the home in Louisville. With the help of Marcus's veteran buddies, the congregation at Shawnee Baptist Church, and Carrie Emeline's family, the process is completed in one week. They leave the selling of the home in the capable hands of Mr. and Mrs. White, and a realtor who is a member at Shawnee Baptist Church.

Early in January 1975, Marcus and Carrie Emeline sign the papers for Marcus to adopt Drew. He is now Andrew Michael Taylor, and Marcus's son.

At the end of January, Carrie Emeline says goodbye to her school, her church, and Mr. and Mrs. White. Marcus says goodbye to Pastor Mattingly, Harry, and the veterans' group. They stay at Carrie Emeline's family home in Franklin until leaving for Bellingham.

The home in Louisville, Kentucky sells to the first family that views it. In February, 1975, the Taylor family moves to Bellingham, Washington, and they sign the papers on their new home: the three bedroom log cabin on the lake.

In March, Marcus and Sally became the joint owners of their parents' restaurant.

In June, with the help of his father and the pastor at the Bellingham Baptist Church, Marcus begins a veterans' group at the church for veterans suffering with PTSD. One year later, Marcus establishes another group in Seattle, Washington, ninety miles away.

On October 15, 1975, Carrie Emeline gives birth to another daughter: Heather Christine Taylor. For this birth, Marcus never leaves his wife's side.

Author's Notes

I have never before written a book that portrays some events that happened in my own family, as I have done in *Christmas Pact*. My brother, Specialist Four Gerald Martin Staats, was killed in battle on 26 February, 1970. The events that took place in *Christmas Pact* on that day regarding Andrew and Jerry were the exact information that was provided for my family by the United States Army on that fateful day. Jerry was buried the day following my nineteenth birthday, and he was my only brother. March ninth was the date that my father, mother, and I were meeting Jerry in Hawaii for R&R, so I included it in Andrew and Carrie Emeline's story. The Valentine's Day flowers were my brother's final gift to our mother. Like Carrie Emeline, my mother refused to throw them out until the flowers were long dead.

If you are ever in the area, you can visit the grave of my brother, and other military veterans from many different wars, at Memorial Park Cemetery on North Dixie Drive in Dayton, Ohio. There is a military circle straight to the rear of the entrance of the cemetery, and Jerry's grave is on the North-West side of the military circle. God bless all our veterans.

I would also like to add that the United States Army uniform worn by the model on the cover of *Christmas Pact* is my brother's dress uniform from when he was stationed in Germany and later Vietnam. The uniform is approximately forty-seven years old (as of this original writing in 2015). My mother passed away five weeks before the original release of *Christmas Pact* in 2015. Unfortunately, she did not have the opportunity to view the cover picture before she died, but she knew about the story in progress.

Although my books are works of fiction, I do like some real people to "visit" my stories.

Dr. L.F. Beasley was a practicing physician in Simpson County, Kentucky from 1934 until he retired in April, 1975. He served in WWII beginning sometime in 1942. He made house calls until he retired, delivered many babies, and conducted many surgeries. He died in 2011 at the age of 103. His mind was good; he drove his car until age 99, and played golf into his late 90s! He did not like his given names, therefore he went by his initials L.F., and so I will not reveal his given names either. (Information provided by his daughter Barbara Beasley Smith of Franklin, Kentucky)

Other "visitors" to the story are my husband, Robert E. McLemore's parents, Nettie Sue Harris McLemore (currently resides in Bowling Green, KY) and James (Booker) E. McLemore (now deceased). Also, my husband Robert E. McLemore visits the story at age sixteen.

I added Mr. and Mrs. White to the story who happened to be my own son's caregivers in Dayton, Ohio during the years of 1977-1979. Ralph and Eldena White were a wonderful old retired couple, and they are now both deceased. Although, they were not related to us, my son did call them Grandma and Grampa White, since they took care of two of their grandchildren, also.

Christmas Hotel, the first book in the *Christmas Hotel* series was inspired by an article from January, 2008, in the *Franklin Favorite*, the newspaper in Franklin, KY. The article spoke about a diary left behind in the now razed Keystop Motel in Franklin, KY. The diary, dated 1873, possibly belonged to a young girl named

C.E. Bazell from Rock Camp, Ohio. An Ohio assistant librarian traced the diary to a girl named Carrie E. Bazell who lived in Rock Camp with her parents until the late 1800s. Carrie Bazell died March 20, 1884 at the age of twenty-one, according to a brief obituary.

In 1922, a local Baptist church started a mission at the corner of 38th and Market in Louisville, Kentucky. On March 29, 1923, that mission became known as Shawnee Baptist Church. Over the next forty-nine years, church attendance declined from four hundred to just sixty. As a last effort, the deacons called Lonnie Mattingly, a young man from Bowling Green, Kentucky, to be their pastor. Energized with a renewed focus, Shawnee Baptist Church soon began to grow again.

Mt. Vernon Missionary Baptist Church is an actual church in Simpson County, Kentucky. My husband's great-grandfather, Bailey Peyton Harris, around 1873 or 1874 donated the land, acreage carved from his own farm, for Mt. Vernon Missionary Baptist Church. Nettie Sue Harris McLemore, my mother-in-law and the granddaughter of Bailey Peyton Harris, is still a member.

And the work of righteousness shall be peace;
and the effect of righteousness quietness and
assurance forever.
Isaiah 32:17

Reviews are always appreciated. If you so desire, please post an honest review at Amazon.com and Barnes and Noble for *Christmas Pact*, and I thank you!

As of this Writing

Explore these resources for more information about PTSD in Veterans.

VET CENTERS
If you are a combat Veteran or experienced any sexual trauma during your military service, bring your DD214 to your local Vet Center and speak with a counselor or therapist — many of whom are Veterans themselves — for free, without an appointment, and regardless of your enrollment status with VA.
http://www.va.gov/directory/guide/vetcenter_flsh.asp

UNDERSTANDING PTSD BOOKLET
This eight-page booklet explains what PTSD is, provides information and resources on support, and shares real stories from people who have dealt effectively with PTSD.
http://www.ptsd.va.gov/public/
understanding_ptsd/booklet.pdf

VA'S PTSD PROGRAM LOCATOR

This site will allow you to search for PTSD programs located near you. If you are eligible to receive care through the Veterans Health Administration, you can enroll in one of VA's PTSD treatment programs.

http://www.va.gov/directory/guide/ptsd_flsh.asp

For Family Assistance

FOCUS ON THE FAMILY:
Phone: 800-232-6459 Web Site
www.focusonthefamily.com – or
Email: help@focusonthefamily.com

FAMILY TALK:
Phone: 877-732-6825
Website: www.drjamesdobson.org

DEPRESSION HOTLINE:
Crisis Call Center
Phone: 800-273-8255

DRUG AND ALCOHOL HOTLINE:
The National Alcohol and Substance Abuse
Phone: 800-784-6776

SUICIDE PREVENTION HOTLINE:
Phone: 630-482-9696

ABUSE: PHYSICAL, VERBAL, AND SEXUAL
HOTLINE:
Rape, Abuse Network
Phone: 800-656-4673

ANGER MANAGEMENT HOTLINE:
Crisis Call Center
Phone: 800-273-8255

Christmas Pact Discussions and Questions for Book Club

In the following questions please either answer for yourself or try to see the situation through the eyes of a young woman you know well.

1. How do you feel about Carrie Emeline's whirlwind twelve-day romance with Andrew, knowing there was a good chance he might later be deployed to Vietnam? Would you have married a man that quickly, knowing the possible consequences of him getting wounded or being killed?

2. Before Andrew was killed, Carrie Emeline planned to meet him in Hawaii for his R&R. Would you have attempted such a trip, even with a nurse, when eight months pregnant? We know Carrie Emeline was in love, but do you consider it to be a foolish decision on her part?

3. Following Andrew's death, Drew was born four days after the funeral. Carrie Emeline was thrust

immediately into motherhood. However, years later, Andrew's death then hit her hard, and she realized she never allowed herself the time to grieve. How would you have handled the grieving process?

4. Carrie Emeline believed the lie Marcus told her about the Christmas Pact, and wanted to obey the wishes of Andrew. Although she was skeptical, she did want Drew to have a loving father in his life. She knew that Andrew and Marcus were good buddies. Would you have trusted Marcus? Carrie Emeline had no way to prove what he stated regarding the Christmas Pact. All she knew was that the addresses were exchanged to look up the families. Her address was written in Andrew's handwriting. Would you marry a man who was not a Christian under these circumstances?

5. In the beginning of Marcus's strange behavior and nightmares, Carrie Emeline did not know about PTSD. However, she did ask him to get help. How would you have handled the situation when he didn't seek help?

6. Marcus had a controlling behavior toward Carrie Emeline, and at times he treated her more as his child than his wife. What would you do in

such a situation? Do you think this stemmed from his childhood, the army, or both?

7. When they vacationed in Bellingham, Washington, Marcus reconnected with family. The nightmares also subsided. If you had been Carrie Emeline, would you have suggested moving to Bellingham?

8. On the morning Marcus caused bodily harm to Drew and Carrie Emeline, would you have handled the situation as Carrie Emeline did? Would you press charges on your husband, get a restraining order, and change the household locks? OR would you have found a way to support him? Carrie Emeline now had been reading up on PTSD and knew Marcus showed the signs. Would you have stood by your husband, or put your children first, as did Carrie Emeline?

9. Think of all the chances Marcus had been given to accept the salvation of the Lord Jesus. He grew up in a Christian home; Andrew witnessed to him; Carrie Emeline invited him to church; and there was the radio preacher he was drawn to listen to on two different occasions; and Pastor Mattingly; and the man in the park who Marcus later suspected was an angel. Do you think

Marcus was afraid of salvation, and that's why he continued to run from the Lord? What do you think was the deciding factor when he admitted he needed Jesus?

10. When Carrie Emeline was finally persuaded by Christopher to meet with Marcus and her parents at Christmas Hotel, she was very antagonistic. Would you have been more or less judgmental and understanding toward Marcus?

11. After hearing Marcus's testimony of salvation, would you have allowed a man like Marcus back into your life and into the lives of your children?

12. Do you think Carrie Emeline made the right decision to leave her home state and family, and move all the way to Bellingham, Washington, to help Marcus?

**Sneak Peek of Christmas Love and Mercy
Book Five of the Christmas Hotel Series.
Enjoy!**

Prologue

Thursday
December 01, 1988

Chris tiptoed into the bedroom to check on her. She lay on her back, sleeping with a slight smile on her sweet face. She had kicked off the covers, so he straightened the quilt and tucked her in. His mother had made this quilt over a period of eight months. With a chuckle and the inevitable hug, Mom said, "It's my first quilt. I want you to have it. You're my youngest and my last, so you get my practice quilt."

Chris smiled, remembering the conversation. His mother had been his rock all through his growing up years. He loved his father, but there was something special about a mother's love. Her love was always unconditional. He didn't give his parents a great cause for alarm, but he did engage in a few teenage pranks.

Although Chris and his nephew Brian were six years apart in age, and he being the older, they were the best of friends. On Halloween night, back in '71, when Chris was sixteen and Brian was ten, they toilet papered the trees of his biology teacher's home. Of course, as the older boy, he was the one to get in trouble.

"You did that why?" questioned his father in a stern voice. "Your teacher, Mr. McKinley paid me a visit. You were spotted by Lori Anna Stanley, who you know lives next door. Lori Anna thought it was funny, but her parents James and Carol Ann were not pleased. After all, Mr. McKinley is their neighbor. What do you have to say for yourself, Christopher Joseph Wright?"

Chris hung his head. He knew he was in deep trouble when either parent used his full name. "I'm sorry, Dad. I'll clean it up."

"You will do just that, *and* you will apologize to Mr. McKinley. I told him you'll also handle chores around his house after school three hours each day for a week. Therefore, there will be no work or pay at Christmas Hotel that week."

When he arrived to clean up the mess, of course Brian was a no-show to help him. Chris saw three-year-old Lori Anna standing behind a bush, watching him. Chris placed the ladder against the tree, climbed up, and began removing the paper. Thankfully, it didn't rain or snow or he'd have a serious mess. As he threw down the shreds of toilet paper, Lori Anna stepped away from the bush, picked up the shreds, and stuffed them in a large garbage bag Chris had left on the ground. He looked down and smiled at his little helper. She looked up at him and returned a smile, displaying her dimples. Her mom must have given her one of those home perms, because her normally straight black hair was in little ringlets all over her head. *What a little cutie.*

The phone rang, interrupting his reminiscing from the past and abruptly jolting him back to the present. He stepped out of the room, quietly closing the door. "Hello," he said into the receiver. "Yes, Mom, she's asleep. Yes, I'm okay. I'll probably take off a few days from Christmas Hotel. I think Mr. Hanover, Mr. Adams, Mr. Thompson, Mr. Clark, and of course you and Dad can make certain all shifts are covered. I just need to be here *and* at the hospital."

"I understand, son. Please let me help you more. You're wearing yourself out and spreading yourself too thin."

"I'm fine, Mom. I love you."

"I love you, too. Never forget that."

Chapter One

Lori Anna Stanley

*"I wait for the LORD, my soul doth wait,
and in his word do I hope."*
Psalm 130:5

One year earlier
Tuesday Morning
December 01, 1987
"Hey, Uncle Chris. Did you just snap our picture?" Brian had been snuggling on a bench in Franklin's town square with his wife Christine.

Chris laughed, throwing back his head for a good guffaw. "I'm just photographing my annual Christmas pictures of the square. My, my, a picture of you snuggling with Christine will make a great picture for your little one someday. *And* quit calling me uncle. I'm only six years older than you."

"I know, but I just want to remind you now and then that you're getting old."

"Thanks a lot."

Christine smiled and rubbed her rotund belly. Her coat no longer completely closed; she appeared to be wearing a couple of bulky sweaters underneath.

Brian jumped up. "Give me the camera, Chris. Let me take *your* picture for a change."

"I don't think so, buddy boy. This is the latest Canon model. It's the RC-760 released this year. My parents gave it to me for my birthday in September. I know how camera-challenged you are. Why you couldn't even use my Polaroid from the sixties. You cut off everyone's heads."

"Ha, ha. I was a kid. By the way, why aren't you at your desk at Christmas Hotel? Since when does the senior manager have time off?"

"I do schedule a day off now and then. What about you? Shouldn't you be doing your detective stuff? Aren't you working on a big case?"

"It's all under control," Brian said with a smug grin, and returned to his seat, hugging his wife closer.

They all turned when a camera flashed nearby. A young woman snapped pictures about twenty feet away, and a well-trained Golden Retriever sat at her feet. When the girl walked a few paces, the dog obediently followed and then again sat at her feet. Despite the chill of the December morning, she wore no coat; just a bright green sweatshirt over black sweatpants tucked into her tall, furry boots. A multi-colored knit hat covered her head, but her straight black hair hung to her waistline. Every time she spun around for another picture, her long hair followed in a swinging motion around her lithe, petite figure.

Chris watched her, mesmerized. She gave extra special meaning to the phrase poetry in motion. She appeared to be around twenty, so he knew she was too young for him. It didn't seem right, a thirty-two-year-old man ogling such a young woman. However, he couldn't stop watching her and the dog. The dog anticipated her every move.

Brian jumped up and ran his hand in front of Chris's eyes. "Earth to Chris. Don't you know who she is?"

Finally, and reluctantly, Chris turned back to Brian. "I guess not. I thought I knew everyone in Franklin." He cocked his head. "Yet, there is a familiarity about her."

"You dunce," Brian said, landing a friendly smack to the side of Chris's head. "That's Lori Anna Stanley. She's James and Carol Ann's daughter. She's been away at the University of Louisville for the past two years, but she recently transferred to Western Kentucky University. I hear she's working part-time at the *Franklin Favorite*. Maybe that's why she's taking all the pictures. I think you've been cooped up at Christmas Hotel too much. You need to get out more often, so you can know what's happening."

Lori Anna, thought Chris. *It's even worse than I thought. I'm gawking at a nineteen-year-old.* He turned back to Brian, but he had rejoined Christine on the bench. Brian and Christine met three years ago, married two years ago, and now had a baby on the way. Chris watched them laugh together, and Brian rubbed her very-pregnant belly. He turned back toward Lori Anna, but she and her dog had moved to the next block, snapping more pictures. *All my siblings are married with children. They were married by my age. What's wrong with me, Lord?*

Three hours later, Chris returned to the square, this time munching on his lunch sandwich and drinking a Coke. He had gone home to pick up his German Shepherd, Fritz. After seeing Lori Anna on the square with her dog, he realized his day off should involve Fritz. Finishing his sandwich, and tossing Fritz the last bite, he threw the wrappings in the trash receptacle. "Okay, boy, get ready to catch the Frisbee!"

Fritz pranced around in excitement, jumping

and trying to steal the Frisbee from Chris's hands. Chris reared back and threw the Frisbee about twenty feet high, at a distance of about forty feet. Fritz ran and caught it with practiced ease. Chris and the three-year-old shepherd had been playing catch with a Frisbee or a ball from the time his dog was just two months old. At the third throw, a golden retriever jumped, caught it, and the throaty laugh of a woman rang in his ears. Fritz tried to grab the Frisbee away from the dog, but the dog ran from him.

"Here, Bella, bring it to me." Lori Anna laughed when she took it from Bella and threw it. Fritz sat and cocked his head, and then he looked back at Chris. As if to say, "What gives, Master?"

Bella brought the Frisbee back to Lori Anna, and she in turn handed it to Chris. "Sorry, Chris. Bella wanted to play, too."

Chris checked out Lori Anna. She had put on a warm car coat and had on knit gloves, but no knit hat this time. Her long straight hair remained loose and hung down her back. One side fell over her eye, and she quickly tucked it behind an ear, still smiling at Chris. She didn't wear the big-hair teased look most women of the eighties sported. Obviously, she didn't follow the crowd. He liked that about her, because he didn't follow the crowd either. He still wore his brown hair shorter than most men his age, and he bore no tattoos. She had the cutest dimples. She was so small, not over five feet tall. She could easily walk under the outstretched arm of his six feet two inch frame.

He realized he was staring. "Uh ... not a problem, Lori Anna. I see Bella likes to play Frisbee, too. I think Fritz was just a bit confused, but he seems okay now." The dogs were running, jumping, and playing together.

"So, Lori Anna, you haven't been home for a while. Did you recognize me this morning when you were snapping pictures?"

"Yes, but I didn't want to intrude on your time with Brian and Christine. They seem like a very happy couple. I've been gone for a couple of years, and I'm trying to get reacquainted with everyone."

"They *are* happy. As you could see, Christine is very pregnant with their first child."

"Do they know if they're having a boy or a girl?"

"No, they decided they wanted to be surprised."

During a lull in the conversation, they turned to watch the dogs playing.

"Bella is two. How old is Fritz?"

"He just turned three. His lineage has been in our family since 1954, before I was born. First with Lydia Grace's first dog Bullet and then his son Gabe. Fritz has cousins all over Simpson County."

Lori Anna smiled and motioned to a nearby bench. "Why don't we have a seat and watch our dogs play?"

"Okay." *Now what*, thought Chris, as he sat by her on the bench. *She's nineteen. I can't be attracted to her. However, she doesn't appear to be a giggly teenager. She seems very mature.*

"So, Brian told me you transferred from the University of Louisville to Western Kentucky University. Why the switch?"

She smiled again, flashing even, white teeth. "I forget how quickly news in a small town travels."

"I'm sorry. I didn't mean to pry." Chris knew his face reddened. It always did to his mortification. Maybe he was being nosey.

"Oh, no, it's okay," she said as she touched his arm.

He felt the electricity shoot through him. *Okay, what am I doing? I'm sitting on a park bench in the square, and anyone in town who's nearby will see us. She's right, news does travel like wild fires in a small town.* He noticed a surprised expression cross her face. *Does she feel it, too?*

"I was only teasing," she continued. She removed her hand from his arm. "Actually, I missed the small town atmosphere. Louisville was just too big for me, and I also wanted to be closer to my parents. Dad hasn't been well lately, and Mom's been worried about him. She did get him to quit the long-distance trucking. The short-distance runs permit him to be home nightly. In her words, 'That allows me to keep an eye on him.'"

She paused for a moment to watch the dogs. Then, "With me attending classes in Bowling Green and working for *The Franklin Favorite* newspaper here in town, I can help out, too." Pausing again, she remarked, "By the way, I noticed you're into photography, too. I saw you with your camera this morning."

"Yeah, I've been taking pictures since I was a kid. It's been one of my dad's many hobbies, and through the years we've used photography as our special time together. I suppose I grew up with a camera in my hands. My dad's camera collection is huge. I think he has cameras back to circa 1920. However, I haven't been paid for photography, like you. It makes me the amateur and you the professional."

"I've not been a professional very long. The paper just hired me in September. I've only been into photography about ten years. I received my first camera at Christmas when I was nine."

The age difference struck him again. *Nineteen-year-old Lori Anna has been using a camera ten years, and me about twenty-eight years. Good grief, I need to get far away from her.*

He rose. "Well, Lori Anna, it's been a pleasure seeing you again. Please tell your parents I said hi." Did he see disappointment on her face? "Oh! I should let you know Christmas Hotel now has a darkroom in the basement. I added it about ten years ago. If the paper office is closed and you need pictures developed in a hurry, please feel free to use it. Just tell the manager on duty where you'll be. We also have a full gym down there too, along with separate men's and ladies' lockers and shower rooms. It's really for the guests, but the town's people are welcome. Both are available twenty-four/seven, three hundred sixty-five."

She rose with him. "Thank you, Chris. I'll probably take you up on both of the offers." She turned toward her dog and called, "Come, Bella," and Bella ran to her, with Fritz at Bella's heels.

Chris walked to his 1986 black Ford F-150 pickup parked at the curb across from Christmas Hotel. Opening the passenger door, Fritz jumped in and sat on his side of the front seat. As Chris climbed in, he looked toward Lori Anna. She was heading in the direction of her parents' home. The lonely feeling gripped his heart.

Available November 01, 2019

www.ingramcontent.com/pod-product-compliance
Lightning Source LLC
Chambersburg PA
CBHW071150250626
47159CB00001B/42